JACK THE RIPPER: THREADS

Jay Hartley

Copyright © 2021 Jay Hartley

All rights reserved.

ISBN: 9798483238751

CONTENTS

Part 1. Breaking Dawns

Part 2. Killer Instinct

Part 3. Evil Walks

Part 4. Polly Nichols

Part 5. Annie Chapman

Part 6. Elizabeth Stride

Part 7. Catherine Eddowes

Part 8. Mary Jane Kelly

Part 9. Five Sided Triangle

Part 10. End of May

Part 11. Trials and Tribulations

Part 12. Setting Suns

DISCLAIMER

This story should be treated as a work of fiction. Some scenes are based on actual, documented events. The dialogue and narrative have been created for dramatic effect. This book should not be regarded as a historical fact, for now.

In memory of Florence Elizabeth Chandler.

PART 1

Breaking Dawns

9 November 1888

Miller's Court, Whitechapel

The unforgiving stench of death could make one feel painfully alive. Within seven months, like the gutted corpse of the whore in front of him, James Maybrick too would be dead.

At that moment, he did not care for his own fate. He cared only for that moment. A wave of exhilaration and euphoria had overtaken his senses.

It was around 2:00 a.m. James surveyed his work with a mix of pride and awe. The concoction of heavy metal drugs and harsh alcohol was now rapidly wearing off. The fog was starting to clear. The foul smell was cutting through like cheese wire.

A few hours earlier, things had been somewhat different in the Horn of Plenty pub. The drink had been flowing, and spirits had been high—despite the late rain. It was there that he had spotted her again.

It wasn't the first time he had laid eyes on Mary Jane Kelly. She was often in the Ten Bells, where he had spent numerous Friday and Saturday evenings. There, he slowly and progressively raised his levels of hatred and contempt towards the fallen women of Whitechapel. They came and went from pub to pub, selling their filthy wares. Aided by arsenic, beer, and gin, James would take his time to work up the right level of loathing and disgust. There was always a time of night when Jack felt more comfortable than James.

James and Mary Jane had shared a brief encounter in the Ten Bells a couple of months prior. She was a pretty girl with a soft Celtic accent—not short, porcelain-white skin with rosy cheeks, a hint of freckles, blue eyes, and dark-red hair. She never seemed to be with a bonnet. A free soul. Buxom and well proportioned. Mary was not like the others. She was young, spirited, and exhaling life. Or at least she did. However, just like Florie, she too was delicate but damaged. They both flowered all too quickly. She was fighting for sunlight in a place of darkness. She was entangled in a wild and brutal garden ravaged by nettles and weeds. This was not a place for her. She needed to be liberated, and liberated she had been. She was preserved in immortality, like a fly in amber.

A few months earlier, back at that public house, and whilst in a drunken state singing some old Irish ballad, she had accidentally bumped the gin in James's hand. This led to him spilling it on his very expensive overcoat. A quick apology was met with quiet and controlled dignity.

"It's quite all right, my dear, it's merely but a drop. Please, continue."

James remembered that she gave him a cheeky curtsey before bellowing her song's remaining verses with vigour. He noted even then, for a whore, she had an unusual charm.

It was either fate or fortune that their paths should cross a third time. This time, James would not miss his opportunity. She truly deserved to become Jack's masterpiece.

James stood there in the grime-caked hovel, staring at this collection of oozing flesh and organs as the rain continued to gently kiss the paper-thin windows. He had achieved his aim. This vital young woman had been stripped of all her humanity, reduced to nothing more than slabs of meat. Nothing more than all of us really are.

He had already removed her heart and wrapped it in newspaper to bring it with him. Jack would enter her heart in death.

Only an hour a two earlier, she was singing drunkenly again, this time "Pick a Violet from My Mother's Grave." A beautifully poetic end that Jack could not have planned better for her.

Just one last job to do. James put two fingers in a congealing pool of blood gathering on the bed. With his digits soaked in her blood, he unceremoniously leaned over the corpse of Mary Jane Kelly to paste the initials *F* and *M* on the panel of the partition door. A little clue for the police to find. He wondered if they would also see the *F* carved into the flesh of her left arm. They were probably too blind to see any of the funny little clues he had left along the way.

The crimson smell of drying blood and the rotten odour of foul faeces had a sharp ability to sober up even the most robust constitutions. It wouldn't be too long now before sunrise—time to leave this place. Jack's work was done. James must go.

His hat and coat lay on top of Mary's clothes that he had neatly folded just after he cut her throat open. As he put his trophy into his bag, something caught his eye with a glint. He spotted a key under the bed, half buried under a scratchy old blanket. He reached down and picked it up. On his way out, he wondered if it was the same key Kelly claimed she had lost. As he left the room and closed the door behind him, he tried the key. Indeed, it fit the lock. With that, he dropped the key into his pocket and exited the passageway of Miller's Court, back out to the chilly embrace of Dorset Street.

Despite the cold of the night, James felt only heat.

*　*　*

30 May 1850
Paradise St., Liverpool

Almost forty years before the notorious murders of Whitechapel lived an eleven-year-old boy in Liverpool fascinated with death and human anatomy. Morbid thoughts occupied this boy's mind from a young age, ever since he found out he was named James after a brother who died just a few months old.

James was anxious. The intrigue was becoming all too much for him. At 29 Paradise Street stood the Liverpool Museum of Anatomy. It marketed itself with the slogan "Man Know Thyself." It had not long opened, and ever since it did, James had been desperate to see for himself what lay inside. He had lost count of the number of times he had passed the doors trying to peek a look inside. One time he even tried to sneak in behind a fat man, but he was promptly spotted and ejected.

Everything about this place captivated him. What strange sights existed behind those velvet curtains?

It was late afternoon, and the sun still beat strong. James had conscripted his younger brother Michael to see if they could find a way to sneak inside. In their short trousers and neat haircuts, the two boys lingered directly opposite this palace of wonder. Michael, aged just nine, did not share his brother's enthusiasm.

"James, why are we here?"

"We are going to try and get inside over there. We need to find a way in."

"I don't want to go in there."

"Stop being a baby. Do you want the world to know you are a baby? I will tell everybody Michael Maybrick is a baby!"

"I'm not a baby!"

"Good. So you need to help me."

James grabbed Michael by the hand, and the young men traipsed across the cobbled street, avoiding carmen hurtling past on their ponies and traps at breakneck speeds. They reached the double door entrance. A sign on one side clearly said, "Strictly No Children." James was not concerned by such rules.

"James, it says no children. We are children."

James exhaled a hulking sigh. "Some of us are babies though, are we not, Michael?"

Michael pouted.

James pulled the door handle down and slowly opened it to

snoop inside. Through the gap, he peered in. He could see a ticket booth where a bored young man was reading a book. James scanned the room. He could see a large, dark entrance to what looked like an exhibition space. James got an overwhelming sense to find out what was in there. He had to know.

Suddenly, a voice boomed from behind them.

"James and Michael Maybrick—you step away from that door right now!"

The boys turned around to see their father, William, darting towards them from across the street.

"What on God's earth are you doing? That is no place for any self-respecting adult, let alone young boys! You will come home with me right now. You shall be punished for this—what were you thinking!"

"I'm sorry, Papa," yelped Michael as he started to sob.

James was expressionless. All he could feel was an overwhelming rush of disappointment. The old man could stop him from seeing what was inside there today, but he could not prevent the inevitable.

One day he would see what secrets this enticing Pandora's box held. He was certain of nothing else.

∗ ∗ ∗

25 October 1856

Paradise St., Liverpool

The fascination with death only grew as James got older. His school friends were able to source books that featured so many weird and wonderful drawings of the human body. These books were to become James's most prized possessions. Sometimes the urges would overtake him to satisfy himself. He saw things in the human body others did not.

The previous day, he had turned eighteen years old. The only thing he could think about amongst the niceties, cards, and presents was visiting the Liverpool Museum of Anatomy. The birthday treat he was most excited about was this. He had even spent the past few months cultivating a wispy moustache to assist in his desire to pass as an adult. Whilst his friends were thinking about drinking alcohol and courting women, James was more interested in seeing displays of actual human organs.

It was Saturday mid-morning. The delights that lay beyond the darkened windows and large French doors were tantalisingly close. He waited outside the entrance for a few seconds to gather his composure. Just as he did several years earlier, he stood here contemplating what was in this place. Now he would finally get to know.

James took a deep breath and threw open the doors. He confidently strode up to the middle-aged man standing at the ticket booth. A man on a mission.

The attendant took a brief moment to consider this patron's credentials.

"Yes, sir?" the attendant asked.

"I would like admission for one adult, please."

Immediately James was served.

"That will be fourpence, sir."

James took out his suede drawstring purse and took out fourpence from the birthday money he had accumulated. He placed the money on the counter.

The attendant returned a small paper ticket.

"Enjoy the exhibition, sir."

James nodded and moved towards the thick velvet rope dividing the foyer from the excitingly dark room. His heart was racing. Sweat gathered under his hat. The anticipation was almost too much. He passed the rope.

As he entered the room, James was amazed. All his senses were tingling. The scents of smoky candlewicks and cleaning alcohol wafted through the air. The room was almost pitch-black. He was the only one there. Perfect.

Gaslights and wax candles illuminated the numerous cases, models, and jars all around. He had never felt such sensations. His throat was dry with anticipation.

There were multitudes of displays presenting the various wonders of the human body. James started to scan the room slowly in awe. He did his best to absorb all that he could see. There were jars filled with organs. Muscles hanging from skeletons. All sorts of beautiful sights. He drank it all in.

The start of the exhibition display was pedestrian. Dull explanations about the planet and chemical processes. Then something about food. This wasn't very interesting. James wanted the good stuff.

As he meandered along the prescribed route, he quickly spotted miniature human body models with the skin removed. There were real skulls of newborn children. There was a female pelvis, malformed. James felt a tingling of arousal. This was more like it.

The following display demonstrated the life cycle of humans. It showed various examples of a foetus in the stage of development. Then a delightful jar of an exposed uterus. This was followed by a display of a stillborn child whose dead body had been cut open to reveal its inner workings. It was wonderful.

The following collection had wax models of two female breasts—dissected cleanly as if they were two pieces of bread sliced from a freshly baked loaf. The cuts were perfect. They looked so lifelike. The level of detail fascinated James.

One particular glass display in the corner of the room drew his eye. As he edged closer, he could start to make out the words on the placard. It read, "Extensive venereal disease of the female reproductive system." This one was truly delicious.

Inside this large case was a collection of organs, decayed and slightly rotten. James was almost overwhelmed with the sexual feelings dominating him. He was fully aroused and was glad of the room being so dark. He stared intently at all the details the display had to offer, committing it to his memory. The need to release all these built-up urges was now too much. He needed to go home and satisfy them.

James knew he could now enter the museum freely and decided

to make a return visit soon. He quickly exited the exhibition space and scurried back towards the double door entrance. James opened the doors and moved out onto the street. The musky, death-filled air of the museum was instantly replaced with the walloping smack of horseshit from the bustling street.

James squinted at the sky as the sunlight hit his eyes.

The darkness had altered his vision.

* * *

12 July 1858
Bishopsgate St., City of London

The city greeted him with the foulest smell he had ever had the displeasure of experiencing. It was strangling all it touched. The suffocating reek of excrement and death.

London was the epicentre of the commercial world. Ships by the dozens constantly pulling up and down the River Thames with goods from the furthest reaches of Her Majesty's great empire. Spice, coca, tobacco, coffee, and more. The scents James hoped to savour were not there. Instead, something most foul welcomed him to this new world.

T&J Harrison imported brandy from France. They started their business originally in Liverpool over twenty years earlier. They had ambitious expansion plans and had secured a new shipping route into London's Docklands. The sun never set in the British Empire.

Business never slept. Import, export, buying, selling—it was a constant cycle of opportunity. This new role he found himself in excited him. When James learned of the opportunity to join their newly created office in the City of London as a clerk, he could not be more enthused.

It was Monday morning, and he arrived at the shared office building, close to Liverpool Street. He was jarred by the funk that wafted in the air as he strolled from the station. He quickly opted to walk with a handkerchief over his mouth. A thick cloud of bilious odour was enveloping London.

James entered through sizeable double oak doors. He found a clerk sitting inside at a desk, also with a handkerchief over his mouth.

"How can we help you, sir?"

James was just nineteen years old but wanted to be accepted as a man. He put away the handkerchief and puffed his chest out.

"I am James Maybrick. I am here to start my employment with T&J Harrison."

The clerk looked down at a sheet of paper in front of him. He opted to keep his handkerchief in place.

"Ah, yes. Room 20 on the third floor. You may go up."

James could not help but ask. "What exactly is that stench?"

The clerk looked at Maybrick, baffled. "This is the first you have encountered it, sir? It is from the Thames itself. It has been with us for months now. It is getting worse due to the heat. Many are calling it 'The Great Stink.'"

It was not unlike rotting eggs but much more sulphuric or fermented. It was really scratching James's throat now. There was absolutely nothing great about this smell. He could barely concentrate.

"It is most certainly unique. Thank you," said James as he headed towards the staircase.

He trundled up two long flights of stairs before he reached the second floor. James strolled down the corridor before arriving at the correct room. He tried to clear his throat and then knocked twice.

A smartly dressed older man opened the door.

"You must be the boy, Maybrick? I am Thomas Harrison. Come in."

"Thank you, sir."

James was surprised at how small this room was. It contained just two desks and two chairs facing each other. They were tightly packed in among numerous drawers and cabinets. It was very different to what James was expecting. A little claustrophobic. Not a great combination with the putrid air. There was a small window that was too high to see anything but fragments of displaced light. It was firmly closed. Probably for the best.

"You may leave your hat and coat on the back of the door."

"Yes, sir."

James did as instructed and then took the chair opposite the now-seated Harrison.

"What we do here, Mr. Maybrick, is simple. We ensure our

product arrives on time from one port to another. It may sound simple, but I assure you that nothing is ever plain sailing in the world of shipping. That is a little joke."

James did not find the remark amusing but still offered a polite smile. Harrison coughed and then continued.

"You will get used to the smell. I have. Now, I am expecting you to be bright enough to listen to instructions carefully. To have the foresight to see the challenges ahead and the hindsight to learn from your errors. This is a fast-paced business, Mr. Maybrick, and your mind must be equally as quick. I trust you understand?"

"I do, sir. I shall listen intently and speak sparingly."

Harrison smiled.

"Good lad. You are learning already!"

Despite the repulsive fog wafting over London, James remained upbeat. Today was a good day. It was the first day of James in business, and what a man of business he would be. He would learn all he could from Thomas Harrison. He wished to be a master of commerce, and nothing would now stand in his way.

Filth or no filth.

* * *

2 February 1860

Fenchurch St., City of London

James watched her through a window dusted with sleet. The cold wind tingled the bristles of his moustache. The light inside glimmered on her long golden hair. His gaze was transfixed from the safety of the shadows across the street.

He had seen her many times before. She worked in Dewdney's Hair Jewellers close to his office. A plain girl but still pretty. She seemed very quiet. James wondered if that was why he was drawn to her. She was not like the wenches of the local public houses. He always felt dirty after engaging in their services. This one seemed pure and innocent. James was intrigued.

It was early February, and the cold air blanketed the cobbles with invisible ice. The shop window was dripping with condensation. James was wrapped in a thick overcoat and was wearing fine leather gloves and a woollen scarf. He trod carefully as he entered the shop and the bell rang.

The other woman in the shop greeted him. She did not interest him.

"Good morning, sir. You may not be aware, but we cater for ladies only."

James barely made eye contact. His attention remained on the quiet one.

"I am not here for custom. I wish to speak with that woman over there."

The shopgirl looked slightly confused. Then she too switched her attention.

"Sarah Ann, do you know this gentleman?" she asked.

"No, I do not, Ms. Ellen. What is your business, sir?"

James smiled and moved towards Sarah Ann.

"Please do not be alarmed. I wish only to speak with you for a few moments. Would that be agreeable?"

Ellen looked at her colleague for her approval. Sarah Ann nodded in the affirmative.

"It seems she is willing to spare you some minutes, sir. Please do not keep her occupied for too long. We are trying to run a business."

Ellen slunk off to the far corner of the shop, keeping one eye on this stranger. James edged closer to Sarah Ann.

"Sarah Ann? That is a rather charming name."

She offered a soft smile in response. "Thank you, sir," she replied in her light Northern lilt.

James stared at her intently, just smiling. "Forgive me, madam. I do not know my manners. My name is James Maybrick. I am a senior shipping clerk at a fine French brandy company. I work just a few yards from here. I have passed this shop on many occasions, and well, the most enchanting thing in the window is always you."

Sarah Ann blushed. "Whilst that is very kind of you say, sir. I would struggle to find that to be true."

"It is true. There is something about you I find interesting."

"Interesting? How could you? We don't know each other."

"I propose we change that. Why don't we take a walk along the Thames and become acquainted?"

"In this weather, Mr. Maybrick? I think we both would most certainly catch a chill!"

"Well, it would be worth it. I am a significant man in this city.

You would do well by being on my arm."

James knew he might have exaggerated his status a little. His ambitions were far greater than being a clerk for an old brandy merchant. The city was bursting with international merchants from all sorts of trades. A role more befitting of his ambitions would no doubt emerge soon.

Sarah Ann pondered in thought. James continued his sales pitch.

"I am also a great conversationalist and very charming. Indeed, I believe your mother would simply adore me!"

Sarah Ann laughed. "Well, you have sold me, Mr. Maybrick. You need not worry. My mother passed many years ago."

"I am sorry to hear that."

"Please don't be. It was a long time ago now. I still have family in Sunderland, but I am very much at home in London now."

"I did think your accent was not local. Being from the North myself, in my case Liverpool, perhaps that is why your spirit attracted mine?"

The young couple smiled at each other, and James then jolted back to reality.

"I am late for work! I must leave. We are taking that walk tomorrow after work. I shall meet you here at 5:00 p.m. I will expect you to be ready and waiting!" James darted towards the exit at pace.

"Well, Mr. Maybrick, I expect I shall see you then."

At the door, James pulled the tip of his hat down to bid farewell and left.

As he briskly trotted out into the frosty chill back towards the direction of the office, he sensed Sarah Ann was looking on. Now she was watching him through the window.

"She is mine!" he declared.

* * *

14 August 1868

Bromley St., Stepney, London

The room was small, and the air was dry. The chatter of passers-by was the only noise heard within the past five minutes. The silence between them was as thick as concrete.

James stood at the end of the bed. Sarah Ann had not moved since he entered the room. The curtains were closed, and she was wrapped in a quilt. The room was lit only by the flickering light of a candle almost extinct on the bedside table. This modest house had been the home for James and Sarah for a few years now. It was not theirs but shared with her aunt and her husband.

"Sara Ann, I know you are upset, but I have no choice."

More solid silence.

"I must return to Liverpool. My work dictates that I can no longer live in London. Besides, you will be far better suited to staying here with your aunt."

James had seen his career progressively improve over the past few years. After leaving the brandy business, he soon found himself specialised within the world of cotton. More than half of the world used British-made cotton cloth products. The advanced technologies developed from many years of linen and wool production had given Britain an industrial edge over its counterparts. James was now an emerging name within the industry. Now almost thirty, he had just accepted a position as a commercial clerk for a leading cotton merchant, based at Albany Hall in Liverpool.

Sarah Ann's wall of silence crumbled.

"Go then, James! Abandon your wife! Leave me behind like the damaged goods I appear to be!"

James straightened his back. "You must stop being so brutal on yourself, Sarah Ann. It is not your fault those children did not survive after birth."

James said the words to offer comfort, but he did not believe that at all. He entirely blamed her for their deaths. It was not because he wanted them to survive. That would mean being more committed to her. James was more surprised that the woman he had managed to spend the past eight years of his life with was so barren. She was weak physically and weak mentally. After each death, she would spend weeks on end in this state, curled up in her bed. James did not have the patience for such self-pity.

"Why can I not come with you?" she sobbed.

James had been over this a hundred times. The desperation and neediness she expressed sometimes could be immensely irritating.

"My piggy darling, we have discussed this. My work requires me to focus on the critical tasks at hand. You do not know anyone in Liverpool, and I will be working all hours. You will be far more comfortable in London with your family instead of being alone in a city with which you are unfamiliar. Besides, it would help if you had adequate time to recover from the losses you have experienced. I have arranged with your aunt to ensure you will be well kept for financially in my absence."

Sarah Ann added more concrete to the silent wall.

"It is not like it will be forever," added James. "I will be returning to London regularly for visits, and when everything is settled in Liverpool, I shall send for you."

James was looking forward to showing his mother how he had blossomed into a well-respected man of business. Michael's musical success was one thing, but the real mark of a man should be judged by the powerful company he kept. Professors of music would not be able to open the doors James could.

The wall tumbled again.

"You will forget me, James. I know you will. Why would you come back?"

James moved around to the side of the bed and got down on both of his knees. He looked directly at Sarah Ann. He gently stroked her face and spoke in a soft tone.

"You are my wife, piggy. You are the only woman that matters to me. I promise when things are right, I will come back for you. Do not despair. I promise I shall return."

They were not legally married. James did pay someone to

perform what looked like a marriage ceremony for all intents and purposes, but it was not in any way, shape, or form legal. It was convincing enough for Sarah Ann to believe it was. In turn, it was easy enough for her to convince her family. A modest ring and a charming tale, and she was his. Manipulation was a skill he had mastered since then.

Sarah Ann gave a gentle smile as James continued to stroke her face.

"You promise?"

"Oink oink—I promise!"

They both laughed. James got up from his knees and climbed under the blankets, fully clothed.

"What are you doing, James?"

He started to kiss her. She started to giggle as he put his hand under her chemise.

"My aunt, she will hear us!"

"I shall give you both something to remember me by then. Consider it a parting gift!"

James kicked off his shoes and pulled his trousers down to his ankles. Within seconds, he was inside her.

With his career in the ascendancy and the social circles starting to open up, it was simply not worth James putting at risk everything he had been working for to become public about Sarah Ann. He did care for her, of course. She was simple and asked for little, but clearly, she would not be suitable for the world he was carving out for himself.

As he gave Sarah Ann a leaving gift she would not forget, he could not help but be more aroused by the deception.

It made the honey all the sweeter.

PART 2

Killer Instinct

30 June 1870
Anfield Cemetery, Liverpool

On a crisp summer's morning at the end of June, the Maybrick brothers solemnly observed the coffin of their father, William, being lowered into the freshly dug grave. For a few moments, it was deftly silent, aside from a distant crow cawing.

The vicar drew in a large breath.

"We therefore commit his body to the ground, earth to earth, ashes to ashes, dust to dust, looking for that blessed hope when the Lord himself shall descend from heaven with a shout, with the voice of the archangel and with the trump of God, and the dead in Christ shall rise first."

Their mother, Susannah, of course, was not present, as was the custom. Anfield Cemetery was one of the newest in the area and was thoroughly modern. With three elegantly designed chapels and numerous entrance lodges, it was more than fitting to become the final resting place for their father.

The unassuming guilder and eldest brother, William, was present. He had opted for a simple life just like his namesake parent. He married at twenty-one and remained in Liverpool.

Then there was James, the recently returned influential

businessman with a decade of experience gained from London's beating heart of commerce. He was also a recent inductee to the St. George's Lodge of Freemasons, a prestigious accolade in itself. James was the first of the brothers to visit America.

Also at the grave was younger brother Michael. He too was successful, but in the arts. He was starting to travel extensively across the land with his work. Michael had always been fawned over by his mother because he could hold a tune and play the odd instrument, much to James's disdain.

In attendance too were the youngest brothers, Thomas and Edwin. The two of them had also found their way into the cotton trade; James would be quick to point out, less successfully so.

The vicar uttered the final words of the ceremony. Then, as prayers were offered by those present, James could not help but fix his gaze upon Michael.

How could our parents feel this so-called "artiste" had more to offer the world than I? A pigeon-livered choir boy who does not have what it takes to survive in the real world. Perhaps one day, I will commission him to write me a jolly little jig. It's about all he is useful for, he thought.

James had been back in Liverpool for almost two years. Michael's continued absence would only strengthen James's advantage with their mother. The sooner he disappeared again, the better.

Michael must have sensed his brother's stare. He made his way over to James as proceedings drew to a close and the crowd began to thin.

"Dear brother, isn't it with such sorrow we lose father this way?"

Michael asked.

James felt Michael had some nerve. Who paid for the care of their father when Michael was swanning around singing songs and tickling piano keys?

"Indeed, little brother, it is. Those of us who were able to be here with him until the very end still cannot believe he is gone."

Michael did not wait long to reply.

"Those of us who were able to share some of his best years with him, such as I, would be inclined to agree with you, brother."

James could feel a surge of anger rush through his veins, a feeling he had not had as strong since childhood towards his sibling. Such as when Michael told James that he was named after another brother called James, who had died in infancy. Michael had overheard his parents discussing it once. He did not hesitate to let James know that he was a mere replacement for another by the same name.

"Indeed, a sad loss for us all," James replied with teeth gritted.

This musical fool seemed to believe he held some equal status. If it weren't for the fact that his mother would be so upset, he would have no qualms in giving Michael a physical education on the subject of respect. It was clear to James he was long overdue. Providing such a lesson was not an option for now.

"We should return to the house. I'm sure Mother would wish to be furnished with the fullest details of the ceremony," Michael concluded.

James felt a sense of smug superiority over his brother. Michael should appreciate his place in the pecking order and remain there. It would not be a sensible ambition to challenge him.

With their father now gone, their mother would not always be around to defend precious Michael.

***

6 October 1874

Harbormaster Club, Norfolk, Virginia

Despite it being early October, James was impressed by the mild weather the city of Norfolk was experiencing. It was as fresh as spring. As he sipped at a straight bourbon, a light salty breeze gently caressed his skin. He sat on the outside deck of the private member's club overlooking the bustling port. It was dusk, and the boats were still thronging in and out. Some of those ships would be carrying his raw cotton back to Liverpool. James swelled with pride at his achievements.

A well-dressed man appeared at the table.

"Mr. Maybrick?"

James turned his head, then quickly stood up to shake his guest's hand.

"Mr. McClain. Please take a seat."

"Thank you," replied the American.

"What will you drink?"

"I shall have the same as you, sir."

James signalled the waiter to come over.

"Two bourbons!"

"Tell me, Mr. Maybrick, how are you enjoying Norfolk since your arrival?"

After sixteen years of lining the pockets of others, this was now his time to put his own needs first. It felt exciting. He was in America for good. James knew that setting up a branch office of Maybrick & Co. in Norfolk—the company he had formed with brother Edwin just three years prior—would be a masterstroke.

"I am finding it most enjoyable. What is there not to like?"

"Our city is very much enjoying a boom. The port, as you can see, has never been so busy. The recent Norfolk & Portsmouth Cotton Exchange opening has attracted many talented traders to the area, such as yourself. Our lodge has never had so many applications."

James had understood the value of having Masonic links and access to that network throughout his business life. Through this network, it was suggested he should open an office in the United States in the first place. Now he wanted to be firmly part of the local lodge. Therefore, he needed to be nominated as a member. Michael McClain was the worshipful master of the Norfolk Lodge. James was speaking with the right man.

"I am a proud Mason, Mr. McClain, and I have been a loyal and committed brother in England since I was a young man. I am a member of numerous lodges, all of which I do not doubt will endorse my application. I have nothing but respect for all of our ancient traditions."

"That is inspiring to hear, Mr. Maybrick. Our lodge is a chartered lodge with the Grand Lodge of Virginia, which has seen two of its past members become presidents of the United States. One of which was none other than George Washington. Should you be successful in joining our organisation, you will be amongst some of the most esteemed company our city, and indeed the state, has to offer."

"It would be nothing short of an absolute honour, Mr. McClain."

James collected social contacts like they were postage stamps. Being part of the Freemasons was like being given unfettered access to a post office.

"As you know, Mr. Maybrick, it is not my decision alone. However, I believe you would be a fine addition to the lodge, and I would have no hesitation in nominating you as a member. It shall be down to the other members to validate your application."

James knew how this worked. A nomination from the worshipful master was all but a cast-iron guarantee.

"I cannot ask for anything more, Mr. McClain, and I offer my immense gratitude for the privilege of your nomination."

The Mason smiled and sipped at his bourbon.

This exciting land of opportunity and pioneering spirit. Optimism was the overwhelming trait all Americans seemed to share. Only in a land like this could an engraver's son from Liverpool earn his fortune based on entrepreneurial endeavour alone. It was all rather very un-British, but James was never wedded to the idea of staunch patriotism.

Money, power, and status were far more attractive.

The two men sat in silence for a few moments, watching the ships come in and out of the harbour.

"Tell me, Mr. McClain, did you receive the contribution for the building work of the new Masonic Temple?"

"We did, Mr. Maybrick. We are very grateful for the generosity."

James smiled. He really did enjoy business.

Brothers would always look to make good men better.

* * *

9 March 1877

Howard's Brothel, Norfolk

Mary Howard was her name. The madam of the whorehouse where James found himself. The air in the brothel was thick with the scents of many perfumes. It was sickly sweet, like being dunked in a barrel of potpourri and sugar. It just about masked the smell of musty tobacco that also wafted through the large townhouse. James could hear an old piano clinking out a jolly tune. It was busy.

He had had a good day on the exchange. The trading season was drawing to a close, and business had been excellent. It was Friday. He was in a cheerful mood and ready to have some fun.

James had spent supper with some other traders in town. From there, he then went to a local members' club to continue the jollies. Most of his acquaintances left around 11:00 p.m. James was not ready for the night to end. So he ventured down to Howard's brothel to see where the night would take him.

Pretty intoxicated but still functioning, James knew what he wanted. He had decided he would finish the day by giving some little whore a taste of his power. She would thank him too.

The selection of whores this night was limited. James was yet to engage. Instead he continued to drink red wine whilst sitting comfortably in an overly flashy maroon leather chesterfield chair. He felt imperial. Tonight he would take his time. They must be deserving.

To be taught a lesson by Sir Jim should be treated the same as that of a privilege, he mused. *Do they not know who they are dealing with?*

He was no ordinary customer. He was supremely powerful, and they would get to feel his power as intimately as one possibly could.

I would desire to strangle one of the whores as I'm punishing her, he considered. *Watch the colour drain from the bitch's face as she took the full force of my power. How that would excite me so!*

He was quickly jolted back to reality by Mrs. Howard.

"My dear Mr. Maybrick, it is always a pleasure to make your acquaintance. It is a wonderful evening, is it not?"

James was not too pleased with being taken away from his dark inner thoughts. He quickly realised the situation required social graces.

"Indeed it is, Mrs. Howard. Much like the many ladies you have available."

Howard gave a broad smile. "As you well know, we very much

aim to please, Mr. Maybrick. Should any such lady require your attention, do not delay in alerting me so."

Howard then floated across the room to speak with another lost soul looking to kill boredom with elicit excitement. Then, from nowhere, appeared a whore he had never seen before. A redhead. Young, pretty, and stout. She looked like the type of whore who could handle what James had to offer. She would do very nicely.

"Mrs. Howard?"

James alerted the whore master. Within seconds she was sitting beside James on the chair next to his.

"Mr. Maybrick, which girl has caught your eye?"

James stared at this young woman and surveyed her like a lion would study an unsuspecting wildebeest. He had her in his sights and was ready to pounce.

"The redhead over there, how much?"

Howard briefly looked around and quickly spotted the focus of James's attention.

"Ah, yes, that is Sue-Ellen. Good choice. She is fairly new to us and comes with high recommendations. For her, we would require two dollars. Would that be agreeable?"

James didn't even attempt to haggle; his mind was set.

"It is, Mrs. Howard."

"Very well, I shall get her ready for you now."

Howard drifted over to the young auburn-haired girl. James watched on as she spoke with Sue-Ellen, who briefly looked over at James as agreement terms were explained. The girl flashed an awkward smile towards him before making her way to the numerous bedrooms on the upper levels of the house.

Howard returned to James.

"In five minutes, please proceed to room 4 on the first floor. Sue-Ellen will take care of you from there. As usual, please settle with the door upon your departure. Enjoy, Mr. Maybrick, but please be careful not to damage our goods. It's somewhat harder to sell bruised fruit."

That remark almost amused James.

"Mrs. Howard, I am a gentleman, and as such, she will be returned to you as sold."

James remained seated as Howard left. While he finished his drink, thoughts of what he would do and how hard thrilled him so much he could not help but smile. He was excited. This was going to be fun.

Sue-Ellen was almost certainly guaranteed not to return as sold.

* * *

18 June 1877

York St., Norfolk, Virginia

Blister-like but painless, the lesions around his manhood were spongy and uncomfortable.

James had noticed the numerous sores over a month before. He had hoped that nature would deal with the inconvenience. Nature did not deal with it. It had gotten progressively worse.

Concerned this could affect his virility, he knew he needed medical assistance. James knew Dr. Ward was also a fellow Mason. He felt that such an ailment required the kind of discretion that only a brother of the lodge could provide. Therefore, he believed Ward was a man that could be trusted and was fetched to attend to James's urgent need.

James was living with an American from Memphis by the name of Nicholas Bateson, and both men were very much enjoying the life that single and successful men employed. They shared a townhouse on York Street. Their servant, called Thomas, maintained the property, washed and pressed their clothes, and ensured his masters were fed their daily meals. James occupied the room at the very top of the stairs.

It was a little just after 10:00 a.m. when James heard the front doorbell sound from his bed. The servant answered the door and, after a brief exchange, led the doctor up the three flights of stairs towards his bedroom. After a couple of polite knocks on the door, James permitted them to enter.

"Yes, come!"

The door opened, and Dr. Ward entered. James and the doctor knew of each other, having frequented the many members' meetings the newly built Masonic Temple had held.

"Mr. Maybrick, it's good to see you again."

The physician took the wooden dressing table chair and moved it towards the bed, where he sat.

"I wish the circumstances were different, Doctor. Nonetheless, I do appreciate you attending to me at such short notice."

"No problem at all, Mr. Maybrick. So how may I be of assistance?"

James creaked his neck and released a slight cough.

"You see, Doctor, I believe I have something quite unusual in a place quite . . . private."

Realising that James was referring to his genitals, Dr. Ward moved swiftly to reassure his patient.

"I feel I must stress that as your doctor, as well as a fraternal brother, anything that should arise from today's examination will be held in the strictest of confidence. It will never be public. My job is not to judge one's morals, Mr. Maybrick, but to assist as best as I can in ensuring the correct remedial care is offered."

With this information in hand, James began to relax a little.

"I appreciate the vow of discretion."

"I will need to see the problem. Would you mind lifting your gown to the waist? I will then move the bedding gently down."

James did as requested, and the bedsheets were moved slowly down the bed by the medical man. James focused intently on the picture on the wall of the far side of the room.

After what seemed an eternity, the doctor examined the infected area and began lifting the sheets back up to give his patient his modesty back.

"Well, Mr. Maybrick, I'm afraid it is not good news."

"What is it? Please do not coat the truth in sugar."

The doctor took a deep breath.

"You have what is known by many as the 'French disease.'"

Maybrick contorted his face in response.

"The what?"

"In medical terms, you have contracted syphilis. The condition is spread when a diseased woman infects a man through the act of procreation. There is no cure, and the best thing we can do is prescribe you a mix of medicines and hope they can reduce any further symptoms, or at the very least delay them."

James snapped.

"Fucking whore bitch!"

"Mr. Maybrick, I would advise against any form of overexcitement at present."

The doctor opened his bag.

"The challenge with this disease is that whilst we know there is no known cure, the symptoms could be somewhat erratic. There will be times you will feel fine, and there will be times when you will not."

"What type of symptoms?"

"Well, it varies wildly depending on the severity of the infection. It could range from blotches of the skin to paralysis to insanity and even death itself. There is no way of knowing how bad the infection may be. I will leave you some medicines that you can start taking immediately. I will also supply you with a prescription. Now, I cannot issue a prescription with no prior reason. I would be in dire trouble if I did. I wish to state on your medical record that you have contracted malaria with your permission. Would this be agreeable?"

James was still seething over the news that one of Howard's whores had given him this disgusting disease. It took a few moments before he answered.

"Of course, Dr. Ward, whatever you feel is most wise."

The doctor left a bottle of mercury tablets and Fowler's solution on his bedside table.

"Now, Mr. Maybrick, please take one mercury tablet three times a day with meals and no more than five drops of Fowler's solution in a day. I will write you a prescription for quinine to support the malaria diagnosis. We will assess your condition again in two weeks."

James was lost in his thoughts. The doctor cleared his throat in a bid to break James's daydream. It worked.

"Sorry. Thank you, Doctor."

James then rang the servant's bell above his bed.

"Thomas will escort you to the front door, Dr. Ward. Once again, your discretion is most appreciated."

The doctor nodded. He then stood up, picked up his bag, and returned the chair to its original position.

"For what it is worth, Mr. Maybrick, you are not the first person in Norfolk to have contracted this ailment, and I very much doubt you will also be the last."

It doesn't feel much like comfort, thought James.

At that moment, the servant arrived to usher the doctor back downstairs. James stared at the medicines on his bedside table. He was now infected from whores and would have to take these ghastly medicines for who knew how long.

He couldn't help but think of the phrase he once read in one of the many periodicals he consumed. It read something along the lines of "A night in Venus could lead to a lifetime on mercury."

The planets had not aligned today.

* * *

13 March 1880

SS Baltic, *Atlantic Ocean*

It was early evening aboard the SS *Baltic*. The ship was the height of modern luxury travel. The spacious berths included a servant bell and steam heating.

This is a much more civilised way to travel, thought James.

He was pretending to enjoy the company of the characterful General John G. Hazard in the grand saloon. The room was richly carpeted throughout, with numerous stained-glass windows running from floor to ceiling. Large mirrors adorned the walls to give the impression of more space. The generous skylight above poured in purple-tinted rays of the setting sun.

James had taken a considerable amount of arsenic earlier to keep his senses sharp. He wasn't sure how much he had taken since coming aboard. James was continuously surprised by how much of the stuff he could tolerate. Since his "malaria" diagnosis, he had become more and more reliant on this toxic powder. Its potency kept him sharp and made him feel physically better. At times even invincible.

It was the second day of this six-day trip. James was intrigued and bored by the general in equal measure. He had come across him earlier in his career during the formation of the New Orleans Cotton Exchange. It happened by chance that both men boarded the same steamer from New York to Liverpool.

The general had an endless repertoire of battlefield stories from his career fighting for the Yankees, particularly during the Civil War. It was, however, his subsequent career in the American cotton industry that James had always respected more. Those battles were far more interesting to him. He felt that on a social level, both were great men of equal stature. It was proper that he should spend time in such eminent company. Always the opportunist, James believed that perhaps the general could be of use to his ambitions at some point in time.

Perhaps what James hadn't bargained for was for that moment to arrive sooner rather than later. Amid another anecdote around army manoeuvres, appearing from nowhere were two well-dressed ladies James instantly sensed were of American high society. The two men stood up in respect as the ladies approached their table.

"Now, General, you wouldn't be telling tall tales about the war again, would you?"

The general took her hand and gave it a respectful kiss. "Well, Baroness, you know me. I am a man of honour and courage. No tales of mine suffer from a fear of heights. Please forgive me. My guest and associate, Mr. James Maybrick Esquire—a prominent trader in the cotton industry. James, this is Baroness von Roques."

The baroness gave James a courteous nod.

"It's a pleasure to meet you, Baroness."

She then proceeded to introduce the younger woman, "This is my daughter, Florence Chandler. We are presently on our way to Paris, where we have a residence."

Impressed by the stature of the women, James immediately sensed an opportunity to add to his network of socially beneficial contacts.

"Why don't you ladies join us? I'm sure the general would have no objection?"

James awaited the general's response.

"Indeed not. It would, of course, be a pleasure as always."

The baroness smiled at the men.

"Well, it would simply be the absolute height of rudeness to reject such an invitation now, wouldn't it?"

With that, the two men pulled out a chair for each of the ladies to sit down at their luxurious Italian marble table. As the group settled, a waiter arrived for their drinks order. James decided to take the initiative.

"The general and I will have bourbon, and please bring a bottle of your finest champagne for our guests."

The opportunist in him was taking over. This could be potentially lucrative one way or another.

"Why, thank you, Mr. Maybrick."

"Please, I will hear nothing of it. It was not every day I get to enjoy such illustrious company."

The baroness launched immediately into a conversation.

"Florie's late father, William Chandler, was mayor of Mobile, Alabama. Being a cotton man yourself, Mr. Maybrick, you will, of course, appreciate the city's importance in the cotton trade?"

The waiter started to put the drinks on the table.

"Indeed I do, Baroness. Ports such as Mobile play an important part in my business interests. Your former husband must have been well admired to achieve such a prestigious status?"

James sipped at his freshly poured crystal tumbler of bourbon.

"He was. His family were very influential in the city. When William died suddenly, the family quickly spread some rather nasty and idle gossip, which I, for one, can only assume is reflective of the deep-seated fear of the North that many Southerners seem to harvest so readily."

The general decided to push a little. "With the greatest respect, Baroness, did you not then go on to marry a Confederate captain after your first husband's passing?"

The baroness was unfazed. "That's correct, General. I did indeed. Captain du Barry was a great support to the children and me during that difficult time. A fresh start in Georgia was good for all of us."

She paused to sip her champagne.

"However, it was not long before Frank was requested to represent the cause in Europe. So we took a Blockade Runner out of Savannah, and just as we got to the Bahamas, he became ill very quickly and died. For one husband to die on me so suddenly is unfortunate. Two? Well, that is simply the worst of all luck, I can assure you, Mr. Maybrick!"

"Indeed."

James was increasingly curious.

"May I enquire, Baroness, if I may be as so bold? How does one navigate such incomprehensible tragedy?"

The baroness took a moment before replying, "Mr. Maybrick, one does not have a choice in such matters. We must continue in the belief that God Almighty himself has something better planned for us."

James knew at that very moment that Baroness von Roques was not all that she seemed. She was a formidable woman in many ways.

"Of course, my most recent marriage to the baron was very much a welcome event in mine and the children's lives."

I'm sure it was, James thought. He wondered where the baron was.

"May I ask, is the baron accompanying you on this voyage?"

The baroness shuffled in her seat. "He is not. He was travelling across Africa at present. I'm sure our paths will cross again soon."

James had never heard of something as quite extraordinary as the tales of many husbands the baroness told. Either her luck was as unfortunate as she claimed, or perhaps this woman had done whatever was needed to survive. If so, the level of ruthlessness involved in such endeavours was hugely intriguing to James.

"We have yet to find a place where we can lay our family foundations for the future. Finding one place where we can all settle is proving to be harder than anticipated."

The baroness placed a hand on Florence's arm.

"My son and I are very much at home in Paris. Florie has never really expressed a preference, have you?" The baroness directed her focus towards her daughter.

"Indeed, Mama, I'm happy if you are so."

James hadn't taken much notice of Florence until now. She was not unattractive. She had fresh, rosy cheeks and a slightly pale complexion; rich, dark-red curly locks; and a fine figure. Young, but that was not always a bad thing. He soon found himself imagining her in the bedroom doing all manner of things.

The baroness quickly broke his fantasy.

"Tell me, Mr. Maybrick, do you have any children?"

After a slight hesitation, James responded, "Alas, I do not, Baroness. I am a bachelor. My work kept me far too preoccupied with such pursuits. However, I am acutely aware that I should perhaps start thinking about my legacy sooner rather than later. As your history has shown, life can be taken away quite abruptly."

The baroness offered a wry smile. "Well, aren't you a rare curiosity? A successful and handsome businessman who is still not yet wed?"

James quickly picked up the inference that perhaps there was a more obvious reason for such a circumstance. He wanted to debunk any such notions of his masculinity promptly.

"It is no more than simply having not found the right woman yet."

After a few moments of silence, James could sense the baroness was thinking intently.

"Mr. Maybrick, would you be as ever so kind as to escort Florence to the upper deck for some fresh air? I feel some sea air would do her a world of good. Perhaps even take some time to get to know one another a little?"

Florence shot her mother a look of disdain that James did not miss. The baroness shot an equally bold look back.

"It would be an honour and pleasure to do so."

With that, Florence resigned herself and quickly adapted to this newly created situation her mother had crafted.

"Shall we, Mr. Maybrick?"

James smiled. "Please, call me Jim, Ms. Chandler."

James got up from the table, walked over to Florence's seat, and pulled out her chair for her in chivalrous custom. As the pair linked arms and headed for the nearby staircase, James thought this could be the start of something most gratifying. He always knew the general would deliver at some stage, and becoming part of American high society could now be within reach.

It was all very butter upon bacon, but James was not afraid of the taste of excess.

* * *

1 May 1880

Mount Pleasant, Liverpool

This room was small but well maintained. Sitting on a wooden chair by the bed, James found himself staring out of the window. He watched a tiny sparrow perch itself on a branch of a silver birch. The curtains were slightly drawn to keep any bright shards of light at bay, but he could still see the stationary bird. The air inside smelled of lavender. All the Maybrick brothers were here. James's mother had just died, and he felt nothing.

Michael knelt at the bedside, holding his dead mother's hand against his face, and started to sob.

"Dearest Mama, your grace and wit will be sorely missed by all who knew you."

James now stared at Michael. It was mildly interesting that he should have a completely different view of their mother. James would not be missing Susannah. She was nothing but a bitch to him.

William came over and placed this hand on Michael's shoulder as he continued to sob like a baby. He always was such a baby. James looked around and noted Thomas and Edwin behaving appropriately—standing upright with no ounce of emotion. The correct way to behave on such occasions.

"I shall call for the doctor," asserted Thomas as he left the room.

Michael's sobs were starting to subside. After a few moments, he placed his mother's hand back on her chest, stood up, leaned over, and kissed her on the cheek.

"Sleep well, Mama."

James almost felt a wave of vomit gush up from his stomach. This outpouring of emotion was very unmanly, but James always had his suspicions that Michael was not a typical alpha male. He was a showman. Today he was giving all present a royal performance. James felt obliged to offer something.

"God rest her soul," croaked James.

Two months earlier, not long after James disembarked from the steamer from New York, he had come to this same boarding house. He'd informed his mother of his intention to marry an eighteen-year-old Southern belle with links to American high society. He naturally assumed that she would be pleased. It was quickly made apparent that she was far from being so.

Unknown to James, his mother was aware of his relationship with Sarah Ann Robertson. How she knew of this and for how long, he did not know himself. James suspected that Edwin, the only brother who knew of Sarah Ann, must have told Michael, and he, in turn, ran blabbing to their mother.

Susannah made it clear that she thought James's behaviour was immoral.

"That poor woman in London believes she is your wife! All that creature has already suffered, and you plan to add even more woe and sorrow into her pitiful situation? Have you no heart? I sometimes wonder if you are even capable of any genuine affection for anyone or anything. I'm ashamed that a son of mine can behave in such a cruel and selfish manner. I am disgusted."

Her words still rang loud in James's ears as he stared at her lifeless body in front of him.

However, he would have to admit that the timing of her death was fortunate. The wedding date was set for just a few months from now. Proceedings would have been slightly awkward if his mother planned to be difficult over the whole affair. Such concerns existed no more.

Michael took a handkerchief from his inside jacket pocket and wiped away a few stray tears from his cheeks.

"I wish to handle the arrangements for her funeral," asserted Michael. "I trust this is agreeable with you all."

All the brothers presented various indications of approval, except for James.

"Are you sure that is wise, Michael?"

Michael was slightly taken aback by the comment. "Whatever do you mean?"

James straightened his back in his chair and gently clasped his hands on his lap. "Mother's death has affected you rather profoundly. Would taking on such extra stress be wise? I only ask as a brother concerned for his brother."

Michael had heard this melody many times from James. An attempt to undermine and belittle him. James would not get any advantage over him today.

"Well, James, as much as I find your concern rather touching, I am competent and able to handle such a thing. You need not worry for me, dear brother."

James smiled. "Very well, that is settled."

Michael straightened his jacket, patted William on the shoulder, and left the room.

After their father passed, Susannah's drinking had escalated. She had always enjoyed a glass of sherry. Indeed, of late, it would have been rarer to see sober. As such, she was much faster and looser with her tongue. She was offering home truths daily like they were peppermints. Many of which were directly aimed at James.

Michael could take care of the funeral arrangements. James never quite understood why she had such hate for him. At least he survived, unlike Alfred and the James who came before him. It wasn't his fault they were too weak to survive. Perhaps there was something to the idea that weak women produced weak children.

His mother deserved some credit though; she did give birth to him after all. She wasn't totally useless, but he was glad the bitch was now dead.

James sensed an opportunity to be the new head of the family. He must surely be the natural successor. He had no concerns that William, Thomas, and Edwin would not fall into line. Michael might take a bit more applied pressure.

Michael would soon learn to accept his place in the new order one way or another.

James felt free as a bird.

* * *

19 July 1880

St. James's Church, London

It was a bright day. The sun was toasting the London pavement, and the birds were chirping in chorus, befitting for the day that was in store.

St. James's in Piccadilly was a pretty but modest church by West End standards. In the heart of the capital, its location set it apart from the others that could have been considered. Its fashionable setting befitted such a momentous occasion.

James waited impatiently outside with his best man, Michael. Both men were wearing their perfectly tailored wedding suits, with the only difference being that James sported a navy long-tail jacket, while Michael wore a more subtle grey tone. They were both wearing white waistcoats, navy neckties, and lavender doeskin trousers. The sun's rays bounced off their shiny black leather shoes.

They greeted the guests as they arrived one by one. James felt a sense of opportunity. The same tingling feeling he had had when entering America for the first time. Would he not be once again enjoying the fruits of this great land this very night?

James was invigorated. Why would he not be? He was about to marry a woman over twenty years his junior. It would also give him access to some of the most sought-after social contacts in America. The baroness had indicated that President John Quincy Adams was an ancestor. He was graduating to a whole new level of social class. Many reasons to be chipper. Now that the potential bump in the road with his mother was no longer a concern, he was bullish about his future life with Florence Chandler. That deserved a quick pick-me-up of medicine before coming outside.

James was acutely aware that not everyone was so positive about this marriage. Michael, for one—but he had dismissed it as jealousy. James was constantly dismayed that his younger brother could gain access to some of the most exclusive clubs and lodges in London yet James's influence and affluence could not acquire equal status. Now the tables were turned. James was entering the high society of America, and Michael could not bear to see James rise. Michael could only dream about these social circles. James's sense of smugness and superiority over his brother had indeed returned in abundance over the past few months. America was proving to cater to all his ambitious desires.

Michael had indicated to James that he felt his older brother was making a fool of himself. He also claimed he was a little embarrassed asking others for favours to get a local church to facilitate this wedding. It had all made him feel rather uncomfortable. James was from Liverpool, and Michael felt this was all a little excessive. James thought it was necessary and imperative. He wanted the baroness to believe that James Maybrick Esquire, son of a gentleman, was a man who had the best contacts in London. Except they were Michael's contacts. James never let such frivolous details concern him. Perception was everything.

With all the guests now in the church, James and Michael were given the signal that Florence's carriage was close. It was time. The two men entered the small ecclesiastical building and ambled their way towards the altar. The church had been decorated elegantly with the freshest flowers adorning both sides of the aisle. The gentle scent of orange blossom tickled James's nose.

Meanwhile, Florence was just outside the entrance with her brother, Holbrook.

"I fear I am making a terrible mistake, dear brother. I do not love this man."

Holbrook took a deep breath. "I understand that, sister, but this is not about love. Those quaint notions of such a thing are left to fairy tales. This union is one of convenience. Mama has been very clear. It would be best if you had a financial insurance policy. This marriage will provide you with that. You are a woman now, which means you must do your duty as such. Surrender those childlike ideas. Embrace the opportunity this provides you. It is the best option for you now after, well, you know . . ." Holbrook ended his sentence abruptly.

"Say it, goddamn it! After I gave birth at sixteen years old? That is what you meant. Don't let the cat hold your tongue, Holbrook!"

Florence began to cry. Holbrook swiftly took out a handkerchief from inside his jacket and wiped away his sister's tears.

"Beautiful Florie, hush, I do not mean to cause you upset or distress, but you have a chance to make something of your life. I care only for your well-being."

Florence started to settle down. After a few moments, she regained her composure.

"Very well. If this is to be my fate, then so be it." She took a series of deep breaths before linking her brother's arm. "I am ready now."

For what seemed like an eternity, James waited for the arrival of his American bride. Then suddenly the grand organ burst into song. It was Pachelbel's *Canon in D major*. James knew the time had come. He had not been in any way nervous. That remained so. He thought that perhaps there should have been some feeling that would have stimulated him, but it had not arrived. No matter—this was business on a personal level.

Florence glided her way to the altar. With the absence of her father, it was her brother who was giving her away. She was head to toe in pleated satin and white lace. The dress was made at the exclusive House of Worth in Paris. No expense was spared for this bride. An exercise in ostentation. It would only suit to boost his credentials with his new extended family. An investment James believed would pay dividends long-term.

He could not help but think about the great royal weddings of the past. The merging of great houses that came together to create a dynasty. This could be one such dynasty.

As he loudly said his vows with gusto, his mind wandered to a darker place.

"I, James Maybrick, take you, Florence Chandler, to be my wife to have and to hold from this day forward, for better or for worse, for richer and for poorer, in sickness and in health, to love and to cherish, and I promise to be faithful to you until death parts us."

All the time he uttered these words, he thought of taking her in the way he loved to take all women. Tonight, she would experience the whole Sir Jim experience. He had not had a virgin since Sarah Ann.

Licking his lips, his anticipation for blood and tears was tantalising.

PART 3

Evil Walks

22 August 1884
Beechville, Liverpool

The sun lay over Liverpool like a warm blanket. James sat alone in the dining room, nursing a china cup of breakfast tea. Despite the comfort he found himself in, the sense of loss suffocated him. He somehow found himself back in the city where he started.

The beautiful house he now lived in was rented but was in an affluent location. James had known the Janion family for many years. He was to have married Matilda Janion at one stage, but it was not quite the union of status he was aiming to achieve. However, the two remained friends over the years. She had since married and become Mrs. Briggs. This was her house.

As he took a slow sip of his warm tea, careful to avoid drenching his moustache, he stared at the letter he had just finished writing to the Norfolk Cotton Exchange to announce his resignation. That was that—his American dream was officially over. The Maybrick business would continue in America with Edwin now living the life James already sorely missed. The life he had been building for the past decade was no more.

James felt strangled with disappointment. Life was now achingly pedestrian. His grand visions of the future had not materialised.

The business side was satisfactory enough. It was right to leave Norfolk as soon as coal became the dominant commodity, but was he right to leave America altogether? The sensible thing was to focus on his business back in Liverpool. His married life, however, was far from satisfactory.

Deception was a skill Caroline von Roques had mastered in her years of many husbands. The family had no money, no valuable connections, and minimal land. To make matters worse, the woman he'd married was damaged goods. James was sold faulty merchandise. You could not return these goods. Worst of all, it seemed Michael had been right. James was a fool. These parasites needed James more than he needed them. He had been hoodwinked.

James knew from the wedding night that all was not right with Florence. She was not a virgin. He knew Sarah Ann was because she had bled when they consummated. Florence did not.

James recalled how he challenged her immediately afterwards.

"You are not pure, are you, Florie?"

He remembered how long she took to reply, lying on her side with her back to him.

Eventually, she croaked her response, "No. No, I am not. My first love was a boy from Atlanta when we lived with Frank. Our passions had overcome us."

There was another pause.

"I was with child, and I had the baby. I had to give it up. Mama said it was for the best."

James got up from the bed, grabbed an empty champagne flute from his bedside table, and threw it against the opposite wall. Florence remained unmoved in the bed, still with her back to him. His face was beetroot red.

"Neither you nor you whoring mother thought it pertinent to tell me this before we got married?" he roared. "No, of course not. Why would you? Scheming bitches looking for a quick shilling, like gutter whores! Let me tell you right here and right now, Florence, you will not be getting a goddamn penny from me. You can tell that to your fucking whore of a mother as well!"

James put on his clothes in a rush and left the hotel room, slamming the door behind him.

After a day or two to calm down and reassess the situation, James felt he would give his young wife another chance. They met for dinner, and Florence apologised. There were was no conspiracy to mislead him, she assured him. She also claimed she had become besotted with him. He knew this was not true, but he was happy to let her pander to his ego. Only he, the baroness, Holbrook, and Florence knew of her secret.

"Florie, you must never speak of that child to another soul. You must promise me!"

Florence agreed.

Initially, James decided to split their time equally between Norfolk and Liverpool. For a while, a change of scenery did help. The more Florie obliged to demonstrate her obedience to him, the more he would offer her security and comfort. In many ways, this type of handling gave James greater control over his young wife. He rather liked that power. James insisted he monitor all her letters to her family, and she obliged. This level of influence he enjoyed.

Then, she provided James with a son. James Chandler Maybrick was born. Florie had proven herself useful after all by giving him a son and heir. Earlier this year, they decided that it was best to call just one country their home. Liverpool and England it was to be.

Now they were here in this house. As comfortable as it was, it could not be any more reflective of suburban monotony. The repetitiveness of routine that he had hoped to avoid was now in full flow. James had become just another grey man with another grey life. The medicine was one of the few things remaining that offered him any form of excitement. His desire to keep pushing his resistance levels continued to inspire and surprise him in equal measure.

James considered paying Sarah Ann a visit in London. That might be interesting. Florie had avoided her wifely duties where she could, much to his disdain.

To feel anything other than the numbness of boredom would be better than this.

* * *

2 December 1887

Beechville, Liverpool

* * *

James was aroused. He didn't quite know why, but he was. He could still hear her crying across the landing. Something about her pain was particularly delicious. Even when he was punishing those whores until they cried, the sensation was not as good as this. Her tears were making his desires tingle, and he was doing everything he could to not act upon them.

The argument they had just a few moments before was the most intense they had ever had. Florie had found out about Sarah Ann. She didn't know her name, but she knew he kept a mistress in Liverpool. James was not about to furnish her with the full historical details.

The dullness of every day had been too much for James. On a trip down to London three years earlier, he had met up again with Sarah Ann. Initially, it had been quite awkward. James knew he could use the excuse for business in America for much of his absence. He then used the malaria story, gifted to him by Dr. Ward back in Norfolk, and expanded upon it. In his version, he had been suffering severe episodes of paralysis regularly. This seemed to garner sympathy from Sarah Ann. After a while, it was like old times. They reminisced. Before the day was over, James booked them into a hotel where they consummated their reunion.

James was once again living a duality. He was enjoying the deception, and once again, he had the edge. Two women, unaware of each other. Each believed him to be the dutiful husband. Suddenly the grey days were not so grey. Unbeknown to Florie, he had rented a house on the west side of Liverpool near his office.

He had set up a small but comfortable home for him and Sarah Ann. She had fallen pregnant twice since she moved to Liverpool. Of course, like in London, her barren body could not sustain them. But this time, she reacted with much more acceptance than before, much to James's relief.

Health was something that did genuinely concern James. It was not all fiction. The bouts of chills and burns he was getting throughout his body were still quite bad. The more medicine he took, the more the symptoms persisted. The doctors were useless. The level of arsenic he could now tolerate was more significant than any other man he knew. He dared not tell anyone the truth of just how much he could handle. No one would believe him.

It was late on Friday night, and James had been in the city at his club. He had consumed a fair amount of whisky and arsenic. Florie accosted him in his bedroom as he was undressing for bed. She told him she knew all about his mistress. A friend Florie did not name said they saw them together the previous week in Liverpool. She asked if that was where he was tonight. He did not answer.

"Is this the way your wife, mother to your two children, should be treated, James? Publicly humiliated by her husband?"

She was apoplectic with rage. James was not going to let this all go one way. It was about time she showed some feistiness. He was excited.

"Well, perhaps if you opened your legs more, you would not drive me to such things!"

For that comment, he received a vase thrown at him. It missed.

James was feeling energetic. The last dose of medicine had given him a significant boost.

"You want to get physical, Florie? I can get very physical, very quickly."

James started to undo his waistcoat buttons. It was at this point Florence fled the room. He tried to grab her as she sprinted out through the door and into her room across the landing. James raced after her and could hear the lock click behind her. He banged on her door.

"You forget, Florence, this is my house. They are my children. The dress on your back is mine. Everything you own is mine. You are mine. I do as I please when I please. Don't you ever forget that!"

James could hear her sobbing hard on the other side. He smirked.

After a moment, he moved within an inch of the door and began to whisper, "Florie, my darling. You chose to have separate bedrooms. Such decisions come at a price. If you do not like the cost, then you know what you must do."

He retreated to his room. Listening to his young wife crying uncontrollably, James was feeling once again all-powerful. He sat at the chair in front of his dresser and looked at himself in the mirror.

He was smiling from ear to ear.

*　*　*

3 March 1888

Battlecrease House, Liverpool

It was a beautiful spring afternoon. The air was filled with scents of the garden, earthly cut grass and sweet chrysanthemums.

It was the first one at their new home called Battlecrease House. Another rented property, but that did not concern James. It was a setting befitting his status.

The children ran around the vast back garden under the watchful gaze of Nurse Yapp. They even had a small lake and a couple of peacocks roaming the grounds. James was pleased to see the children so happy. Florence too was seemingly in better spirits these days. She wasted no time directing the staff to rearrange the furniture and decor more to her liking. Battlecrease was a significantly larger property than the last, and finally, James was starting to feel a genuine sense of achievement.

He sat in his wrought-iron chair on the patio and sipped on some freshly made tea.

What man would not wish for such a life? he pondered.

James's mind wandered to the idea of playing cricket. It would not be long until the new season started. Being so close to the club could also bring more social engagement opportunities. Perhaps even persuade some of the more illustrious figures from the exchange to venture this side of the River Mersey. He wondered if "Mr. and Mrs. Hammersmith" would likely venture this far east of the Wirral. Probably unlikely. They spent most of their leisure life with the Wirral Hunt.

James enjoyed giving people funny nicknames. "Mr. Hammersmith" was George Bridge—a senior member of the exchange. James resented how his colleagues fawned over George Bridge, credited for importing luxurious Egyptian cotton. He got lucky. Still, despite his distaste for the man and his wife, James had to be part of his circle in some form. On numerous occasions, James had tried to insert himself into George's social calendar, only to be seemingly thwarted at every turn by his wife, Eleanor—the bitch!

James knew she was fond of Florie. Perhaps his young wife could defrost the ice queen a little. He really should be more involved with the hunt. Unfortunately, despite being a keen rider and a club member, James did not show his face there as much as perhaps he should. Hunting foxes seemed relatively trivial compared to real life.

The combination of medicine and sunshine made James feel amorous. Perhaps he would visit Florie tonight. It was about time she engaged in her wifely duties. It had been far too long. She owed him after all he had done for her lately.

Maybe she would fight him off. That would only serve to make him enjoy it even more.

* * *

21 March 1888

Battlecrease House, Liverpool

*　*　*

James was semi-naked in the bathroom, having just commenced his daily wash routine. It had taken him by complete surprise, but it was there. He knew exactly what it was. The same soft bubbles of skin that had been gone for almost eleven years were now back on his manhood.

A volcanic rush of anger surged through every sinew of his being. The eruption came. He could not contain it. James let out a massive roar of rage and smashed the mirror he was looking at into a hundred pieces with his fist.

Within seconds there was a knock at the bathroom door. It was Nurse Yapp.

"Mr. Maybrick, is anything the matter, sir?"

Slowly the flood of rage dispersed as he clung to the bathroom sink, head bowed down. He did not reply.

Again came Yapp, "James, do you require assistance?"

After a few deep breaths, he regained his composure and stood up straight.

"No, Alice. I'm fine. I just cut myself shaving."

Yapp was not convinced. "Very well, sir, I shall leave you be."

James knew what it was. It was the same wretched disease he had back in the days of Norfolk. He had only been with Florence and Sarah Ann of late. For all of Sarah Ann's flaws in keeping her offspring alive, James knew that he had complete and utter dominance over her. She was not the issue. So that left one.

He sat down on a nearby chair.

"The whoring bitch!" he growled.

No wonder he was not feeling his best over the past few days. His slut of a wife had passed on the dirty pox. No doubt letting herself be taken by one or more of the young bucks sniffing around her lately. After all that he had done for her, this was how the bitch repaid him.

"I need more medicine."

He knew his physician would not increase his dosage without reason. James wished this to remain private. He did not know if he could trust his present doctor. James could not bear this information ever finding its way to the numerous lodges or clubs where he was a member. The subject of ridicule and amusement, he refused to be. He would need to find a supply himself.

As for that treacherous bitch, she would need to be taught a lesson. Having a child so young should have been all the evidence he needed to know that his wife was just another whore. Why did he not act then? He was too Samaritan. He was taking pity on the fact that she was so damaged. And this was his reward?

In the end, all whores were the same. They did whatever it took. Once they smelled the money on you, they would infect you one way or another.

"Oh, how the world would be better with fewer whores!" he considered.

He would be lying if he were to deny that such illicit behaviour did not also thrill him. Who was this whore master that had turned his wife's head?

"I would love to see the look in his eyes as I punish the bitch as she has never been punished before," he imagined.

James hadn't realised he was grinning.

*　*　*

28 March 1888

The Old Post Office, Liverpool

"Absolute whore!" James muttered in anger before taking a swift gulp of gin.

He sat alone at a worn-down table in this small city public house. Dingy, dark, and deserted, it was a comfortable and familiar spot. James had been coming to the place now known as the Old Post Office since he was young. Right now, James needed familiar.

The bitch was out there with her new whore master.

Nurse Yapp had given James information that Florence had an appointment to meet someone in the nearby Whitechapel district for a coffee. He left work at noon and marched over to the area to see if he could spot his young wife with her illicit lover. It did not take long before he caught sight of them—laughing whilst they drank their coffee. They were laughing at James, no doubt. How dared they laugh at him!

James did not wish to see more. He shuffled the short distance down to this place for refreshment.

Who was this man she had the gall to be so open with? He looked like a man with money. An older man. Naturally, that was her type. The scheming bitch. James would wager she would have dropped her drawers at the first sign of money. The whore would have made it far too easy for him. No doubt she offered herself to him on a plate. Pathetic.

James felt the only comfort right now coming from the idea that her new whore master might well be suffering from the same disease she gave him. He smiled.

"Even the sweetest fruits can turn sour," he considered.

The mother was a whore; of course, the apple would not fall far from the tree. James's mind was fuzzy. He was tired of whores. Whores were no more than just diseased animals. He was extremely tired of this damaged whore. Whores were an infestation. With any infestation, you needed the most potent remedies. A rat-catcher would be lauded and appreciated for cleaning the world of such vermin.

So many whores.

* * *

14 April 1888

Horwich, Greater Manchester

Horwich was in the middle of nowhere. James was tired of visiting these tiny towns that somehow shoehorned their place into the general Cottonopolis area. A phrase James detested anyway. On this particular visit, he had come to speak with a small mill about their desire for a cheaper supply of raw materials. Despite it being a

Saturday, he was pretty glad to be away from home.

The volume the proprietor was suggesting was pitiful to James. He had found himself incredibly bored by such meetings. To make matters worse, he was seeking a credit arrangement, which irked James even more.

The weather was cold and wet. Manchester could be rather dreary at times. Much like Liverpool. James spent the previous weekend in Manchester city centre with his brother Thomas. He had seen a number of whores walking the streets and was very tempted to act on his impulses. The medicine had made him strong, but he had not yet the courage to act. This weekend, even though the pains were back, things felt a little different.

Once the meeting concluded, James could not muster the urgency to return home. Despite the depressing weather and location, it was infinitely better than going back. Things at Battlecrease were arctic. His illness led to him taking much more medicine, but it was not reliable. The constant swing between pain and power was happening daily. Now his nerves were becoming affected.

The move into the new house did not solve their problems. Florie had whored herself out and given him the dreaded disease again. She was also overspending, unaware of James's knowledge of such. A whore only cared for money. The bitch thought she was cleverer than him.

"We shall see who is the clever one!" he contemplated.

James asked the mill owner which hotel would suit his wife for a weekend retreat. He informed him of the Crown Hotel. So James decided he would stay overnight and see if the town got any more attractive at night. He checked himself into the Crown, which was just a ten-minute walk from the train station. He ventured into the station as he passed to buy his ticket for the morning. A night in "Whore Itch" it would be. How very apt.

He checked in and was shown to his room on the upper level. It was a simple room. A modest but comfortable-looking double bed dominated the room. It had a large window that overlooked the main junction outside. He had everything he needed. James then decided he would take an afternoon nap to revitalise the senses.

James awoke from his slumber just as dusk was luring the sun into its grasp. He checked his pocket watch on the bedside table. It was just after 4:00 p.m.—time for supper. After promptly redressing and a quick dose of medicine, he ventured downstairs to the public bar. The landlord was a rather bulbous and stern-looking chap with a dark-red face.

"What will be your poison, sir?"

"I'll take a beer, please, landlord."

James looked around the pub. It was pretty busy this early of an evening, which surprised him. As he sipped his beer at the bar, he could not help but notice a very loud and drunk woman cavorting openly with her male friend.

"Rather a little early to be so sozzled, would you not think, landlord?"

The burly man behind the bar also gave the woman a

disapproving look. He leaned in close to James as if to confide.

"The man she drinks with is not her husband. She makes a wittol of the poor soul. A good man is Thomas Hodgson. I would wager he had no idea Jane's even here. She does as she pleases, that one."

James took another sip of beer. "Poor fellow indeed."

As James sipped the remainder of his beer at the bar, he kept looking over at the woman. The bitch had no shame. Whoring herself out for a few drinks with anyone gullible enough to finance her desire. The world needed fewer of these "women," and a husband deserved more from a wife. James finished his beer. He had seen enough. He bade goodbye to the landlord and felt a need to settle his stomach.

After a short stroll down the main street, James found a small shop that served local pies. He decided he would take sustenance here. Half an hour later, he finished his meal and decided to visit one or two pubs along Church Street. The first he spotted was the Brown Cow. A charming village-style pub. A warm fire and not too busy. He stayed for two beers before deciding to move on. A short walk further up, he found himself in the more prominent and grander Black Bull. He was a little taken aback to see such a wide range of ales. It would simply be rude not to sample one or two. The pub was bustling and was one of the more popular ones within the town.

After two or three local ales recommended by the landlord, James felt a little more relaxed. He decided that he would now move on to gin. He had discreetly taken a few dabs of his medicine through various points of the evening. He was feeling strong.

James took a look at his pocket watch. It was just after 7:30 p.m. He decided he would head back to the Crown. He could not help but think about the drunken whore earlier. He wondered if she was still there, whoring herself in front of everyone. As he drew close to the hotel and was about to open the door, he could see two figures drunkenly stumbling across the way, holding each other up. They were walking down the hill. It was indeed the same couple from earlier. He didn't know why, but his immediate instinct was to follow them.

As they steadily walked on laughing, arm in arm, James kept his distance. The rush of not being seen was thrilling him. They continued downhill, taking a turn across the road. It was dark. Only a few cottages lined the road. The lack of light was proving useful. It was not long before the couple reached some woodland. James continued to follow, remaining to keep a discreet distance. The couple had a brief look around. Once they were happy no one was looking, the man unclipped his braces, and his trousers dropped to the ground around his ankles.

James crouched slightly behind a bush to avoid detection. The excitement of watching this unfold was tingling all his senses. He felt aroused but also had an overwhelming feeling of anger.

"The whore!" he kept repeating over and over under his breath.

The man lifted the woman's dress at the front and had her pushed up against a tree. She wrapped her legs around him. James watched intently as the man grunted and groaned his way through a few minutes of hard thrusting. The man let out a muffled cry of satisfaction before quickly pulling up his trousers and reattaching his braces.

"I'll head back now to the Crown," the man hollered.

James noted that the man spoke in a thick Yorkshire accent.

"Give it five minutes before coming back up," the man added.

The man hurriedly walked off, past the bush where James was hiding. The woman was now alone. James waited a couple of minutes just watching the whore tidy herself up after the event. He felt like he was witnessing a feral animal in the wild.

Then suddenly, the urge overtook him. James stood up from behind the bush and confidently strode his way through the trees. The woman could now see him and was startled.

"Who goes there?"

"Please, madam, I did not mean to scare you. My name is Mr. Smith. I am with the parish council. Are you aware this area is not open to the public on an evening?"

The woman, being a little worse for drink, screwed her face at him. "You are trying to tell me the parish don't want folk down here at night, and they sent a man in suit down to stop them?"

James smiled and moved in closer.

"That's right, madam. I know it might seem a little peculiar, but the parish worries such behaviour will attract, well, unsavoury types to what is a beauty spot." James was now very close to her. He leaned in and whispered into her ear, "After all, who wants whores spreading their filth everywhere?"

He suddenly grabbed her by the throat and started to strangle her as hard as he could. James pressed his thumbs deep into her neck. She desperately tried to release his grip, but within seconds, she blacked out. He then took the shawl around her neck and yanked it as tightly as he could, throttling whatever life he could from her whilst she was blacked out.

James pulled her across the wet grass to the muddy bank where there was a nearby stream. The drop was around twenty feet. He dragged her down the muddy bank by her tightened shawl. As they reached the foot of the bank, he pushed her face-first into the shallow pool of water. For a few seconds, she became conscious again. James kept her face firmly pressed into the water. She splashed in vain, but James was too strong. Within a few moments, she was gone for good.

He had done it. James had killed a whore. The feeling he was experiencing at that moment was sensational. He quickly turned her over, untied her shawl, and unwrapped it. He removed it and then tied it loosely back on around her neck. This would appear as an accident. The drunk bitch simply fell into the ravine.

Suddenly, another feeling overcame him. James undid the buttons on her dress and pulled the top down to reveal her breasts. He then unbuttoned his trousers and gratified himself into the water. The furious act was no longer than a few seconds. The rush was too much.

James quickly tidied himself up and positioned her back facedown into the water. He pulled himself back up the bank and onto the grass. He had wet mud all over his shoes and on the bottom of his trousers. As he crossed the wooded area, he grabbed as many loose leaves as possible to wipe the caked soil off his shoes and trousers. He could clean himself up fully back at the hotel.

James chose to walk back the way he came, checking if any souls were around, but none were. He went back up the hill and crossed the junction. James's heart was pumping, and the energy was racing through his veins. As he walked back through the door of the Crown, he felt a sense of invincibility. He could see the Yorkshireman at the bar drinking with another man.

James smiled as he slowly ambled up the stairs.

PART 4

Polly Nichols

29 March 1880
Guildford St., London

The house Edward Walker lived in with his son was tightly packed in a long, terraced row with other small red-brick worker cottages. It might be cramped, but in this part of London, to have such privacy was a luxury.

Edward, however, was exhausted. Twenty years earlier, his wife, Caroline, had died from consumption. Since then, he had worked hard to keep his children, Mary Ann and Edward Jr., safe. He did so by providing the money from his work as a blacksmith for food and board. It was physically gruelling work. His body was broken from pure graft.

Mary Ann, who preferred to be known as Polly, took on the woman's role from a young age. The cooking, cleaning, and maintenance of the home became her duty. She did so with due care and diligence. Edward often regretted that he didn't marry again for Polly's sake. The burden placed on one so young felt unjust. The truth was, he had never recovered from Caroline's death. It was unlikely he ever would.

Now Polly was here in her brother's house. She was thin and drained, her cheekbones sharply cut. The lines of stress gathered on her forehead like strings on an old violin. Her clothes were raggedy and scruffy. She looked defeated.

Edward Jr. and his family were not home. The hush of peace was unusual. Father and daughter sat at a tiny well-worn wooden table with two equally shabby chairs in the kitchen. He was not prepared for what Polly had to say.

"I have left William."

"Do what? What do you mean you have 'left' him? He's your husband, for god's sake. You can't leave him!" Edward was perplexed.

"He's not a good man, Pa. He had been taking the affections of another, our neighbour. I've had enough of it all." Polly started to sob. "The cruelty is too much to take. I can't bear it anymore. I fear my sanity is leaving me."

Edward took a moment to digest the information. "I'll have a word with him, maybe knock a few shades of sense into that thick skull of his."

"You'll do no such thing, Pa! You're not a young man. I can't bear the thought of ever returning to that place. She is welcome to him as far as I'm concerned."

"What are you going do, Poll? I mean, do you want to stay here?"

"No need. I have a friend who has a bed for me over the water. I'll stay there a while. I'm not here for me. I'm here for the boy." She paused for a moment. "He doesn't get on with his father, and I know you will be a great influence on him."

"Of course, he can stay here no problem, Poll. I'll take care of him."

Polly broke into a rare smile. Edward noted to himself how long it had been since he saw his only daughter smile.

"What about the others?"

Polly's face became sullen again.

"Well, if his nibs wants to play happy families with Rosetta Walls, then he can do so with her children and mine. Let's see how they get on trying to raise all of them under one roof. Anyway, they will be better off with him. Until I can get myself sorted somewhere else at least."

"You sure you're going to be all right?"

Edward was concerned for his daughter. Polly reached across the table, took her father's hand, and clasped it in both of hers.

"Don't worry about me, Pa. You take care of the boy, and keep an eye on the others for me, will you?"

"You'll always have a home with me, Mary Ann. Never forget that, regardless of what happens."

Polly offered another rare beam. "I know Pa. It will all be all right, I promise."

Polly tiredly pulled herself up to leave. She strolled around the table to give her father a peck on the cheek.

"I'll be back soon."

As she shuffled her way out of the kitchen, Edward had a foreboding sense that it could be some time before he saw his daughter again.

*　*　*

* * *

19 December 1887

Lambeth Workhouse, London

Lambeth Workhouse was a godforsaken institution of cooking, laundry, and despair. The two-storey pale-red building sprawled over numerous acres of land. A factory for the unfortunate. Polly hoped she would never have to return to this place. The wafting aroma of cleaning alcohol was as harsh as she remembered it from her last visit.

Polly and her accompanying policeman were just inside the entrance, standing on the public side of the dark oak counter. On the other side stood the workhouse master, ready to complete the necessary paperwork.

"Name?" the master asked in a tone that radiated weariness.

"Polly Nichols."

"Creed?"

"Christian, sir"

"Age?"

"Forty-three."

"Have you ever been admitted into this workhouse previously?"

"Yes, sir. This will be my third time."

The master gave a disapproving look.

"A regular? Welcome back," he uttered without any hint of sincerity. He scribbled down his notes.

It was not her preferred choice on any of the occasions. The first time, she was admitted into the infirmary due to illness. The second time was out of pure hunger and desperation. This time was courtesy of the boys of the Met giving her a persuasive shove through the door.

"What is your marital status?" he continued.

"I have been left abandoned by my husband."

Polly knew that the workhouse would most likely try to follow up with William and ask him to pay maintenance for her. As she left him, she was entitled to nothing. It was worth a try.

"Previous address?"

Polly gave her father's address.

For a few months in Camberwell in '83, she had lived with him after he moved out of her brother's house. Old Edward was not too fond of the company Polly was keeping, and as a grown adult, she took much offence at being treated like a child. After a colossal quarrel, she grabbed what she could carry and left.

"Reason for entering the workhouse?"

This time, the policeman replied, "Vagrancy and destitution."

The constable was right. Polly was homeless and without any money. She had been sleeping rough in Trafalgar Square on and off for a few months. December in London could be a brutal place. The wind was no place for the weak. It also found itself as a regular home to many waifs and strays with nowhere else to turn for sleep.

Despite being cruelly exposed to the elements, it was still a beacon for those with nowhere else to go. It was a beacon to Polly. On good days she could make money begging near the National

Gallery. She only concerned herself with making quick money to pay for drinks. If she could make a few shillings to cover lodgings as well, even better. When days were a little more challenging, she would fall back on selling the odd tiff here and there. Needs must.

"Nearest relative?"

"My father, Edward Walker."

Her only ambition at this stage in her life was to numb the pain as much as possible. Numb the pain of all that was lost. The most recent pain in her life was the death of her brother, Edward. He went up in a ball of flames after an accident with an oil lamp in his own home. Polly only found out from a family friend. After their fallout in '83, Polly did not see her father again until Edward's funeral in June. They did not speak then.

The master proceeded to give further instructions.

"You shall go through the door over there marked 'Women.' From there, a female attendant will take all of your clothes and personal possessions. You will then be examined for any signs of disease or infection. You will take a bath. You will then be issued with suitable workhouse clothing. You will be placed in the receiving ward to await your formal admission. As you are no stranger to this place, I'm sure you are fully aware of the process."

Polly offered a sombre nod.

There was so much more pain. Her mother's death. Her brother's death. Her cheating husband. Loss of contact with her children. Loss of contact with her father. All of it hurt. Perhaps some more time in this place would help distract her. Alcohol had taken that role until now.

"Thank you, sir."

Polly meandered along the corridor to the door marked 'Women.' The policeman waited and watched. As she slowly clinked open the door and entered the hallway to hard labour, she could not help but think how history had a funny way of repeating itself.

Except she could not find any reason to smile.

* * *

12 July 1888

The Grapes, Wandsworth

The Grapes public house on Fairfield Street stood proudly on the corner. Like a lighthouse for the lost. It was why Polly found herself here, with only the thick mahogany bar keeping her upright. She had been here for a while. It was a busy spot, bustling with locals. Polly liked how clean and modern it was. It was almost a pleasure to be this plastered.

A stout man with a thick scruffy brown beard approached her.

"Hello, lovely. You here all on your lonesome?"

Polly was struggling to keep her focus.

"I am always lonesome," she replied.

She didn't mean it to sound as melancholic as it did, but it was her most natural response. The stranger did not seem to register her pain.

"How about I buy you another drink?"

Polly never turned down a free drink. Ever.

"Gin for me, please, sir."

Having accrued several months of good behaviour at the Lambeth Workhouse, Polly was delighted when Mrs. Fielder, the matron, had organised her domestic employment. It was as a live-in servant for Mr. and Mrs. Cowdry in Wandsworth. Mr. Cowdry was a clerk for the police, and Mrs. Cowdry was very active in the local community. They were both Baptists and believed in the temperance movement. It was felt by all those concerned that such a household would be suitable for Polly's health and future well-being.

Now she found herself in their local public house. The landlord poured Polly and her new friend a fresh glass of gin.

The stranger introduced himself, "The name is Smithy. I'm a bricky."

Polly smiled. "That rhymes!"

Smithy offered a dry smile. "What about you, sweetheart, what's your name?"

"Polly."

"You local then, Polly?"

"I live with a family as their help, just down the road there."

Polly had been in residence at Ingleside since May. The cleaning and cooking were not unlike what she was used to earlier when she maintained the home for her brother and father. It was something she was used to and found as second nature.

"This family, they all right?"

"Yeah. Nice people, really. Too nice, probably."

For the first few weeks, things were going well. The couple were pleasant. The work was relatively easy by workhouse standards. Before long, monotony started to creep in. Polly decided to alleviate some of that boredom when the family were away by writing a letter to her father earlier that day. She knew how he worried about her. Polly wanted to assure him that she was well and on the right road. It would be a fresh start for them both. Let him know that this family were a good influence on her. She took the letter and sent it on from the local post office.

As it left her hands, Polly started to think about what it would be like to have just one drink. This must have been the longest she had gone without a drink for a long while. After all, her people were away, and she was at a loose end. Her father would get word she was okay. It would be just one drink. What harm could it do? Who was to know? She had on her a few shillings she had made since working there. Then she saw the Grapes.

"You not very nice then, Polly?"

Polly hiccupped. "I think I am a good person. That should be enough, shouldn't it?"

Smithy just smiled.

One drink with Smithy turned into two, two turned into three, and three turned into four. Polly was intensely drunk. She had lost count of the number of gins she had had. Despite being ten sheets to the wind, she was enjoying his attention.

"Time!" roared the landlord. "Everybody out!"

Smithy and Polly were part of the last few stragglers.

"Let me just finish this last drink," Polly pleaded.

Polly downed the last of her gin as Smithy started to lead her out onto the street. Everyone else had gone. It was just them on the road. The mild air was pleasant. The loud clunking of the pub door locking behind them was the only sound.

"Come with me," Smithy asserted.

Despite being very drunk, Polly did not enjoy the dark nature of Smithy's tone.

"No, I think I shall go home," she replied.

"You're coming with me."

Smithy grabbed Polly tightly and dragged her along the pavement.

"You are hurting me!"

"Shut up, bitch."

They reached a narrow side alley that ran by the back of the pub. Smithy hauled her down the alleyway before getting about halfway down.

"What are you doing?" Polly asked in her drunken stupor.

Smithy said nothing whilst giving a quick glance up and down the alley.

Suddenly, he slammed Polly up against the wall. He put his hand over her mouth to stop her screaming. He swiftly lifted up the front of her dress. Within seconds, he had pulled his trousers down. She tried to fight him off, but he was too strong. She no longer had the strength that she once did.

"You have been asking for this all night, you fucking whore!" he spluttered angrily into her ear as he forced himself inside her.

After a few minutes of violent thrusting, Smithy let out an angry grunt. He had finished. Polly was in a state of shock as he pulled up his trousers. He then spat in her face.

"Fucking slut!"

With that, Smithy scurried off back into the direction of the main street.

Polly sank to the floor and started to cry. It took a little while for her to recover her composure. Eventually, she regathered herself. She stood up and rearranged her clothes. Polly wiped her eyes and started to slowly shuffle her way back to Ingleside.

When she arrived back at the residence, she noticed that the couple had still not returned. Still sobbing and worse for drink, Polly decided at that moment that she needed to leave.

"What was all this for?" she asked herself.

She was just was not strong enough to break the chains of the demon drink. Its claws were firmly gripped onto her soul. The drink had made her this way. Weak. She was worthless—less than worthless. The devil had won. She didn't belong here. Who did she think she was fooling?

She gathered as much of Mrs. Cowdry's clothing as she could physically carry, including a black velvet bonnet. She would head back east and somewhere more familiar.

In darkest London, the blackest of souls could find solace in the company of others who were also searching for a comforting shard of light.

∗ ∗ ∗

30 August 1888

Middlesex St., Whitechapel

Nathan's coffee shop on Middlesex Street was a rather intimate place. Small wooden tables and rickety old chairs. It was early evening, and the place was busy enough with traders and passers-by. The aromatic cloud of freshly brewed coffee floated in the air.

James approached the counter where a raven-haired woman was busy piling cups on a tray as steam kettles boiled away behind her on the stove.

"I am looking for a Ms. Nathan?"

The woman looked up at him. "Who might you be then?"

"My name is Mr. Smith. I saw your advertisement for private lodgings, and I wish to enquire of its availability."

"It's still available. I can take you up to look at it if you want?"

"Please, madam."

The coffee house owner turned and addressed a young girl in the back of the kitchen.

"Rosie, I am just showing a gentleman the room upstairs. Keep an eye on things here, will you?"

"Yes, Miriam," the small voice replied.

Miriam Nathan lifted up the latched countertop and led the way.

"Follow me, please."

As they exited the front of the shop, there was a black door beside the entrance of the coffee house.

"If you decide to take this room, you will be lodging with myself and my brother's family."

She opened the door with a key she pulled from her dress pocket. As Ms. Nathan plodded her way up the narrow staircase, James closed the door behind him and followed her up.

It had been five months since James squeezed the life out of that Manchester whore Jane Hodgson. The Yorkshireman was arrested and charged with her murder. By extraordinary circumstances, the trial was held in James's own city, Liverpool. He was a little disappointed that the Yorkshireman was found to be not guilty. That would have been a further layer of enjoyment.

The room was the closest one to the top of the stairs. James noted the convenience. She ushered him inside. It was dark, cluttered, and very basic. A wrought-iron single bed, a simple wooden chair, a meagre oak wardrobe, and a single sink in the corner fill the room.

"So, what do you think, Mr. Smith?"

James smiled. "It is perfect, Ms. Nathan. How much?"

"Two shillings a day. How long will you be looking to lodge for?"

"I would like to take the room for three months. However, I will not be here most of the time. The nature of my work means I travel extensively and erratically, so I will pay for the security of knowing the room is available as and when I need it during this period. Would that be agreeable?"

"It is a rather unusual request. If you pay in advance, then I should have no issue with the unique arrangement. What is it you do, Mr. Smith?"

"I am a travelling salesman. I will happily agree to your terms. I can pay now if that suits you?"

"Absolutely, Mr. Smith, the room is yours."

Since that weekend, James could not help but fantasise about killing again. Florence was no doubt being defiled by all manner of men by now. Whores never stopped spreading their filth.

James had constantly been thinking about how he could commit his next brazen act upon an unsuspecting bitch. This was all Florie's fault. She had driven him to this with her slut ways. Now all whores must pay.

James chose Whitechapel, London, to mirror the fact that he spotted the bitch with her whore master in Whitechapel, Liverpool. He loved his funny little word games. James also knew this area well from his earlier career in the City of London. Back then, he would often visit the dirty whores and give them a unique brand of Sir Jim punishment. This time, the penalty would be death.

James pulled out a wad of pound notes.

"So we are saying around ninety days at a shilling a day? By my calculations, that is around four pounds and ten shillings? How about I pay you five pounds?"

Ms. Nathan's face beamed. "That will do nicely, Mr. Smith."

She handed him the key as she plucked the money from his hand.

"I shall leave you, Mr. Smith. I hope you will be most comfortable."

Nathan clunked the door behind her as she left James alone to get familiar with his new London residence.

James sat on the bed and started to contemplate what was coming next. He pulled up the leather bag he had been carrying onto the bed. He took out the hunting knife that had been concealed. Cloaked in its own leather sheath, the knife was drawn out and examined closely.

As a member of the Wirral Hunt, he had a perfect way to obtain a knife without raising any suspicion. James acquired it under the guise of deer-hunting. He had since become obsessed with this piece of Sheffield steel. Around ten inches in length and around two inches in width, it had a handcrafted mahogany grip. A tool of beauty. Acid to the face would not be the same.

James started to wonder what it would be like to feel their internal organs against his skin. He immediately knew from that moment on, he was going to open them up. The excitement of this idea alone was enough to arouse him.

"The whores shall have their filthy innards exposed to the world, for all to see their rot first hand," he muttered.

The general had once told James about how Yankee soldiers would slit the throats of Confederates quickly and silently. They would grab the enemy from behind, hand over their mouth to muffle any screams, and then run a blade across the artery in the neck. The fool even showed James the position on both sides of the neck. They should have their throats cut first.

The plan now was to have a few drinks in some of the nearby pubs. Time to start laying bait. James was already dosed up on his medicine. He was ready. The excitement was almost too much. He knew what he had to do next.

He must go hunt.

* * *

31 August 1888
Flower and Dean St., Whitechapel

Polly was drunk. She told herself it was to help her stay warm. Polly found she was drunk more often than she was sober these days. The days had blurred into months. The life she once knew as a married mother of five seemed a long time ago now, especially on a night like tonight. Her clothes were rain-soaked, and goosebumps covered her skin. She had seen better summers in London, that was for sure. Often, she found herself thinking about the past. Tonight was one of those times. More reasons to keep warm.

Her memories were just fragments now, like a puzzle with missing pieces. Over eight years earlier, she had turned her back on Peabody Buildings and that life with a husband and children. Things had not blossomed for her since then. Drifting from workhouse to workhouse, doss house to doss house didn't feel much like existence.

Now here she was sitting in the kitchen at this particular dossing spot, The White House. Polly knew it must have been sometime past 1:00 a.m. That's the time they finally kicked people out of "The Frying Pan." The deputy of the lodging house had just caught her in the kitchen. That was all she needed. The deputy had run out of patience and was letting her know.

"You need to pay up your 4d, Polly, or get out. You can't be sitting here."

"I ain't got no money."

"Then you need to go and find some or sleep somewhere else."

Polly pointed to the velvet bonnet on her head. "See what a jolly bonnet I've got now. Save my bed!"

Polly left the kitchen and gingerly made her way to the front door. The cold air slapped her in the face as she stumbled out onto the pavement. So much so she almost fell. Then, after a moment of regaining her composure—and more importantly, her balance—she took a deep breath and began to walk down the road towards Osborn Street.

The rain suddenly subsided as if to catch its breath. Polly decided it would be prudent to walk at a slower pace to carry herself a little better. For nights like this, she was delighted she had sturdy men's boots to keep her upright. She stopped every few yards to gather herself.

As Polly slowly stumbled down Osborne Street towards the junction of Whitechapel Road, she could tell the corner shop was still open. Her vision was blurred, but she knew where she was and where she was going. An innate sense of local awareness. It was the grocer's shop. Using the walls of the houses to keep herself steady, she limped on. Slowly but surely, she got closer to the shop. Outside there was a woman she recognised. It was Nelly Holland, a woman she had co-lodged with up until recently.

"Jesus, Poll, where are you going in that state?"

Still struggling to stand upright, Polly wanted to ask a question of her own.

"Here, Nell, I don't suppose you would have a tipple on you by any chance? Just a swig to get myself right, like."

Reluctantly, Nelly pulled out a small metal flask from inside her dress pocket and handed it to Polly.

"Here, take some of that to warm the old cockles up."

As Polly made her best attempt at opening the flask as cleanly as possible, the church's bells across the road struck 2:30 a.m. She raised her drink to the church bells.

"Cheers to you too!"

After a healthy gulp of hard liquor, Polly clumsily put the screw top on loosely and handed it back to Nelly. She, in turn, took a quick swig and put it back inside her dress pocket.

"Why don't you come back with me, Poll? You can sleep on the floor in the room. At least it will be drier than being out here!"

Polly considered the offer for a moment but then declined.

"I've had my doss money three times today and spent it. It won't be long before I'm back. Anyway, there's a bloke there who has offered to share his bed with me if things don't work out. Thanks anyway, Nell."

Polly elected to continue walking, this time unaided by the wall. She staggered her way eastbound down towards Whitechapel Road.

The famous Whitechapel Road and Whitechapel High Street effectively ran from Aldgate to Mile End. It was the main artery that pulsated through the heart of the area. Polly knew that day or night, there would always be an opportunity here.

As she moved leisurely eastwards, she flashed a smile to the odd passer-by. All of them just kept on walking. Even she could sense that her intoxicated state was most likely putting potential clients off. Still, she would soldier on. Just one more trade and she could head back to the White House with her jolly bonnet in tow.

"You okay, my dear?"

It was a man's voice from behind.

"You seem rather unsteady. Perhaps you could do with some assistance?"

Polly turned around and was a little taken aback by what she saw, or at least by what she could focus on. He was a well-dressed gentleman. The type you would usually see entering the train station of an evening. She realised the station was just a few yards up. For a split second, she thought he must be going home late. Then she remembered it was very late. Maybe after 3:00 a.m.? Still, he seemed like a nice enough chap.

I don't see much danger with this one, Polly considered. Perhaps he could be her last trade?

"That's very kind of you, sir, but the only assistance I need at this time is a financial one. I would be, of course, willing to trade."

"Is that right? Well, perhaps I could be tempted. But tell me, how much for this trade?"

Polly had struck lucky. She was almost convinced he was just a good Samaritan and would be scurrying off at pace in the shock of being propositioned in such a manner. But it turned out he was just like any other man—interested in just one thing.

"Well, I would expect no less than fourpence for a quick tiff, sir."

"Well, in that case, perhaps you could lead me to somewhere a little more discreet so that we can conduct our business with a bit of privacy?"

Polly had secured her final trade. She would get her warm bed after all.

"I know somewhere where we can go!"

Polly linked arms with the well-dressed stranger and walked a little further down Whitechapel Road in the wet and slippery conditions. She guided them down a side alley and over a small cobbled hump bridge that arched over the train tracks. They did not speak. The only sound was Polly's heavy breathing and her footsteps clunking along the pavement. From here, the street became dimmer and narrower.

A few yards further on, Polly took them down an even darker street. There was almost no light now, but that of the moon.

"Just a little further up, we won't be disturbed. You might want to get your money ready."

"Of course. Let me get it from inside my coat."

They unlocked their arms, and he let her continue walking up ahead of him. The thick shadows smothered everything all around. There were no gas lamps to be seen for some distance. Both sides of the road were lined with tiny cottages and a few gates that led to various yards.

Suddenly Polly felt a gloved hand wrap over her mouth from behind. The sudden attack had taken her by complete surprise. She tried to scream, but the glove muffled her voice. She could now feel his body tightly close to hers. His icy breath was rapidly breathing down her ear.

Then his right hand appeared in front of her. Polly could see he had a knife. She knew this was it. She could not escape. His hold was too tight. Her cheekbones felt like they were cracking under intense pressure. This man was out to do her serious harm. She was too drunk to fight back with any strength. She swung her arms around wildly, but it was no use.

All of a sudden, she felt the razor-sharp blade run across the left side of her neck with searing-hot pain. Within a few seconds, a wave of darkness came. She could feel herself falling backwards. It felt like time itself slowing down to a complete stop.

The last thing Polly heard as she hit the floor were the words, "Die, you fucking whore bitch!"

Then she was gone.

*　*　*

31 August 1888

Buck's Row, Whitechapel

The damp cobbles were glistening, coated by the recent downpour. The darkness of the night strangled the street with a pitch-black grip. The silence was heavy.

"What in blazes is that?" Charles Cross asked himself as he approached the crumpled heap on the ground.

He was hoping it would be some discarded tarpaulin. As a carman for Pickfords, such finds were always valuable. It was around 3:40 a.m. As he drew closer, he realised it was a silhouette of a woman lying down on her back in front of the gates of a stable yard. He stopped in the middle of the road and stared tentatively at the lifeless figure. At that exact moment, another man, Robert Paul, across the street, was approaching. Cross called him over.

"Here, I think there is a woman over there," he exclaimed to Paul.

The two men moved closer to examine the body. Cross picked up one of her hands. It was cold as ice.

"I think she might be dead," he declared.

Paul suggested they should sit the body upright.

Cross disagreed. "I'm not touching her!"

Paul gave her a gentle kick to see if she reacted. No response.

"She's either dead or dead drunk," announced Cross.

"I'm already behind time for work," replied Paul.

The two men agreed to leave her and alert a policeman should they pass one.

Around five minutes or so later, PC Neil made the rounds on his beat when he came across the woman lying on the footpath. He promptly turned on his lantern and shone it on the body. He immediately spotted blood oozing from her neck.

"Bloody Norah!"

He looked up and could see another figure at the end of the street. He flashed his lantern multiple times. This initiated an equal response. It was another policeman. Within moments, the figure was in close range. It was PC Thain.

"Here is a woman with her throat cut, call for Dr. Llewellyn at once!"

The constable ran off in the direction of Whitechapel Road. PC Neil continued to survey the body. Another police constable who was alerted by Cross and Paul arrived at the scene. Neil immediately summoned him to get an ambulance.

PC Neil continued to flash his light in and around the body. He was surprised by the lack of blood. Her clothes were disarranged, and her skirt was hitched up to her knees. After a few moments, he used his lantern to search the nearby ground for any clues. There wasn't any.

Directly across the road was a three-storey building called Essex Wharf. The policeman rang the bell. After a few moments, a man appeared at the first-floor window. Neil called up to him.

"A woman has been found dead in Buck's Row. Did you see or hear anything unusual tonight, sir?"

"My wife has been awake all night, and she heard nothing unusual, Constable."

PC Neil returned to stand guard over the dead body. Another policeman arrived on the scene. The new arrival informed PC Neil that he would knock on all the nearby doors to see if anyone had heard or seen anything.

Around five minutes later, PC Thain and Dr. Llewellyn arrived. Thain gave Llewellyn his lantern as he examined the body. He crouched down on his haunches and noticed the wounds on her throat.

"Two deep cuts to the left side of the neck."

Just then, the handcart ambulance arrived. The doctor put his hand on the deceased's bare leg.

"Body is still warm. Move the woman to the Whitechapel Workhouse mortuary. She is dead. I would estimate that she expired around thirty minutes ago. She was murdered here."

The doctor stood up. "I will make a further examination of her at the mortuary."

Neil nodded in acknowledgement. Neil and Thain then proceed to lift the dead body and put it onto the cart. In doing so, all the men were shocked at the volume of blood gathered under her body. All the police officers, except for Thain, started moving the cart to the Whitechapel mortuary. PC Thain remained to guard the scene.

Inspector Spratling was on Hackney Street talking to a loud drunk when a constable grabbed his attention.

"Inspector, you are needed on Buck's Row. There has been a murder of a woman."

Within ten minutes, Spratling arrived at the murder scene and spotted PC Thain. As they both served in the J Division, the inspector recognised the constable immediately.

"Tell me, Thain, what happened here exactly?"

"Yes, Inspector. A woman was found to have had her throat cut in this very spot."

Thain pointed at the pavement where a young man was mopping up blood with a bucket and mop.

"What is he doing?"

"He is the son of Mrs. Green, the next-door neighbour. They wanted to clean the street before daylight, sir."

"Very well. Where is the deceased now?"

"Dr. Llewellyn instructed the other officers to take the body to Whitechapel Workhouse mortuary where he will examine her further."

"Have we gathered all witness statements?"

"We have, sir."

"Then we shall take our leave to Whitechapel Workhouse, Constable."

The two men headed towards Whitechapel Workhouse infirmary mortuary on Old Montague Street. Ten minutes later, the men arrived at the infirmary. The gothic building loomed over the small gravel yard, forcing its ominous shadow upon the mortuary shed.

They saw the deceased's body abandoned on a handcart. There

was no sign of the other policemen.

"Good grief. Where is everybody?" Spratling asked Thain.

"I shall see if I can fetch someone, Inspector."

As Thain headed towards the main building of the infirmary, Spratling removed his notebook and started to write down a description of the murdered woman. A few minutes later, Thain returned with a skinny, older man carrying a set of keys.

"Who might you be, sir?" Spratling asked.

"The name is Robert Mann. I'm the keeper of this mortuary."

"Well, Robert Mann, I think we should give this woman some privacy in death and bring her inside, shall we?"

"As you wish."

The keeper opened the mortuary shed door. PC Thain wheeled the body inside.

"I shall be going for my breakfast now, sir," said Mann.

He left the keys with Spratling and headed back towards the main building.

"Thain, please call for Dr. Llewellyn and remind him to finish his examination, in case it has escaped his memory. Then please return to the scene and search all of the railway arches. It does not hurt to be thorough."

"Very good, Inspector." PC Thain marched off with intent.

Inspector Spratling took his notebook out again and began to record the possessions of the dead woman. He started to empty her pockets and logged the inventory one by one. He noticed rough tears and rips on the front of her dress.

"That's rather odd."

He gently started pulling back the torn fabric pieces, which were soaked in blood at the edges. As he peeled back the layers one by one, he quickly discovered some kind of wound running down the front of her abdomen. Spratling decided the quickest way to see the damage would be to lift the dress up rather than unfastening the clasps on the back.

As he lifted the victim's dress just up past her knees, he stopped dead in his tracks.

"Sweet Jesus!"

He quickly pulled her dress back down again. The sight he saw could not be undone. An eruption of bile surged from the pit of his gut. He darted outside and vomited violently into a nearby hedge.

As Spratling recovered his composure and took deep breaths, he knew this was not the work of any ordinary street murderer. He wiped his mouth with a handkerchief he took out from his pocket. This killer had attacked the very essence of womanhood.

Inspector Spratling could not help but feel that this might not be the first victim, and it might not be the last.

"Evil bastard!"

PART 5

Annie Chapman

20 October 1867
Montpellier Sq., London

It was late Sunday afternoon, and the weather was starting to turn. A chilly wind was beginning to dominate the air. Autumn was firmly here. Today was one of Annie's rare days off.

She was sitting alone in her mother's kitchen in Brompton, near the increasingly fashionable Knightsbridge. She poured herself a discreet whisky into a ceramic cup. Annie knew where her mother hid the bottles and was glad of it today. The house itself was comfortable compared to their previous accommodation down the years. Bittersweet that such a dwelling was only available to them upon the suicide of her father, George. If it were not for his former employer, her mother and her siblings would almost certainly not be here now in this place.

A dark-haired and broad-shouldered man entered the kitchen. This must be the new lodger her mother had spoken to her about.

"My name is Annie Smith. Pleased to meet you, sir."

The man smiled. "John Chapman is the name. Nice to meet you, miss."

Annie didn't realise his surname was Chapman. It was her mother's maiden name.

Perhaps this is some kind of fate, she pondered.

He looked like quite a strong and physical man. Not afraid to get his hands dirty, doing man's work. He also appeared to be from simple means. She was curious.

"Tell me, Mr. Chapman, your accent does not appear to be local. Where might it be you are from?"

"It is true, Ms. Smith, I am not from London. I come from the county of Suffolk in the country. Do you know Suffolk?" John seated himself at the table.

"Alas, I do not, Mr. Chapman. I know very little of the world outside of London."

She had been working in domestic service now for well over a decade. It was a good job, and it kept her occupied well enough, but she had never harboured any desire to see the world. Now, at the age of twenty-six, Annie knew far too well that she was approaching an age where marriage would become less of a possibility for her. A lifelong commitment to domestic service was not something she hoped would become of her.

Annie got up and took another cup from the cupboard. She placed it in front of her guest and took the bottle of whisky out from under the table.

"What would a countryman such as yourself be in doing in the city at this time?"

She poured him some whisky and then retook her seat. Annie placed the bottle under the table once again.

"Thank you, Ms. Smith. I am a coachman. I grew up around

horses. It was always my life's desire to be a coachman. The best opportunities for work in such are in London. It was why my brothers and I all left the country and came to the city."

John took a sip from his cup. The couple sat in comfortable silence for a few moments, nursing their drinks tentatively.

"Please forgive my candour, Ms. Smith, but I was wondering if you were married or presently courting?"

Annie was a little surprised that this country boy was not so shy after all.

"You are forgiven, Mr. Chapman. No. Indeed, I am neither married nor courting."

After almost demolishing his drink with a large gulp, John decided to follow up on his initial question. "I have meant to take a long walk in Hyde Park since I arrived. I understand the lake is something to be admired. Would you be interested in accompanying me on such a walk?"

Annie did her best to attempt at being coy.

"Well, Mr. Chapman, with the weather being as it is at present, I would envisage the walk might not be as long as you may think!"

They both smiled.

This was the first time that the opposite sex had shown Annie any interest in a long while. She was both flattered and excited by it. She did not know where this could lead, but she was hopeful.

"Cheers!"

The two clinked their cups together. To Annie, the drink did not feel like a remedy today but rather something to savour.

* * *

* * *

26 November 1882

St. Leonard Hill Farm, Windsor

The clock ticked on the mantlepiece. Time marched on. It waited on no man.

There was no pain a human could feel more than the loss of a child. Annie could feel she was still present in the room, but everything had drastically slowed down, except for the ticking of the clock. As each second passed, the dripping sound of lost time reverberated in Annie's head.

She was aware people were talking, but the words were no longer coherent. They were just long, drawn-out background sounds. All she could hear was the clock. It felt like her grip on her mind had somehow become loosened, like the top of a jar. She was physically there, but Annie was in an altogether different place.

"Thank you, Doctor," John croaked through a crackling voice.

The doctor had arrived to declare that their daughter was officially dead.

"It appears the brain fever she was experiencing escalated very quickly. Her young body was not equipped to counter its rapid effects. I am very sorry for your loss, Mr. and Mrs. Chapman."

Annie remained utterly still.

The physician continued, "You should contact an undertaker to assist in the funeral arrangements. Naturally, I will handle the medical certification."

In reply, John gave a solemn nod of acknowledgement. The medic collected his bag, hat, and overcoat from a nearby table. He nodded a silent farewell and left.

The couple had married in Knightsbridge, just two years after they first met. For almost a decade, they stayed mainly in West London for both of their work. That was until John was offered a position with Josiah Weeks at St. Leonard's Farm last year.

John now stood in painful silence. Then slowly, he started to limp around the room, turning the photographs in their frames over. His focus was on the task at hand. He saw the clock on the fireplace and went over to prevent it from ticking any further. John stared at the ornate clock face, seeing Annie's reflection in the glass.

She had not moved from the same spot from when the doctor informed her that Emily, her beautiful twelve-year-old daughter, was now gone. This was the fifth child of theirs to die.

"I would ask where were you, but we both already know the answer." John remained facing the clock. "Your child ill with fever was being tended to by a woman whom she barely knew. She died in the presence of a woman who was not her mother!"

Annie broke from her spell to speak, "John, I'm so sorry."

Without warning, John swiftly grabbed the clock from the mantlepiece, spun around, and threw it against the wall beside where she was standing. It shattered into a thousand pieces. Annie was still unmoved.

"Sorry?" he screeched.

John darted towards his wife with a raised clenched fist. He stopped directly in front of her, voice dripping with vitriol.

"You have no idea what being sorry is, Annie." He then punched the wall beside her. "You are not fit to be a mother. You are a slave to the drink, and that is your master. You know of nothing beyond getting your next drop. Go back to your master, you are no longer welcome here!"

There was a moment's silence.

"Get out, get out now!" barked John.

Annie looked directly into John's eyes. "As you wish." Without hesitation, she turned and slammed the door behind her as she left.

A few moments passed before John dropped to his knees, crying and howling uncontrollably. A small cripple boy and another young girl emerged from the other room. They were John and Annie Jr., the last two surviving children of the Chapmans.

"Papa?"

The girl ran to her father and hugged him. John looked up. He quickly regained control of himself by wiping away his tears and standing back up. John straightened out his clothing and calmed himself down completely. He took his daughter's hand and then made his way over to the boy.

"Come, children, we must say goodbye to your sister."

He took both of his children's hands and ushered them back into the next room.

The clock ticked no more.

* * *

***

18 January 1887
  Oxford St., Whitechapel

Annie was standing in the kitchen of John's brother's lodgings on Oxford Street in Whitechapel. The room was sepia-tinged and dingy. It smelt of stale tobacco.

Annie was stunned. She couldn't believe it. She knew he had not been well of late, but she honestly thought he would get better. Now she had just been informed that her husband was dead.

"He got worse over Christmas," George explained. "He died on Christmas Day."

Annie did not reply.

"We did try to find you for the funeral, but no one knew where you were, Annie."

Annie knew where she was. It was not anywhere worth knowing.

"He said he was heartbroken when he saw you last. He got worse very quickly after that."

Annie had only seen him less than a month earlier. She walked down to Windsor to confront him for stopping her money. Despite the bitter cold, she was motivated by the fact that she was penniless. Without any warning, the ten shillings a week she was relying on had gone. Anger was her energy and her warmth. In the five years they had been separated, John had rarely been late in putting her money order into the post office. It was very much out of character.

After two days walking through the countryside west of London, she finally made it to Windsor, the town they made their home after John's new employment as a coachman.

After asking around in a couple of his favourite pubs, Annie had finally located him in his new lodgings on Grove Road. However, she was shocked to see the door answered by an older woman who claimed she was nursing John.

He was bed-bound and sleeping. As she entered his room and gently awoke him from his slumber, his face lit up when he saw that it was his estranged wife before him.

"Annie? Is it really you?"

"Yes, John, it's me . . . your Annie."

His smile was short-lived as the memories of all the pain this woman had caused him over the past twenty years came flooding back. His tone rapidly changed.

"What are you doing here?"

"The money, John, you stopped the money."

John sighed and turned himself over with his back to his wife. "Of course, the money."

Annie moved closer. "We had an agreement, John. I need it. I have commitments that must be met. You gave me no warning!"

John exhaled an even deeper sigh this time. "There is around thirty shillings in the top drawer of my dresser. Take it and be gone!"

Annie stared at him for a minute or two, wanting to say more but couldn't. She was paralysed. Nothing she could say could undo the pain she has caused him. Annie went to the dresser and took the money from the drawer.

"Thank you, John."

Still, with his back to her, he gave her some further instructions.

"You're in Whitechapel, I hear. See my brother George on Oxford Street there in the New Year. When I'm better, I will make arrangements for your money with him. But please go. I must rest now."

Annie could feel a small tear run down her cheek. A quick brush away with her hand, she then quickly composed herself and made her exit.

On the trek back through the countryside towards London, she could not help but remember their life together. There were some happy times, despite the constant grief. The death of children was never something you could ever really prepare to experience. It was tough losing Emily in particular. She had just gotten to twelve, and by then, you would hope they were strong enough. The drink did not make the pain any less so. It just put it off a little while.

When she arrived back at Dorset Street, she found Sivvey, the man she was living with, drunk and asleep in bed. Annie gave him a gentle nudge to wake up.

"Annie, you're back? Did you get the money sorted?" he asked wearily.

"He will not give me any money until the New Year." Annie opted not to mention the thirty shillings.

With that, Sivvey got up, filled his bag with all he had, and stumbled out of the door. Not even so much as a goodbye. It didn't concern Annie much at all.

Now here she was, standing there in a state of shock.

"Do you want some tea, Annie?"

Annie did not want tea. She needed something much harder.

"Thank you, George, but I think I need to go."

Annie slowly traipsed out of George's lodgings and out onto the street. Where she was going, she had no idea. She was even more lost now than she had ever been. The only other person who had gone through the same heartache as her was no longer here.

Despite their separation, Annie always felt comforted that she knew where he was when she needed him. That comfort was no more.

Annie decided to do what she always did when she was overwhelmed. Find the nearest pub. At least the comfort in the drink was still there.

***

10 August 1888

Commercial Rd., Whitechapel

The Commercial Road of Whitechapel was bustling. Shops, food vendors, kids chasing each other, sweet sellers, shoe shiners—it was all life. Anonymity amongst the flurry was something to be savoured. However, today, Annie was not anonymous.

She knew instantly that he had seen her, but it was too late.

Annie wanted the ground beneath her to open up and swallow her. Perhaps the devil himself would drag her down to the depths of hell? She felt she had been knocking on the door long enough. Now would be a perfect time.

"Annie!" The man scuttled across the cobbles to talk with her. "Look at you. You do not look at all well, dear sister!"

It was her brother, Fountain. He was named after the captain of the regiment their father loved so dearly. He was right. She knew she did not look well. Annie had not felt well for a very long time. Where would she even begin to explain all that had happened to her since they last saw each other? Would she talk about the children she had lost? Would she talk about her dead husband? Would she talk about the bruises upon her face from fighting women in pubs? Would she talk about the shame of reducing herself to selling her body at times? Finally, she decided to speak of none of it.

"I would say it is good to see you, Fountain, but it is obvious you have not found me at a good time. You need not concern yourself with my safekeeping or welfare. I am not your burden, little brother."

Annie's preferred mode of dealing with the judgements of others was to protect her pride.

Fountain exhaled a huge sigh. "Annie, you seemingly forget that I am family. You cannot lie to me. I am like you. We are cut from the same cloth. We both need to be free of the wretched drink. I will not give up on you like I would hope you would not give up on me.

By God's grace, our souls can be saved!"

Annie had grown tired of this rhetoric. It was meaningless and unhelpful. Alcohol had given them both tonic against their pains, more than any book could. God might wish to spend some time in her battered shoes. Perhaps his grace would be more prompt.

Annie raised her hand and gently held her brother's cheek.

"I know you mean well, brother. I have no desire for salvation. I want to be left alone. Would you please not tell Ma you have seen me? She will only worry."

Fountain went to hold her hand against his cheek, but she withdrew it swiftly and moved to walk away. As Annie took just a couple of steps forward, Fountain caught up with her and grabbed her shoulder. He gently pulled her around to face him.

"I do not have much, but I would like to give you some money, sister." He reached inside his jacket for his purse.

"Fountain, please do not pity me with your charity."

He pulled out an old cloth drawstring bag and untied it. He then emptied it upside down into the flat of the palm of his other hand. There were two shillings. He offered them to Annie.

"No!"

Fountain took her hand and immediately put the coins into her palm then closed her fist tightly.

"Speak no more, sister. I will hear no more of it. This is not pity nor charity. Consider it as a brother simply paying back a small amount he owes to a loving sister."

Annie was caught by surprise by Fountain's words and was

momentarily speechless. Then, after a short pause, she reached to touch his face again, this time with a smile.

"You are a good brother and more than I deserve."

Both stood in a moment of silence with each other, at peace with their bond as siblings. Fountain then suddenly cleared his throat, straightened his back, and let go of Annie's hand. She, equally as quick, removed her hand from his cheek.

"You take care now, Annie." Then he walked a few steps backwards before turning to go on his way.

She could not help but watch him as he walked away in the opposite direction. Then, after a deep breath, she turned on her heels and carried on with her own journey.

As she walked on alone again through the thronging hustle, a sense of something lost overwhelmed her. She had lost so much in the past few years. She could no longer see the nuances of which pain hurt her most. Instead, the endless pain felt like one enormous throbbing beat, which only alcohol could soften.

The Ten Bells it was.

* * *

3 September 1888

The Home Office, London

It was uncomfortably silent. The two men sat in their seats in the waiting area of the home secretary's office. Both bolt upright, stiffened by their respective resolve. The tension was palatable. The situation had finally concluded after months of discussion.

James Monro, the assistant metropolitan police commissioner, was a Scotsman, lawyer, and spymaster. He had been delicately cultivating a clandestine network of informants and intelligence gathering in his battle against Irish terrorism. Warren wanted Monro to share this information with him as his superior. Monro was not receptive to such a request. This work was for the Home Office. He could no longer find a basis on which he could continue working alongside Warren. Thus, tensions had come to a head.

Sir Charles Warren was a former general in the British Army and was a surprise appointment to the Metropolitan Police position two years prior. Despite his relative success in the military, Monro felt that he was far better placed to become the new police commissioner. However, he was overlooked for Warren. The relationship had hardly started on the best footing.

Charles Warren was a proud military man and Welshman. He took great pride in his achievements. His view on the likes of James Monro was not incredibly endearing. Monro had never fought in a war or led men to battle. How could a man who had spent most of his life in books and offices understand what it meant to lead men? The Metropolitan Police force needed discipline and structure. In Warren's mind, the police were not much different from the troops. Troops needed routine procedures and strong leadership—all of which had been lacking under the previous commissioner. The likes of Monro were part of the problem.

Henry Matthews had been appointed home secretary only a few

months after Warren was installed into his position. The two men also had a tense working relationship, notably after the disaster known by the press as Bloody Sunday the previous November. Matthews had no great admiration for Warren's methods or military ways.

The silence broke when a clerk emerged from the home secretary's office.

"The home secretary will see you now, gentlemen."

Warren jumped up and obliged with urgency. Monro casually stood up, dusted himself down, and calmly followed Warren into the office. The two men stood directly in front of the seated Matthews as the clerk closed the door behind them. Warren's eyes were fixed on the wall, with his back rigidly straight, hat under his arm. Monro was a little more relaxed.

"Well, gentlemen, I think we may have a solution we can all be at peace with. As you are both aware, I invited Mr. W. H. Smith and Mr. Goshen to help me adjudicate the numerous points of issue. After much consultation, we all agree that it is clear that a working relationship between your two roles is no longer possible."

Matthews took a brief pause before continuing.

"We have therefore decided to decline the resignation of Sir Charles and ask that he continue in his role as police commissioner of the metropolis. As for you, Mr. Monro, it is with great reluctance we accept your resignation as assistant police commissioner of the metropolis."

Warren afforded himself a brief smile before refocusing his stare directly ahead. Monro's face was taut and strained.

"However, I would also like to formally announce the creation of a new Home Office subdepartment that will have full oversight of the intelligence network, including Special Branch. The department will continue its important work and will be answerable to this office. The role of head of detectives will remain part of the duties of the assistant commissioner, whoever that shall be. I invite Mr. Monro to be the head of this new intelligence department with immediate effect. Do you accept the position, Mr. Monro?"

This time it was Monro who was affording himself a smile. Warren was motionless.

"Indeed I do, Minister. I accept with great honour."

Matthews cleared his throat. "Sir Charles, can I assume you are agreeable to this new arrangement?"

Warren took a moment before replying, "Indeed, Minister."

Matthews sat back and released a big sigh. "Well, gentlemen, now we have a satisfactory conclusion to this whole affair. I suggest we speak no more of it. Let us all get back to the work at hand and focus on our respective commitments. Unless there is anything else, you both may go."

Warren gave a loud "Yes, sir!"

Monro was not quite finished.

"Home Secretary, may I be as so bold as to request your attention for a brief moment. In private?"

Warren turned heel and exited the room. Monro waited for the door to close.

"Thank you, Minister. Firstly, many thanks for the new role. The country must protect its network of intelligence at all costs. I feel this solution was ingeniously constructed. No doubt you had much to do with the idea."

The home secretary was less than impressed with the Monro's charm offensive.

"I do hope that our exchanges going forward, Mr. Monro, will be somewhat more efficient than this one. Perhaps if you could reach your point in a more timely fashion, we can both return to our duties?"

"Indeed, sir. Apologies. I strongly recommend that the Home Office seriously consider the appointment of Dr. Robert Anderson as my replacement as assistant commissioner. A competent and loyal servant of the crown, he worked with me previously in matters of important intelligence against the Fenians. His character is of the finest order. He will truly be a great asset to the metropolis, sir."

The home secretary looked at Monro for a few moments.

"Very good. Your recommendation is duly noted."

Monro smiled and gave a cursory nod before leaving.

James Monro certainly had his flaws, and his ambitious nature was well known. However, the home secretary knew that Monro was someone he could at least work with.

Could he trust him?

Well, that was an entirely different beast altogether.

* * *

***

7 September 1888

Middlesex St., Whitechapel

It was around 10:00 p.m. as James sat on his bed in his lodgings. There was a knock at the door, just as he placed a generous dab of arsenic onto his tongue.

"Mr. Smith, I have left your water outside the door. Good night."

He quickly put the paper packet into his waistcoat pocket and cleared his throat.

"Thank you kindly, Ms. Nathan."

The landlady was a single woman, James had guessed. The coffee shop which the room was over was a busy spot. Ms. Nathan was not a particularly attractive woman. A bit dumpy for James's taste. She must have worked hard in the shop to survive. It could not be easy for a woman to pay her way without a man to take responsibility for her. Florie and the rest of the whores could learn from this woman.

After last time, James felt he needed to be better prepared for any blood on him or his clothing. So he had purchased new clothes in Liverpool, which he packed and brought with him to London. A shirt, some trousers, a waistcoat, and also included were a couple of hats and a selection of handkerchiefs. Now he could mix up his looks to throw any witnesses off the scent, and anything that got bloodied could be disposed of when he returned to Liverpool.

The train journey down afforded some time for planning. James left the exchange a little after 3:00 p.m. to catch the 4:05 p.m. from Lime Street. By 9:00 p.m., he was at Aldgate underground station. James was amazed every time he came down from Liverpool at just how fast he could reach one end of the country from the other. He truly was living in the age of travel.

James had been consumed with thinking about killing another whore again all week. He could hardly think of anything else. The last one was thrilling, but it left him yearning for more. Just as he cut through the whore's chest and down to her quim-whiskers, he had heard some footsteps up ahead in the distance. He had to move quickly to avoid detection. The excitement of opening her up like a ripe peach was not like any feeling he had ever had previously. No medicine had ever given him the same sensations.

Now he wanted more.

James brought in the bowl and jug of water and placed them by the sink. He then moved to the bed to take the knife out of his bag. He withdrew it from its leather casing. The moonlight twinkled off the blade's edge. It really was a piece of exquisite artistry. He placed it back into its sheath and attached it to his belt.

James took a brown felt hat and long overcoat from the old wardrobe and put them on. Again, he was ready for the whores of Whitechapel. Would the whores be ready for him?

＊＊

8 September 1888

Hanbury St., Whitechapel

***

Annie had no idea what time it was, but she knew she was sober. It was starting to get light. There was a soft breeze that stroked her face. The privy she found herself in was not exactly the height of comfort, but it was quiet. Her body ached. Her neck was sore from sleeping awkwardly. She used the shed's wall to take some of her weight as she started to drag herself up. The liquid in her lungs was rising again. She took a few moments to cough up as much as she could. She took another few moments to catch her breath.

It wasn't the first time she had slept rough in the back of 29 Hanbury Street. On several occasions, after one too many rums in the Ten Bells, she would find herself waking up in this exact spot and usually in the same manner. Some quick stretches to shake off the cobwebs and Annie felt she could start her day.

She walked across the desolate yard. She trundled up a couple of concrete steps and then entered through the well-worn back door. She then shuffled through the narrow but bright white passageway towards the front door. Upon reaching it, she opened it and gently closed it behind her. The unique thing about this doss house was that the front door lock had not worked for a very long time. It was a handy spot to know for many reasons.

Annie first heard about it from a mate of Sivvey, who occasionally dossed on the stairs before working in Spitalfields market. She did not fancy that prospect very much, with people trudging up and down the stairs constantly. She appreciated the relative tranquillity of the privy. The chamber pots kept the majority of unwanted disruptions during the night to just rare occasions.

The house's closeness to the Ten Bells was an added advantage. It was one of Annie's favourite pubs. It was always good for an early drink. She could go in there in peace. Most who frequented the place were very much like her. There was an unspoken comfort with each other's company.

The sun was starting to rise higher. Sprays of reddish daybreak spilled through the gaps of the grime-stained brick buildings all around. She stood on the pavement of Hanbury Street, looking around for any other form of life. Annie reasoned it must be close enough to 5:00 a.m. by now. Perhaps she could catch the Ten Bells for their early opening.

Annie rifled through her dress pockets to see what money she had. None. She vaguely remembered being kicked out of Crossingham's lodging house in the early hours. She had no money for her bed as she had spent it all on drink. As a result, she decided to make her way to Hanbury Street to sleep it off. Now she needed a drink. The shakes were starting to take hold. Sober was not her favoured state.

As if by magic and on cue, a man started walking towards her at a slow pace. Their eyes met. He gave a slight nod of acknowledgement that he had seen her. He was dressed in what could be described as a shabby-genteel style. His face was not clear due to the shadow of the dark-brown hat he was wearing. It was like the light would not dare touch his face.

Annie did not like to sell her body for quick money, but right now, she was desperate. She needed to drink before the shakes got worse.

"Fine morning, is it not, sir?"

She forced a smile. The man drew closer and was now standing directly in front of her. His proximity could be deemed as invasive by some ladies. This close, she could see the twitching of the hairs in his carroty moustache. The wildness in his eyes was more concerning. For a split moment, she was worried.

Suddenly, he smiled back. "It is most certainly getting better."

The man's sudden switch to politeness put Annie at ease.

"I will make your morning even better if you choose to come with me for the business."

Just then, a woman walked past. She gave a quick look towards Annie and her stranger. The man remained focused on Annie.

"Will you?"

Annie felt the sale was very close. "Yes."

Annie beckoned her man to come with her. She swiftly turned to re-enter 29 Hanbury Street as her guest followed. Back through the bright white passage and out to the backyard, Annie led her client. She was only just through the back door and into the yard when the man grabbed her from behind. He tried to cover her mouth with his hand. Initially, he missed. Briefly, she let out the word "No!" before her assailant managed to get his hand over her mouth successfully the second time. He had her in a tight grip. Then a knife appeared before her in his right hand. Without even a moment's hesitation, he drew it rapidly across the left side of her throat. The intense pain shocked Annie.

Within seconds, the black void of darkness took her away.

Annie's last fleeting thought was that of relief.

* * *

8 September 1888

Leman St. Police Station, Whitechapel

Leman Street Police Station was the central station of the H Division. It was an imposing five-storey building that dwarfed its neighbours on either side. It dominated the street like a confident bobby strolling his beat.

Inspector Fred Abberline wasn't expecting to be back in Whitechapel anytime soon, yet he found himself back in a place he knew all too well. Dorset born and bred, Abberline was a stout man in his early forties. His thinning hair was sandy, but his whiskers and moustache were thick. He was rarely without his bowler hat and walking cane. It would not be unreasonable to state that he resembled a studious bank clerk more than a well-regarded police detective.

Now he sat opposite his former commanding officer, Superintendent Thomas Arnold, head of H Division. Arnold was an Essex man who, like Abberline, had served in the East End for the majority of his career.

Arnold leaned back in his chair, with his hands clasped behind his head. He spoke plainly and did not suffer fools.

"I'm surprised the Yard has such interest in the demise of immoral unfortunates. As you know, Fred, Whitechapel is filled to the rafters with them."

"Well, Superintendent, the Yard is just concerned with why there have been two, now three, knife murders against them in just a month."

Abberline was settling into his new role at Scotland Yard when suddenly he was asked to assist in the investigations of the recent Whitechapel murders. The sudden spate of murders in the East End meant that Scotland Yard wanted someone on the ground who knew the locals. They might be more willing to give up vital information more freely to someone they knew and trusted.

Arnold shrugged his shoulders and leaned forward.

"Perhaps if these women did not choose such a precarious means of existence, they would still be around to smell the roses."

First, there was Martha Tabram. An unfortunate who was stabbed almost thirty times in a stairwell off Gunthorpe Street. A soldier or sailor was initially suspected of that one. Then just last week was Polly Nichols, who was given a wretched end. The wounds on her neck and body were quite simply from another kind of evil altogether. The Yard was concerned that they might have been by the same killer. They asked Fred to assist and see if there were any connections.

"May I ask what do we know of today's victim, Superintendent?"

"We'll find out together, shall we?"

This very morning, Abberline received a telegram at Scotland Yard informing him of yet another murder of an unfortunate. This one was in the backyard of a lodging house on Hanbury Street. That was now three knife murders on prostitutes in the space of just a few weeks. Even by Whitechapel standards, that was concerning—hence why Fred was here.

Arnold stood up and walked to the door of his office before bellowing, "Reid!"

He retook his seat. Within a few moments, Inspector Edmund Reid, head of CID at H Division, entered. He noticed Abberline and smiled.

"Hello, Fred. You can't stay away, can you?"

Abberline liked Inspector Reid. The rumour was he was an extremely talented singer and magician. Remarkable for such a well-respected officer.

"You jest, Edmund, but sometimes I feel I can never escape the excitement of Whitechapel."

Reid took a seat beside Fred. "I have many days like that."

Arnold was not one for such small talk.

"So, Reid, please enlighten Inspector Abberline and me on today's latest victim. You visited the scene?"

Edmund cleared his throat and proceeded to remove a notebook from his inside jacket pocket.

"Yes, sir. I arrived at the yard of 29 Hanbury Street at approximately just after seven o'clock this morning. Several officers were already present, including Inspector Joseph Chandler. Dr. Bagster Phillips was concluding his assessment of the victim's injuries. The victim was found close to the steps at the rear door of the building leading to the backyard. Her throat had been cut open, just like that of Polly Nichols. In this case, Dr. Phillips believed the killer attempted to try and remove the head completely but failed to do so. Her stomach, chest, and genital areas were cut open and were fully exposed. Not only that, parts of her intestines were thrown over her left shoulder. What also looked like a long link of sausages still attached to her insides was thrown over her right shoulder. I've never seen a scene like it."

Arnold leaned back in his chair again. "He's going further this time it would appear?"

"That's not all of it, sir," continued Reid. "It seemed he took her uterus with him."

Fred and Arnold both stared at Reid.

Arnold broke the silence. "He did what?"

"I just spoke with Dr. Phillips after his post-mortem, and he was able to ascertain that the uterus and part of her bladder were missing. The murderer must have taken it with him."

Arnold was now scratching his head.

"What on God's earth does anyone want with a prostitute's uterus?"

Reid and Abberline could not answer.

"The victim, what's known of her identity at this stage?" Fred was curious.

"Very little. Dr. Phillips ages her somewhere between thirty-five to forty-five. He places the time of death sometime around 3:00 a.m. He believes she was dead a couple of hours before her body was discovered. She seemed she was also not in great health before her murder. An inventory of her possessions has given us some clues, all of which we are pursuing. The main one is officers finding a leather apron in the yard. Detective Sergeant Thicke believes this could be a vital clue. He knew of a Jew named Pizer, who is known locally as 'Leather Apron.' This would be our main line of enquiry at this time."

"Thank you, Inspector Reid. You may return to your duties."

"Yes, Superintendent." Edmund got up from his seat.

"So, no doubt I'll probably see you again sooner rather than later, Fred?"

"No doubt you will, Edmund." Inspector Reid exited the office.

"Her uterus, Fred? What do you make of that?"

The truth was, Abberline could not make anything of that. He had never seen or heard of any other murder like it.

"It is difficult to say, Superintendent. If it was for a medical desire, surely there are better specimens that could be acquired. Not only that, why go to such lengths, such as attempting to remove the head as well? It is all very bizarre."

"Well, the Yard does seem to like the strange ones. As Reid said, I'm sure we will be seeing much more of each other over the coming days and weeks. Anything you need, ask. You know where everything is."

"Thank you, sir."

Fred considered the strangeness of the most recent murder. What was it the murderer wanted? Clearly, it was not money. Could it be revenge? Understanding the motivation would come later; Fred knew the priority was to stop the killing.

Despite Arnold's view, Fred knew these women did not choose their lives. Circumstances and misfortune conspired against them.

They might have lived at the bottom of the barrel, but they deserved better deaths.

PART 6

Elizabeth Stride

21 April 1865
Kurhuset, Gothenburg

The weather was still. Everything was still. The baby lying dead in the cot was still. Nothing but silence. Nothing was moving. Neither wind nor rain. Nothing. Death was here. The world was empty.

Elizabeth Gustafsdotter didn't quite know how she had come to this point or to this place. Her natural curiosity and vivid imagination had outgrown the family farm in Torslanda. At just seventeen years old, this slender and eager dark-haired farmer's daughter went to the big city to follow in the footsteps of her elder sister. She looked for work as a maidservant.

Elizabeth had managed to find it with the Olofsson family, spending four years in their service. It was hard work, but the girl from the country was not afraid of such things. However, after one night of drinking in a nearby inn, it was enough for the family to terminate her employment immediately. She had broken the terms of the servants' agreement.

Since then, the past year had taken her to depths she never knew was possible.

In particular, the last couple of months had had a hugely

profound effect on her. Since learning of her pregnancy, the possible father threw her away like an old handkerchief. Elizabeth was on her own.

Unwittingly, she had become a victim of trafficking. He had seen Elizabeth with her belongings crying near the church on the very same day she lost her position. The church doors were locked, and he seemed so friendly.

"Hey, miss, are you okay?" she remembered him asking her.

"No, sir, I am not. I am desolate and without work. My employers just kicked me out onto the street after four years of service!"

He sat down beside her and offered her handkerchief from his jacket pocket.

"Please, take this. It will all be okay, I am sure."

Elizabeth took the handsome blonde stranger's handkerchief and began to slow down her sobbing.

"Thank you, sir. This is most kind."

"Please, it is nothing. My name is Karl Ericksson. What is your name?"

"Elizabeth. Elizabeth Gustafsdotter."

Ericksson smiled at her. "That is a very beautiful name. You are very beautiful."

Elizabeth smiled back. She was taken aback by such a compliment.

"I live not far from here. I have my own lodgings. It is not much, but if you need somewhere to stay for a few days whilst you find a new position, you are more than welcome."

Elizabeth could not believe such a nice man would come to her assistance like that. She was naive.

"That is most generous, sir. However, I do not have any money for food or board. I'm sorry."

Karl was beaming from ear to ear. "You must not worry about that. I am sure we can find a suitable arrangement."

When they arrived back at his grubby room above a chandler shop, Karl did not waste any time getting what he wanted from her. He was not so gentle after all. The fact that he gave her alcohol and food confused her. She was not sure if she should stay.

After a few days, he introduced his "friends" and asked her to "look after them." Elizabeth was made to sleep with many men. Night after night. Day after day. This went on for many months. When it was apparent that she was pregnant, she was once again discarded to the streets. Alone and scared, she needed to survive somehow.

Elizabeth found solace in vodka. The man in which she put her trust so cruelly abused it. Vodka made her forget. Forget the days. Forget the nights. The truth was, she had no idea who the father was.

A few weeks earlier, she was picked up by the local police and forced to register as a prostitute. As such, she was subjected to a degrading medical examination that led her to this place. They told her she had syphilis and required treatment. That was how she ended up in this horror hospital. They put their lotions and potions inside her. Now her baby lay dead in front of her.

At just twenty-one years old, Elizabeth was already exhausted by life. Men could not be trusted. Authority could not be trusted. Nothing could be trusted. Death might have just spared the poor baby girl the cruelty of life.

Elizabeth got out of her bed gingerly, still in agony from the pain of giving birth to a baby already dead. As she moved close to the cot and stroked the cold, blue face of the infant, she could not help but cry.

"Goodbye, my sweet girl."

* * *

10 July 1866
Swedish Church, Wapping

The Lutheran Church in Wapping was like a slice of Sweden in the East End of London. It did not fit in with the local surroundings, but then neither did Elizabeth. The building stood within its own grass square. The mix of circular and square stained-glass windows demonstrated its unique Scandinavian style perfectly. The angular bell tower greeted visitors as they approached the narrow oak door entrance. This place was both familiar and strange to Elizabeth.

The priest noticed her coming through the door. In Swedish, he greeted her immediately from the other end of the long, narrow aisle.

"Hej kära resenär!"

Elizabeth strolled towards him at pace.

"If you do not mind, I would prefer to speak in English. I need the practice," she asserted.

"Of course. When in Rome, as the Catholics would say," replied the priest. "Please come, and sit down." He ushered Elizabeth to join him to sit on the front row.

Sweden was no longer a place Elizabeth could call home. She had no intention of ever returning. It was why she was here. She was seeking to register her permanent residency in London at the behest of her employers.

The experience of Kurhuset left her scarred in more ways than one. Even after losing her baby, she was made to return to that place again twice more. Endure more "examinations." During her October admission, Elizabeth had caught the attention of the good-natured German, Mrs. Maria Wiesner. Maria offered her the chance to work as a maidservant to her family, which she accepted without hesitation. As a result, Elizabeth could be removed from the police records as a prostitute. Once this happened, she was delighted to have the opportunity to improve her circumstances.

"So, how can the Church help you today?" asked the priest.

"My name is Elizabeth Gustafdotter from Torslanda, and I arrived in this city five months ago from Gothenburg."

Elizabeth had started working for the Wiesners in November last. They were a friendly family involved with the Gothenburg Orchestra. Music constantly filled their home. As much as the Wiesners were charming people and had given her a chance of everyday life, the urge to leave Sweden would not desert her.

"So you wish to register your permanent residency in England?"

"Yes, sir. That is correct."

"Well, Ms. Gustafdotter, I need to collect my ledger from the back room. Please wait here one moment."

The priest got up from the pew and paced his way to the door behind the altar.

Elizabeth had initially asked the Church to help transfer her here, which they declined. Then whilst working for Wiesners, she was made aware of a family moving to London and needed a maidservant. She applied for the position and was hired. This was her ticket to a better life outside of Sweden. With or without the Church's help, she would find herself in the most important city in the world.

The priest returned with a ledger book and pen and seated himself back down at the pew.

"Now, can I confirm your religion as Lutheran?"

Elizabeth had not been spiritual for a long time, but she knew how to play the game. Religion had failed her at every opportunity. Their doors were closed when she needed them after losing her position with the Olofssons. They turned her away when she needed their help to leave her wretched life behind. No one offered their prayers when her baby died. Religion meant nothing to her.

"Passionately, sir."

The priest smiled. "Very well, let's begin."

* * *

14 November 1884

City of London Cemetery

The wind whistled through the cemetery like a message from heaven itself, chopping through the leaves and grass. Elizabeth had lost her religion long ago, but one could not help feel some spirituality when surrounded by death. Now forty years old, she was more open to such ideas.

All around John's grave spot were hundreds, if not thousands, more. A simple stone marking with his name, age, and date of death was engraved upon it.

"Is this all a good man's life is worth?" she muttered under her breath.

John Stride was a man of simple means, but he was a man with a history nonetheless.

Elizabeth only held nothing but affection for her late husband. Their marriage did not last, but that was no fault of his. The age gap of over twenty years never really became an issue for either of them. The union was more of a pragmatic friendship than one of raw passion. She did try to make it work. Those years as coffee shop owners in Poplar were hard work, but it offered an element of stability for Liz in a stage of her life when she most needed it. John offered her safety and security.

Not long after registering her residency in London, her life began to unravel once again. The family into which she came into service had terminated her employment after just a year. There were plans for them to move to France and to take her with them. Then it all went very wrong.

Her master's brother, who had a residence nearby, had taken an interest in her. He was married, but that did not stop him. It started as simple, lingering looks. After a while, when he visited, he would find excuses to brush past her. He would often do so quite intimately when nobody was looking. Within a few months, he was fully touching and kissing her whenever he had the opportunity. Then late one night, she was alone in her room in the attic when he came and visited her. Elizabeth was flattered that someone in a higher class would be that attracted to her. So when he pushed himself upon her, she did not protest. She let him do what so many men before had done with her body. The very next day, she was asked to leave the house, never to return.

She was abandoned again by men she trusted—this time in a country with minimal language or contacts. Through sheer luck, she could find service employment very quickly with Elizabeth Bond on Gower Street. It was in a nearby coffee house to her new employer that their paths crossed. Initially, they built a cordial friendship, arranging to meet for coffee and cake. John was surprised that this was a daily tradition in Sweden. After a few months, John suggested they get married and open their own coffee shop with his savings.

Why not? she thought. He was a lovely man who didn't drink and was kind. He was stable. Elizabeth needed something she could call her own. Stability was good. It made sense.

The first few years that followed were challenging but probably the most rewarding for her. Everything started with so much promise. Then as more public houses kept opening, the number of teetotallers kept dropping. The competition was too harsh. They even tried to change their fortunes by moving the shop, but it was no use. John had no choice but to sell the business.

Elizabeth had fallen pregnant several times during their relationship but had lost them all through miscarriage. She could not keep a baby. He was heartbroken every time. Elizabeth couldn't help but think that children could have been the making of her. That place in Stockholm had taken away that opportunity from her with their chemicals and potions. Of course, she could never tell John the truth. It was to be a significant issue in their marriage. John had given so much to his father's business in Sheerness that he wanted something of his own. She failed him. After a few years of trying to reconcile and separating, in the end, they both decided the marriage had reached its conclusion.

Since then, she had been drinking heavily, flitting between workhouse, vagrancy, and the doss house. Ambitions of business, family, and marriage were firmly extinguished. All that remained today was a need for alcohol and survival. The least she could do was be here now. She was giving John the respect and goodbye he deserved, having missed his funeral.

The wind whipped across her face once more as Elizabeth leaned down to the gravestone. She kissed her fingers and then touched the stone before wrapping her arms around herself to protect herself from the brutal elements.

No element was more brutal than life itself.

* * *

6 April 1887

Dorset St., Whitechapel

Elizabeth was tired, despite it being the middle of the day. The drinking and arguing over the past few weeks had caught up with her. She was alone in this small, soot-soaked room. Even more, Michael had locked her in. He did this often when he wanted her to "behave herself."

This time she knew there was an apparent reason as to why. It was to prevent her from making an appearance at the courthouse. If she didn't show for the case, then it would be dismissed.

Suddenly she felt a sharp pang in her left eye socket. It was where Michael had punched her. He put some power behind this one. So much so she even banged her head off the wall as she fell backwards onto the floor. For a short man, he was happy to make his physical presence count when he wanted to.

The fights had always been rough with Michael. His temper could be very hot. Liz was no angel herself. She would admit she would rile him deliberately at times. This time, however, he was keen to ensure she knew her place. Seemingly, this was that place—nursing bruises in a filthy locked room.

Elizabeth got up from the bed and shuffled slowly towards the window, where there was a pail of water. She took a nearby old rag and briefly soaked it in the water before applying it to her damaged eye. As the damp cloth connected with the skin, she winced with sharp pain.

"This is a bad one."

Liz held the cloth tenderly to the bruise and looked out of the window onto Dorset Street. As usual, life was overflowing. As she looked up and down the road, she spotted Michael. He was almost home. She put the rag down and swiftly jumped back into bed. She wrapped herself up in the dusty blankets tightly and pretended to be asleep. After a few minutes or so, she could hear his heavy footsteps clumping their way up the wooden stairs. Then the sound of the key clattering into the lock. Within seconds the door was open before being promptly slammed shut again. She could hear his heavy breathing as she kept her eyes tightly shut.

She felt him sit down at the edge of the bed.

"Liz, you awake?" Without giving time for a reply, he continued, "I know you are. I saw you at the window just now."

She swiftly threw off the blankets and sat up. "So you saw the prisoner then? Is it not you who should be under lock and key, Michael?"

He released a deep sigh as he ran his finger and thumb over his thick moustache. "You know why I did that. Had you have not made a complaint against me for assault, I would not have been forced to keep you locked in this room, would I?"

Liz looked away with her arms crossed.

"Due to your failure to show up at the magistrates' court, the charges have now been dropped. As I said, they would be. This is the end of the matter."

Liz remained still, locked in her stare away from him.

Michael then placed his hand on her ankle and smiled. "Liz, come on. We can be normal again now."

She remained unmoved. Michael then started to rub his hand up and down her leg.

"Come on, girl, let's forget all of this nonsense. How about you throw some rags on, and I will treat you to a few drinks down the Britannia?"

After a few moments, she broke her silence.

"You think I am so weak, Michael, that the promise of drink will replace what you have done to me? Look at my face! The way you treat me at times is worse than that of a dog. I may not have much, but I deserve better than this. Am I so feeble-minded that I am to forget?"

Michael stroked his moustache again. "All right, Liz, calm down. What will it take?"

She gave out a short sigh and focused her attention back on him.

"How about if I promise to try and control my tongue, you shall try and control that temper?"

Without missing a beat, Michael met her offer with a firm agreement, "Done!"

After a moment, Liz smiled. "Oh, Michael. You know no man

means more to me than you, don't you?"

Michael moved closer to Liz. "Say that again."

Liz knew what she was doing and what was coming. In a sultry voice, she whispered to him, "You are the best man I have ever known. No one has ever made me feel the way you do. You know where."

Michael grabbed Liz and threw her down onto the bed. The two then started engaging in a passionate embrace. The heat was overcoming them both.

Liz knew with the fire of his passion also came the fire of his temper. She knew this relationship was not perfect.

For now, it remained a better option than being alone.

**

15 September 1888

Scotland Yard, London

Chief Inspector Donald Swanson was sitting in his new office. The office was bare. It had nothing but a simple chair, a basic desk, a blank writing pad, and a large window overlooking Whitehall.

"Where to start?"

Raised in Thurso in Scotland, Swanson came to London as a young man looking for an opportunity away from his father's life as a distiller. He had no desire to follow his father into that world. Donald was always a good scholar. After a brief period as a teacher and clerk, he answered a job advert in *The Daily Telegraph* for new police recruits. Now aged forty, he had spent over half of his life as a serving policeman.

In the twenty years of working for the police, Swanson had acquired a reputation as a thorough and organised detective. His natural administrative abilities were not all that common amongst his contemporaries. Such skills enabled him to gain an edge in catching criminals earlier in his career when working in the Y, K, and A divisions.

Swanson had been at the Yard almost a year now. His reporting and analysis skills positioned him as an officer his superiors could rely upon for an efficient investigation. One such superior who appreciated Swanson's talents was Sir Charles Warren, commissioner of the metropolis.

Sir Charles had just informed Swanson that he was putting him in overall charge of the investigation into the murder of Annie Chapman, the prostitute found with a missing uterus in the backyard of Hanbury Street in Spitalfields. The decision was made because the newly appointed assistant commissioner and the man in charge of all detectives across London, Dr. Robert Anderson, was on rest in Switzerland. The suggestion was he could be gone as long as two months.

Swanson had been given his own office to conduct his enquiries. Warren stated that Swanson had full authority to see every paper, document, report, and telegram related to the murder. Today a memo was issued to inform the acting assistant police commissioner of such. He would ensure the message was echoed and understood across the CID departments across the whole metropolis.

Swanson was thankful that Inspector Abberline had already been working with H Division on the murder of Polly Nichols and Annie Chapman. Fred's knowledge of the area and these cases would be a valuable start point for this investigation.

"Fred is where I shall start."

Swanson wrote a memo inviting Fred to see him at his earliest convenience. He would leave it with the desk officer downstairs to catch Abberline.

"Now we begin."

* * *

29 September 1888

The Bricklayer's Arms, Whitechapel

The weather was horrific. It was a stormy night. Elizabeth was glad to be in the dry. The rain spattered against the windows relentlessly. Despite still being September, this must have been the wettest summer she had experienced yet in England. She decided earlier she would enjoy Saturday evening spending her hard-earned money from her recent cleaning work.

The Bricklayer's Arms was one of the nicer public houses nearby.

Elizabeth's drink of choice as a younger woman would have been vodka. It was a little harder to get when she arrived in London, so she developed a taste for gin instead. That was what she was drinking when he tapped her on the shoulder at the bar.

"May I buy you your next drink?"

He seemed a little out of place in here. The man was dressed well enough to stand out.

"You may, sir."

With that, he pulled out a suede drawstring purse from inside his jacket. Elizabeth could not help but see the bag overflowing with coins such as florins and shillings. The stranger caught the landlord's attention and ordered two gins.

"How did you know I wanted gin?"

"I didn't. I wanted gin." He then gave a broad smile.

Liz shrugged her shoulders and sipped her drink.

The man moved in closer. "I am sure I have seen you before, have I not?"

Elizabeth was not sure if this was an attempt at flirtation. She now started to notice the features of his face. His eyes looked almost dark red. His pupils were black pinholes, and he was missing his eyelashes. His moustache was a dark-red hue. A man with money but a peculiar-looking gentleman all the same.

"Perhaps. I am the Queen of Sheba, did you not know?"

The man did not seem moved at all by Liz's attempt at humour. He leaned in even closer, this time quite intimately.

"I know what you are."

Liz moved her head back away from his. "If that is the case, sir, then you will know to be so close costs!"

The laughing man pulled back and reached back into his pocket.

He pulled the drawstring bag out again. He took a sixpence and placed it on the bar.

"Tell me, 'Your Majesty,' what does this buy me?"

Without a beat, Liz took the coin and quickly placed it in her dress pocket.

"That will buy you my company here without complaint for a short while."

The man leaned in again and this time kissed her on the neck gently. The warm breath and bristles of his moustache did not make Liz feel at all comfortable. For his sixpence, she knew he needed something for his money. She allowed him to continue.

"Let us go somewhere more suitable. I have more money I can spend."

After a few moments of contemplation, Liz looked towards the pub's door, and the rain was still lashing hard.

"The rain is too heavy."

"Well, let us wait over by the door until it stops."

She gave him a nod of acceptance, and they both then finished their drinks.

As they made their way to the door, the stranger's hands were all over Liz. Through a false smile, she went along with him. They waited at the door for a few moments as the man continued to hug her and kiss her neck. At that moment, two rough-looking men entered the pub and saw the pair canoodling at the door.

"You should bring her in for a drink instead of standing there!" The man was laughing as he passed with his friend.

The stranger remained unmoved and carried on nuzzling on her neck. Liz just politely smiled.

The rain continued to beat down. They were now kissing in between embraces.

A few moments later, the same man shouted from across the bar, "Here, that's Leather Apron trying to get around you there!"

With that, the stranger prompted Liz to leave, and the pair set off into the hard rain. They headed towards Commercial Road, just a short distance away. As they got to the road, a shop canopy had remained open, and a group of people assembled under it to protect themselves from the drenching. It did not look like stopping anytime soon.

The pair stood in awkward silence, alongside the others, protecting themselves from the weather. After a few moments, the man suddenly changed his demeanour to one of frustration.

"This is not as I had planned."

"What exactly do you mean planned?"

The man stared at her for what felt like an eternity. He said nothing. All she felt was an intensity so sharp that it seemed to cut through to her very soul.

He leaned in and whispered into her ear, "It would have been spectacular!" With that, he suddenly set off without as so much as a goodbye.

Liz suddenly felt very uneasy.

If I didn't know any better, I'd say that man had evil in him.

Immediately she placated such fear with her internal logic. All the newspapers had been saying the Whitechapel murderer was most likely a Jew. This man was definitely an Englishman.

After about ten minutes, the rain started to subside, and the clouds began to disperse, as did the crowd under the canopy. Liz decided after all that excitement that she needed another drink. She opted for George IV on Berner Street. It was a friendly and cosy local, and she might bump into a regular she knew. He was always reliable for a few pence and a quick bit of business.

She walked down Christian Street and passed the long row of cottages. After a short stroll, she eventually reached Berner Street. The rain looked as if it was going to hold off. For a while, at least.

Liz entered the pub. She was surprised at how busy it was. She had to negotiate her way to the bar through the swarming crowd.

Rain seems to make people very thirsty, it would seem, she mused.

The landlord almost missed her, but a quick wave his way and she was served. She took out the newly acquired sixpence and handed it to the publican.

"Gin, please, sir."

Within moments she was again enjoying the taste of London dry gin, a taste she acquired after arriving from Sweden. She navigated her way around the bar. There he was—her regular. He was with his wife. Men were all the same. The poor cow had no idea.

Just then, he spotted Liz. She gave a cheeky smile. He smiled awkwardly back. When his wife was not looking, he proceeded to give Liz the nod to go outside. She finished her drink and went out onto the street. She crossed over, walked a few doors down, and waited. After five minutes or so, he appeared and came over.

"You are very naughty, Liz!"

"I was born naughty, as well as you know!"

"I don't have long before she comes looking. Threepence for a tiff round the back of the school?"

Liz pretended to mull over the offer. "Let me think . . ."

Her client was becoming a little impatient. "Ah, come on, Liz, I need to be quick!"

Liz smiled. "It's okay, I promise I won't tell your wife."

Smirking, he moved closer. "You'd say anything but your prayers!"

They shared a lingering kiss. After a quick look around to see if the coast was clear, they swiftly headed towards the boarding school on Fairclough Street.

It was a spot they both knew well. As soon as they got there, he wasted no time. He lifted Liz's skirt up at the front and then pulled his trousers down. It lasted no more than a minute. The transaction was quickly over. The client pulled his trousers back up, and Liz readjusted herself. He then proceeded to reach into his jacket and pull out some coins. He gave Liz the threepence as promised.

"You going back in the George?"

"No, you're perfectly safe!"

He smiled, gave Liz a nod, and then scampered off. As she waited, she could hear what sounded like Russian music riding on the wind. It must be coming from the Socialist club nearby. She closed her eyes and drank in the melody. Music had always had a calming effect on her. After a few minutes, she exited back out onto the street.

Elizabeth decided that she would probably take a wander past the Red Lion on Batty Street. It was now just after closing, and the landlord was pretty prompt at kicking people out. She might pick up a bit of business there.

As she reached Batty Street, she noticed that the place was still very much open. Instead of hanging around, she decided she would go in and have a gin. It was not as busy as the George, but there were still enough people to make being served more time-consuming than she would like. Eventually, she was served. She took her time and sipped her gin at the bar. Looking around, she could see there were a few couples quietly chatting away. Equally, there were several men on their own, nursing the last of their beers. There were people here, but there was very little life. After around half an hour or so, the landlord decided enough was enough. He announced he was closing. It must be around 12:30 a.m. Liz finished her drink and decided that she would head back towards Whitechapel Road.

She left the public house and walked towards Fairclough Street. As she turned the corner, she walked straight into him—the peculiar man from the Bricklayer's Arms. Again, she was confronted with those dark eyes and hairless eyelids.

"Well, well, well . . . we meet again."

Liz was not at all comfortable.

"Yes, it would seem so, sir."

Liz tried to brush past him and walked further up Fairclough Street. She only got a few paces up the road before he raced in front of her. This time he moved in so close that Liz had no option but to put her back up against the wall. He immediately placed his left hand on the wall just a few inches from her head and closed in.

"Where could you be rushing off to now in such a hurry? I believe we have some unfinished business to attend to, do we not?"

Liz was now feeling a little intimidated. She did not like how this situation was developing. She decided to raise her voice a little in the hope someone might hear.

"No, not tonight, some other night. "

The stranger was not convinced.

"Why the change of heart, 'Your Majesty'?"

Nothing good was happening here. She gently pushed him away and continued walking.

Liz could hear the music again. If she could get as far as the club, she could probably shake him off there. Again, she managed to get a few yards ahead before he passed at pace to get in front of her.

"Tell me, is it the money? You know all too well that I am good for it."

Liz was very uncomfortable now. What if this strange fellow was the Whitechapel murderer? There was something not right with this one.

"As I said, not tonight."

Once more, she pushed past him. This time she was able to get to the corner of Berner Street. Again, the stranger managed to get in front of her. This time he started walking backwards. Liz did her best to jostle past him.

"Come now. I know what you are. I do not believe your legs are ever closed for the business. Whores like you never stop!"

They were now almost directly opposite the club. Liz abruptly stopped. Despite the music being quite loud, there was no one around to get their attention. She decided her best option was to try and push her way out of this.

"And you, sir? What exactly is your business?"

A surge of confidence rushed through her veins as if some other force had overtaken her. She was scared, but she was also angry that she was made to feel so afraid.

"I fear your intentions are not genuine. I shall alert for help!"

With that, she made one final push past him. This time it was much more of a shove. Liz tried to flee across the street quickly in a bid to reach the club. To reach safety. Her heart was racing. She hoped she had done enough to deter this dark character.

Just as she got to the open gates of the yard, she felt him grab her around the mouth. She could not breathe. She could not scream. He had one arm under her right arm, and he had a knife in his hand. Try as she might, she could not release his grip. She tried to break free, but it was futile. Quickly he drew the blade across the left side of her neck. She could feel the air in her lungs rapidly dropping.

As the blackness overcame her, she could feel her body falling towards the damp, cold ground as he let her fall. The last sound she heard was Russian folk music.

Then the music stopped.

* * *

30 September 1888

Dutfield's Yard, Whitechapel

The feeling of the knife crossing the bitches' throats was the most sensational. The blade was so sharp it sliced through skin and tissue like soft butter. Watching the life drain from the whores' eyes as they hit the floor was also something to savour. However, ripping them open and feeling their organs slip and slide up against the skin, well, that was truly exquisite. It was the most erotic feeling that James had ever experienced.

He wouldn't get the chance with this slut. It was too public, too exposed. Like the two whores before this one, he quickly rifled through the dress pockets for any money. He found a few coins and put them in his own pocket.

No whore would enter hell with the ill-gotten gains from her filthy ways.

James then remembered that he had purchased some cachous from a street vendor earlier. He took the plain packet from his inside pocket. He put them in her right hand and clutched them tightly.

"Tell the devil your dirty story with sweet breath."

The approaching clunking sound of hooves on cobbles alerted

James that he needed to act. He had no time to flee the way he came. The pony was almost at the gate. He would be spotted. He could see it was darker further into the yard. He got up and dashed into the shadows. Immediately, he spotted a couple of privies that were set back. He bolted into one just as the pony reared up.

"Woah, boy, woah!"

Louis Diemschutz was a hawker who had spent the day selling cheap jewellery in Sydenham Hill. He was returning the cart to the yard when he came across the body of Elizabeth Stride just inside the opened gates. Louis got down from his seat on the trap to get a closer look at the figure lying on the ground. It was very dark. He was unable to tell if the woman was dead or just drunk. He went inside to look for a candle and to alert his wife. James peered around the corner to see the pony unattended.

James took his chance to briskly jog back down the yard passageway, past the pony, and out onto Berner Street. His heart was pounding hard through his chest. He took an immediate right and quickly reached the chandler shop on the corner. Soon he came to Back Church Lane. He could relax a little now. He was far enough away to avoid suspicion.

Each step away from the scene made his heart beat that little less hard. That was close. That was exciting. He needed more. James took out a tin matchbox in which he kept his arsenic. He stopped and took a few dabs of the grey-white powder on his fingers. He took a quick look around and then rubbed it on his tongue.

Suddenly a thought dawned on him. The police might not even

realise the whore was one of his. After all, he did not get to finish his work.

"The bloody Jews will probably be blamed again!"

James paused for a moment, then smiled.

"What if I do another? There shall be no confusion then," he considered. "I might even take another piece away like the last one. Maybe something a little less cumbersome."

A uterus was not the easiest thing to dispose of once he finished his business with it. He would need something a little more subtle this time.

James decided he would head back to his lodgings to freshen up and mix up his appearance. He was excited.

The night was not over yet.

* * *

30 September 1888
Berner St., Whitechapel

The International Working Men's Educational Club on Berner Street was the central meeting place for many radicals in the area. The Social Democrats and anarchists used the building to print publications, organise protests, and host social events for people of the same political persuasions. More often than not, they attracted fresh Jewish immigrants from Russia and Eastern Europe.

These men and women identified themselves as more culturally Jewish than religiously. The more settled Orthodox Jewish population found these radicals unhelpful, as did the British government and Metropolitan Police. The events of Bloody Sunday in Trafalgar Square the previous November was still a raw nerve for many on both sides. Thoughts of revolution did not amuse England's well-established order of things.

Since the last murder of Annie Chapman, the Jewish population of Whitechapel had become the focus of unwanted attention and scorn from much of the local Gentile population, including the police. The whole debacle surrounding "Leather Apron" had left a very sour taste of anti-Semitism. A Jewish man named John Pizer was arrested for simply having the nickname "Leather Apron." Officers found a leather apron at the scene of Chapman's murder and promptly arrested him. It transpired it was owned by one of the lodgers of the boarding house, who left it in the yard to dry. Pizer also had alibis for the nights Polly Nichols and Annie Chapman were murdered.

Now Jews were the focus once again. A murder of a Gentile just inside the property of a radical Socialist club left many of the patrons feeling uneasy. The police were quick to try and link the two events as being connected. This did not go unnoticed by some of the more vocal members of the club, as officers questioned them in the immediate aftermath of the discovered body.

Joseph Freedman was one such radical.

"Do you not find this highly suspicious, Officer?"

PC Hawke was in the process of taking Freedman's statement.

"It is not my job, sir, to ascertain suspicion. I am simply

recording the statements of those present."

"But I was not present, was I? I was here inside the club. I did not see or hear anything."

"Yes, sir, but the body was found outside the club. Which means it is part of the murder scene. As such, we must be thorough and take down everyone's statement. Witness statements are crucial evidence."

"How do you know it was the murder scene? I mean, someone could have placed the body there deliberately to implicate the club. The British government are not receptive to ideas such as ours. I would not be surprised if something more sinister is at play here, Officer."

"More sinister than a woman found with her throat cut, left bleeding to death in the gutter? We may have different ideas of what qualifies as sinister, sir."

Freedman could not but help but feel the Jews would be the ones again associated with murder. This was putting the work done by the Socialists back by years. He could not just sit on his hands and not act. He was trained to be radical when the situation required it. The cause needed action now more than ever. Heroes were made in such moments.

If witness statements were such crucial evidence, perhaps a new witness was required. One that saw a Gentile committing the murder? Joseph's thoughts began to form.

Tomorrow a new witness would give a different story to the one currently being crafted here. Propaganda would replace morals.

It seemed to work for the police.

PART 7

Catherine Eddowes

26 July 1861
Bilston St., Wolverhampton

Wolverhampton, like so many towns across the midlands, had been boosted by industry. The surge in factories was largely thanks to the sprawling canal system that led back down to London. The heavy-sooted smoke of advancement could be tasted in the air.

Bilston Street was reflective of modern times: a patchwork mix of multistorey Georgian houses standing alongside small terraced worker cottages and commercial yards.

Kate was packing all her worldly belongings into an old potato sack. Once again, she was on the move. Her Uncle William was furious. He decided enough was enough and that it was time for "Chick" to find her own way now. William was the brother of her late father, George. Kate was always amazed at how quickly bad news travelled within a family. Who needed a telegram?

"What were you thinking, Kate?" William was pacing up and down the bedroom as she was packing.

"I'm sorry, Uncle. I do not know why I did it." Kate genuinely could not explain.

"After everything this family has done for you. This is how you repay us. You're lucky you are not in front of a magistrate in the morning!"

Such threats did not concern Kate. At just nineteen years old, she felt she had already suffered her fair share of injustice. Perhaps she thought she was owed something and tried to take it. It was not like the Old Hall Works would miss a pen case. She had reasoned to herself that they must make hundreds of these things each day. They would not miss one. Except they did. Prying eyes saw her slip one into her dress pocket. Within minutes she was standing in front of the manager, who made it quick work to release her from her scouring duties with immediate effect.

"Both your father and I have given that place many years of loyal service. They were generous to welcome me back after we all left for London when you were a baby. Our father before us worked there. Our family have a long-standing reputation with the company. It is for that, and for that only, you were not given over to the police. We cannot have you stay here any longer!"

Kate never asked to come back to this place. She had grown up in Bermondsey in South-East London. Yes, she was born in Wolverhampton, and most of her family were from here, but she always felt every bit a Londoner. Her accent was unmistakably London. After her father died, the children that were still alive were all separated. Both her parents had died of consumption. Her father did his best to keep the family together and to provide after her mother passed, but when the illness caught him too, things unravelled quickly. Some of her younger siblings were sent to the local orphanage. A couple of her older sisters went into domestic service. One even got married. She alone was packed onto a train and sent to live with her aunt and uncle in the Midlands. That was four years earlier. Now she was leaving again.

"I am truly sorry, dear Uncle, for the shame my actions have brought upon your good name. Thank you and Aunt Elizabeth for taking me in after my father died. My intention was not to embarrass you, but I see how my actions have done so. Thank you for the past four years, and I hope one day you will find it in your heart to forgive me."

William said no more and watched Kate as she left the room. As the other family members also watched her leave, Kate could not help but get excited about the idea of adventure. There was a sense of release from what was inevitable. She was not going to be just like every other girl in this town. She would not follow the same patterns laid down by the women generation after generation before her. The world was full of interesting people she had not met yet. It was full of exciting things she had not seen yet.

Kate knew of another of her father's brothers, Thomas Eddowes, who lived in Birmingham. He too was regarded as the black sheep of the family. Perhaps he would find affinity with her new outcast status.

This was the first time in Kate's life that the unknown was something to embrace rather than fear.

The story of the future was yet to be told.

* * *

4 April 1869
Cottage Pl., Westminster

Kate could not bear it. Crammed into a tiny one-room lodging in Westminster with her three children, the life she chose was now starting to take its toll.

She could not bear to watch the removal of her dead baby. Harriet was just three weeks old. The poor mite had starved to death. Kate's health of late had not been the best, and she could not give her child the sustenance from her breast she needed. She failed as a mother. Her latest child was being wrapped in blankets and would be taken away by the doctor. The overwhelming sense of failure swamped Kate. It was all too much for her to take. She needed a drink.

A few minutes after the doctor left, Kate grabbed whatever could have any possible value in the cottage. Boots, shirts, blankets—anything.

Kate advocated all her responsibilities to her daughter Annie.

"Annie, please keep watch on your brother. I must go see someone."

She then proceeded to take all she could carry to the local pawnbroker. He, in turn, gave her a small handful of coins for the meagre possessions. Without delay, she headed straight to the Green Man pub, just a short walk away.

The death of a child was not something Kate thought would

ever happen to her. She was painfully aware of death, losing numerous siblings and both of her parents as a child. Naively perhaps, Kate thought her life would be different. She always felt she was different. The life she chose was different. Different, it transpired, was not always better.

She entered the premises as a woman with a single focus. Kate slammed down what little coins she had onto the well-battered, heavily scratched bar.

"Gin. Now please, landlord!"

Aware of Kate, the landlord took just the coins he needed and left the rest there. He poured Kate her drink. Without hesitation, she drank the gin in one fell swoop.

"Same again!"

The landlord gave a disapproving look but again took the coins he needed and poured Kate another drink. This time she took the last couple of coins from the bar and headed to a nearby table to be alone with her thoughts and her drink.

The life waiting for her eight years earlier that she was so quick to leave behind seemed like a desirable proposition right about now. This existence was not the happy one she had hoped for when she departed Bilston Street in a hurry. She made her way to nearby Birmingham, where her uncle Tom and his family took her in. He was a former bare-knuckle boxer and was now a shoemaker. Kate quickly got a job as a metal polisher. After days of hard work, she would often frequent the numerous local pubs. It was around July '62 that she and Thomas crossed paths. This young grey-eyed

Irishman had captivated her.

Despite being a man of abstinence, Thomas went from pub to pub selling penny dreadfuls that he had written. He was an exciting and curious character with his gipsy-like ways. Thomas had caught her attention, and the two got on instantly. Kate was fascinated by his stories of India, where he served in the army before being discharged on health grounds. He was still withdrawing a small pension.

Kate was fascinated with the idea of being a traveller, roaming wherever the wind would take her. She believed there was something romantic to that way of life. Within weeks Kate had left her job in Birmingham and embarked on another new adventure with Thomas.

They went from town to town singing ballads and hawking Thomas's writing. They even went to Wolverhampton for a short period, where Kate's relatives were not as charmed as she was by her new partner. They felt his life choices were most unsuitable for her. Then they always did think that about anything she chose to do for herself.

Exactly six years earlier, she was about ready to give birth to their first child on their travels together. She registered with the Great Yarmouth Workhouse so that she could give birth in their infirmary. This was when Annie arrived. Kate was delighted. The idea of her perfect life was coming together. She did not care much for stability at the best of times. She was very much wed to her vision of a bohemian existence. Laying down rules and roots seemed so ordinary.

It was not long before Kate started to experience the realities of such a life. The lack of money was proving difficult. Kate started to become more and more concerned about her child's health and welfare with the constant travelling. As such, Thomas had to take on more and more reliable forms of labour. This was the start of his temper rages. Thomas was not one for being held down with responsibilities and commitments. He was away again looking for work, leaving her to raise a newborn and two small children alone in London with no money. He had been gone for so long. When he returned, she could inform him there was now one less mouth to feed. She started to cry.

Nobody in the pub offered to comfort her. The afternoon drinkers were consoling themselves with their own issues, looking for the answers etched in the bottom of their glasses.

After a few moments of tears, Kate regathered her composure. She took the few coins left and counted them in her hand. With a quick wipe of tears from her cheeks, she grabbed her glass and returned to the bar.

"Same again, please, landlord."

* * *

17 August 1878

Southwark Magistrates Court, London

The Southwark courthouse was just like any other Kate had been dragged into previously. Dark wood everywhere and reeking of polish. The judge was similar to the others too. Old, harsh, and uncaring.

"This is the second time in as many years that you have been arrested for being drunk and riotous. What do you have to say for yourself, Mrs. Conway?"

Conway was Thomas's surname. They never married, but Kate did use it to give the impression they were. It was just easier.

"I'm very sorry, sir. I have, on occasion, been unable to temper my consumption, and as such, it overcomes me. I then find myself in court before good gentlemen like yourself."

"Perhaps you should strongly consider abstinence as a highly reliable tool to temper your alcohol consumption."

There was a moment's pause.

"Mrs. Conway, the court does not wish to entertain your presence again on such matters. I hereby sentence you to seven days' imprisonment at Wandsworth Prison. That should give you enough time to consider the benefits of abstinence."

The guard promptly marched Kate back down to holding cells as she waited for the other prisoners to be told of their fates. Last year the magistrate at Lambeth gave her fourteen days for the same crime. She was well versed in the process at this stage.

Kate sat alone in her cold stone cell, waiting, deep in thought. The children would be with their aunts. They would be fine. Thomas Jr. was now such a young man. He had been a great protector of his younger brothers, George and Frederick, who both came along after Harriet died to increase the family size.

Their father was taking longer and longer spells away, looking for work. When he did return, there were always arguments. Thomas had a fierce slap on him. Kate often would be bloodied and bruised after such incidents. The rows stemmed mostly around Kate's need to drink. Thomas wasn't there most of the time and had no idea how hard life was for her. What else was she going to do?

Kate and the children had drifted from workhouse to doss house to workhouse again. On occasion, she would be overcome by the drink that she would leave her children on the street to fend for themselves. Usually, a good-natured bobby would find them and eventually get them to their aunt or a nearby workhouse. Kate wouldn't know where they were this time until she was released from prison and looked for them.

This was not the life she thought she was embarking on all those years ago when she left Wolverhampton. Was she brave? Was she naive? She did not know. The only thing Kate did know was that she was exhausted. Despite being surrounded by her children, she felt incredibly alone.

She felt even more alone now.

* * *

30 September 1888

Bishopsgate Police Station, London

Kate had no recollection of how she ended up here. The last thing she remembered was being thrown out of the Three Tuns in Aldgate. Waking up sober in a place she had no memory of being was a common theme. This time, she was just grateful it was in the safety of a police cell.

Kate clearly remembered telling John that she would go and look for some money from her daughter. Again, something that was far more of a habit than she would have liked.

Kate met John Kelly in '81, not long after she had finally decided enough was enough with Thomas. The beatings were becoming far too frequent, and her drinking was getting worse. Kate couldn't quite remember whether he kicked her out or whether she left. When Freddie died in '79, things got even worse. The drink became her only solace whilst Thomas spent so many long periods away.

The on-duty constable was checking the cells every thirty minutes. Kate heard him as he passed her door.

"Here, when am I getting out?"

"When you are capable of taking care of yourself," he shouted back.

"I can do that now!"

No reply from the policeman.

Kate had on occasions continued to abandon the children on the street to go looking for a drink. She would spend a week or so drinking herself in a stupor before eventually reclaiming them from whatever local workhouse took them in. Kate hated Thomas and the life that became of them. It wasn't the children's fault, but she felt short-changed by her life.

Everything came to a head in early '81 when they finally parted ways. Thomas took the two boys, and Annie, then eighteen years old, went with her mother, albeit briefly. Annie found work and left Kate to take care of herself.

When Kate moved into Cooney's lodging house on Flower and Dean Street, she met John. Immediately they found a common passion—alcohol. His character was very different from Thomas, and for that reason alone, Kate felt things were improving. John was much calmer and enjoyed socialising. The pair soon became comfortable in each other's company and very rarely shared a disagreement. The tranquillity of no children, no commitments, and no arguments was something of a comfort to her. Kate felt she was getting closer to being her old self.

John and Kate were rarely with money, but Kate was comfortable with that arrangement. There were no children. They only had themselves to be concerned with. In the last few years, John had been picking up some regular work on the markets, and every season, they would go down to Kent for hop-picking. Kate's drinking was not getting any less, and as a result, without John's knowledge, she would pick up a few quick tiffs here and there for sup money. Kate did not see it as something John needed to know.

Thirty minutes had passed, and Kate could hear keys rattling outside of her cell. She knew that sound. They were letting her out.

"Come on. You are free to leave after you give us your details."

Kate sprung up from the cell bed, despite the throbbing hangover she was experiencing.

"You are indeed a gentleman."

"All right, that's enough. Let's go."

The constable escorted her to the main desk, where the desk sergeant was waiting.

"Name?"

Kate decided to give a false name. "Mary Ann Kelly."

"Address?"

"Six Fashion Street."

"Mary Ann Kelly, you are being released from Bishopsgate Police Station without charge on this occasion. If I see your face in my station again, you will go in front of the magistrate, do you understand?"

"I do, Sergeant. Thank you."

The constable escorted Kate to the door.

"What time is it?"

"Too late for you to get anything to drink."

"I shall get a damn fine hiding when I get home."

Kate didn't know why she said that. John never laid a finger on her. Perhaps the memories of Thomas would never leave her chaotic thoughts.

"And serves you right, you had no right to get drunk." The constable pushed open the swinging door for her. "This way, missus. Please pull it to."

"Good night, old cock."

Kate noticed it had been raining as she walked down the road heading back to Aldgate. The path and cobbles were still damp. It wasn't earlier. She must have been in the police cell for most of the night. She checked her dress pockets. No money. Cooney's wouldn't let her in without her fourpence. Kate decided to head back to the Three Tuns. They might still be open, and she could Norwich a drink off someone.

Kate started to fall back on offering the business to paying customers a few years back, not long after losing Freddie. It was quick money. She tried to do it as rarely as possible. However, today was one such occasion. After returning from Kent with little money from picking, what they had was spent on accommodation for the night. John stayed at Cooney's, and Kate went to the casual ward. Kate went back to Cooney's that morning, and they both agreed to pawn John's boots so they could eat. By the afternoon, they were again without money.

Kate told John she would go and see Annie in Bermondsey to see if she could get some money. However, Kate already knew Annie was not in Bermondsey anymore. She tried knocking her up before they went away to Kent. Annie had moved on and had not left her new address. Instead, Kate decided to head a bit further east so John would not see her. She must have picked up four or five customers, and after each one, she happily went and spent the money on gin. Kate remembered telling John she would be back at Cooney's no later than 4:00 p.m.

After a ten-minute stroll, Kate arrived back at the entrance of the Three Tuns. It was well and truly closed with no sign of life. She banged on the door in vain hope.

"Billy!"

Billy Jones was the landlord who threw her out. Kate waited a few moments, but nobody was coming.

Kate still needed money. Perhaps if she took a walk around, she might find a quick bit of business. Not many around on the High Street. Kate decided to walk up Mitre Street to the junction of King Street. Very quiet here as well. She headed back down Mitre Street and decided she would cut through Mitre Square. She noticed that the square was very dark, particularly in the corner.

That should make a good spot, she thought to herself as she approached Church Passage.

As she made her way down the passage, a man crossed the road directly ahead of her. He noticed her immediately. He waited at the corner as she approached.

"You looking for the business?" she asked. Kate did not wish to be out any longer, so no time for preamble.

The man was wearing a loose-fitting grey jacket, a peaked cap, black leather gloves, and a red neckerchief. He had the outward appearance of a sailor, but his demeanour was more of a clerk. His eyes seemed odd. Like they were red. She wasn't sure, but she thought he was missing his eyelashes. Strange, but he seemed harmless enough.

"It depends. Where?"

Kate could tell he was nervous. This could be the first time he had used the services of women such as her. He was probably just a little anxious. She put her hand on his chest to reassure him.

"Don't worry. I know a very discreet place for us. Just a few steps back this way. The price should be fourpence, and I shall require the money first."

The stranger smiled. He then reached inside his inside pocket and removed a suede drawstring bag. He proceeded to take out some loose coins and handed them to Kate.

"Will that suffice?"

Kate grinned at her customer and put the money into her dress pocket.

"It will, sir. Shall we?"

Kate offered her arm, and the stranger linked up with her. They then proceeded to walk back down Church Passage into Mitre Square. Together they quietly headed for the darkest corner.

"I told you. We shall be discreet here."

They unlinked their arms as Kate moved deeper into the shadows. Suddenly, without warning, she could feel the taste of leather. He grabbed her from behind and had his hand over her mouth. Kate could not breathe. She did her very best to try and break free. His grip was so tight. In a matter of seconds, she could feel something sharp and cold run along her neck with his other hand.

The bastard has cut my . . .

Before she could even finish her thoughts, she was already dead. The end came quickly. The story of her future was now told.

* * *

30 September 1888
Mitre Sq., London

PC Watkins from the City of London Police was strolling along his beat when he noticed something peculiar in the south-west corner of Mitre Square. He immediately spotted something in a heap. His first thoughts were that it was most likely a drunk vagrant who had fallen asleep. He turned on his lantern. As he drew closer, he could see it was a body lying on its back. Now standing over the body, he shone his light directly on it. He physically recoiled backwards in absolute horror by what he saw.

"Christ the Lord!"

Watkins sprinted across the square where he knew a night watchman was working.

George Morris was a former policeman and presently was in the employ of Kearly & Tonge's Warehouse.

"For God's sake, mate, come to my assistance. Here is another woman cut to pieces!"

Morris grabbed his lamp and went with Watkins back to the dead body.

"Jesus!" said Morris.

"Here, take this. Go call for assistance!" PC Watkins gave his whistle to the watchman, who sprinted out of the square onto Mitre Street.

He started blowing the whistle furiously as he raced towards Aldgate High Street. Within a few moments, two officers came to his call.

"Come quick! The butcher has slaughtered another."

Morris and the policemen all raced back to Mitre Square, where they found PC Watkins with the body. The other officers also shone their torches on the body.

"Holy mackerel!" exclaimed one.

"He's done a right number on this one," said Watkins.

"I'll fetch Dr. Sequeira immediately!" said a bobby.

"I will go to Bishopsgate station and alert the inspectors," said the other.

The two officers raced out of the square and found some plain-clothes policemen congregating on the corner.

One of the men, DC Halse, addressed the constables, "What's the emergency? We heard the whistle."

"It's the Whitechapel murderer. He's done it again."

"Where?"

"In Mitre Square."

DC Halse and the other plain-clothes officers rushed to the scene. Watkins and Morris were standing near the body when they entered the square.

"My god, what has he done?"

Halse was visibly shocked by the scene that greeted him. The victim's face was a mess. He had cut the tip of her nose off, and her throat was wide open. There were sliced upside-down V-shape marks on her cheeks. Her clothing was cut to ribbons, and her abdomen was open. All manner of her internal organs was on display.

"Sick bastard!" said one of the newly arrived officers.

A few minutes later, a police constable returned with Dr. Sequeira. The constables shone their lamps on the body whilst Dr. Sequeira squatted down to examine the deceased.

"Well, there can be no doubt the victim is dead. I'm afraid, gentlemen, that is about as much as I can do at this juncture. As this is a murder scene, I do not wish to touch the body."

"A PC has gone to inform Bishopsgate of the murder," informed Watkins.

"We shall wait then for the police surgeon to arrive to decide what we do next with the body."

Just then, Inspector Collard of Bishopsgate Police Station arrived at the scene and addressed Dr. Sequeira.

"Hello, Doctor. We are fetching Dr. Brown. He will be here shortly. Please remain present for the time being as we may require your further assistance."

"Very good, Inspector."

Collard turned his attention to the plain-clothes officers present.

"All of you, go search the locality for anything or anyone suspicious. Head in separate directions. The murderer must not have gone far."

With that, the plain-clothes officers scattered out of the square.

Ten minutes later, Dr. Frederick Brown, the police surgeon, arrived.

"Hello, Fred," greeted Collard.

"Hello, Inspector. I understand the Whitechapel murderer has left us a victim on our side of the fence?"

"Indeed he has. It's not a pretty sight, I can assure you."

Dr. Brown moved closer to the body where Dr. Sequeira was waiting.

"Hello, George. I was not expecting to see you here. Nonetheless, a pleasant surprise. Have you given an examination?"

"Fred. No, only simply to declare expiration. I did not touch or move the body."

"Very good. I shall give a preliminary one now. If you would be as so kind as to take notes as I do so?"

"Of course."

Dr. Brown took out a notebook and pencil from his inside pocket and handed them to Dr. Sequeira. He then crouched down to view the body closer.

"Body is lying on its back. Head turned to the left shoulder. Arms by the side, as if fallen there. Both palms upwards, fingers slightly bent. A thimble lies beside the right hand. Clothes are thrown up over the body with the genital and lower abdomen areas exposed. A bonnet lies above the head. There is great disfigurement of the face. The throat is cut across. Below the cut is a neckerchief. The upper part of the dress is torn open. The body is mutilated, most likely post-mortem. The body is quite warm. No signs of rigor mortis. The crime must have been committed within the past half an hour or forty minutes."

Dr. Brown stood up, and Dr. Sequeira returned the notebook

and pencil.

"Thank you, George. Would you think the killer possesses any anatomical or medical knowledge?"

"From what I could see, I would say not. The incisions are not in the manner of positioning that any reasonable professional surgeon or mortician would cut."

"I am inclined to agree at this point. We shall know more after the full examination."

Both men stood over the carnage left behind of the human life that once was.

"I think you should be able to go now, George. Thank you for your assistance."

"Not at all, Fred. I bid you good night."

Dr. Sequeira doffed his hat, picked up his bag, and trotted out of the square. Inspector Collard spotted Dr. Sequeira leaving and went over to Dr. Brown.

"So, Fred, do you think it was one of his?"

"From the reports I have read, and from what I have seen here, I would be under no doubt. Let us get an ambulance arranged and take the cadaver to Golden Lane to see exactly how far he went this time. I shall do a full examination tomorrow. Good night, gentlemen."

"Good night, Doctor."

Dr. Brown picked up his bag, and he too exited the square. DC Halse arrived back at the scene after his initial search of the area.

"Anything, Dan?"

"Nothing, Inspector. No blood trail, no witnesses, nothing. It's like he just melted into the night."

"Well, the bastard is out there somewhere. Come, let us arrange for the body to be moved to the mortuary."

The two detectives briskly marched out of the Square. Several constables remained to keep public order and to ensure the body remained protected from prying eyes.

Around thirty minutes later, the detectives arrived at Golden Lane Mortuary. The body came ten minutes after that. Two constables lifted the corpse from the handcart and onto the operating table in the examination room.

Just as they laid the body down, a piece of the victim's earlobe fell onto the floor.

"Jesus of Nazareth!" cried Inspector Collard. He then gestured to one of the officers to pick it up.

"You can go now, Constables. You have done more than enough."

The officers left the room.

"Right, Dan, let's take an inventory of her possessions."

DC Halse noticed something immediately. "Sir, her apron."

"What's that, Halse?"

"She is missing a piece of her apron. Look."

He gestured that a significant piece of her apron looked as if it had been crudely cut off.

"Indeed, you are right. Why would he take a piece of her apron with him?"

"I shudder to think, Inspector. Who knows why this animal does any of it?"

"Well, let's get on and make a record of what he left behind. I'm quite sure Acting Commissioner Smith will want to be brought up to speed as soon as possible."

The two men proceeded to document this poor woman's worldly possessions. There was not much to show for a life. Whoever she was, her existence was meagre. Her life was one of hand to mouth.

Now she was tomorrow's newspaper headline. Another name added to the list of wretched souls taken by this horror of inhumanity.

* * *

30 September 1888

Goulston St., Whitechapel

James glanced out onto the street. He instantly spotted the policeman walking in his direction. He slipped back deep into the shadows of the stairwell of Wentworth Dwellings. James waited in silence, holding his breath as the constable passed. After a further half minute or so, he emerged from the shadows. He headed to the wall that could be seen from the street. James gave another glance up and down the road. He was happy no one was around. He pulled a piece of chalk from his inside jacket pocket. James then wrote a message on the bricks as quickly as he could. When he finished, he took a wrapped-up rag from his outer jacket pocket and threw it on the ground, directly underneath the message. He then disappeared back into the darkness of the passageway, which led back out to Middlesex Street.

Around thirty minutes later, PC Long passed the same spot on Goulston Street and immediately noticed the rag. It appeared to be bloodied. He moved in closer and flashed his light on it. It was damp with blood and more.

As he raised his lamp, he caught sight of some writing in chalk on the wall. Long took out his notebook and quickly transcribed the words.

Immediately, a sense of unease overwhelmed him. He nervously checked the stairwells in the dwellings—no signs of blood or any other clues. After a few minutes of searching, he re-emerged back onto the street, where he saw another constable from a different division.

"Constable, over here! I found something."

The officer came over and flashed his light onto the rag. "What is it?"

"I don't know," replied PC Long. "It looks like it's splattered with blood and God knows what else! There is a strange message in chalk on the wall there too."

The constable tried to make sense of it.

"The Jews won't be blamed for nothing? Blimey. I wonder if this has anything to do with the murder in Mitre Square."

"What murder? I did not hear of any."

"I only know as a detective passed and told me. An awful job he did on her—left her in a right mess. Detective reckoned it was around an hour ago."

PC Long decided to take the initiative.

"I'm going to bring the rag to Commercial Street station immediately. Keep watch. No doubt an inspector will come along shortly to investigate."

Around ten minutes later, PC Long arrived at the Commercial Street station and immediately alerted the desk sergeant.

"I think I need to speak to the superintendent. Immediately!"

The desk sergeant sensed that it was important and did not question the PC. He sprinted up the two flights of stairs to the detective floor. Superintendent Arnold had been knocked up because of the murder on Berner Street. Usually, he would be based at Leman Street, but tonight he happened to be at Commercial Street when Long arrived. Within seconds he emerged and made his way to the lobby.

"What is it, Constable?"

"PC Alf Long of A Division, sir. I think you need to see this." Long placed the soiled rag onto the counter.

"Where did you find it?"

"Goulston Street. It was lying at the entrance of some dwellings there."

"Goulston Street? Did you search the area? Was there any sign of blood or a knife?"

"I did a search, sir, but there was nothing. No blood, no footprints, or any knife. The only thing was a strange message on the wall where the rag lay."

"What kind of message?"

"It was in chalk, sir. I made a note of it in my book."

Long pulled his notebook out from his side pocket and began to read what he had written down.

"'The Juwes are the men That Will not be Blamed for nothing.' Do you think it is connected to the murder in Mitre Square, sir?"

"What are you talking about, PC Long? There was a murder on Berner Street, next to a Jewish Socialist club."

"The constable who informed me was very sure, sir. He said it was an hour ago in Mitre Square. He is still at Goulston Street keeping watch at the scene."

Superintendent Arnold addressed the desk sergeant. "Send someone to wake Commissioner Warren. There have been two in one night!"

Just as PC Long and Superintendent Arnold were preparing to leave Commercial Street station, the City of London Police were entering Leman Street station. DC Halse, DC Hunt, and Acting Commissioner Major Smith were looking for some answers. The detectives on the street had heard about Long's find. They wanted their evidence back.

Halse approached the desk sergeant.

"Commissioner Smith, DC Halse and DC Hunt of the City of London Police. We wish to speak to the most senior officer present. We believe you have something important of ours."

The desk sergeant was not prepared for such a visit from senior members of the neighbouring force.

"I'm sorry, gentlemen, but they are all at Berner Street at present."

"Why is that, Sergeant?"

"Well, because the Whitechapel murderer struck there earlier tonight, sir."

The three visiting men looked at each other in surprise. Just then, a PC entered the station.

"There's been another one, Sarge, in Mitre Square! Not only that, but the murderer has also left some evidence at Goulston Street."

The City of London officers waste no time proceeding to make their way to Goulston Street. Around ten minutes later, the three men arrived at Goulston Street to see a lone constable standing guard at the entrance to Wentworth Dwellings.

DC Halse addressed the officer, "Constable, we are from the City of London Police. We need to know what exactly happened here."

"Yes, sir. A bloodied rag was found on the ground just behind me here."

"Where is the rag now?"

"Another PC was here before me. He took it to Commercial Street, sir."

Superintendent Major Smith decided he had had enough running around Aldgate and Whitechapel on a wild goose chase.

"DC Halse, I trust I can leave you to follow this up? I have had enough excitement for one night. I shall return home. You can brief me in the morning."

"Yes, sir."

Major Smith headed back towards Aldgate with Detective Hunt. Halse turned his attention back to the PC.

"If the rag was taken to Commercial Street, why are you still here at the scene?"

"Oh, because of the writing, sir."

"What writing?"

"The writing on the wall there."

The constable pointed directly at the chalked message. Halse had not even noticed it.

"The rag was directly underneath it. The previous officer felt it was important. It said something about blaming Jews."

Halse moved in closer to examine it. He pulled his pocketbook and pencil out from the inside of his jacket pocket and proceeded to write down exactly what he saw: "The Juwes are not the men That Will be Blamed for nothing."

After Halse finished writing his note, he addressed the PC again, "Do not let anyone do anything to this until I return. Do you understand, Constable?"

"Yes, sir."

Halse felt the message was indeed strange. It could be a cryptic clue of some kind and must be photographed immediately. He decided he should head to Commercial Street station. However, he took only a few paces forward before a group of men appeared on the road. They included PC Long, Superintendent Arnold, and

Commissioner Sir Charles Warren himself.

"Who might you be?" asked Superintendent Arnold as they approached the scene.

"DC Halse of the City of London Police. Major Henry Smith sent me. And you?"

"I am Superintendent Arnold, and I'm sure you will already recognise that this is the Commissioner of the metropolis, Sir Charles Warren. What is your business here?"

"I am gathering evidence, sir. There was a murder in Mitre Square a few hours ago. We believe the Whitechapel murderer committed it. We also believe the Metropolitan Police are holding some important evidence from the crime scene that we wish to recover."

Warren, in his clipped Welsh accent, decided to ask Halse some questions himself.

"Well, DC Halse, as I am sure you are aware, you are standing in metropolis territory. This makes this scene our crime scene, and therefore anything from this scene is our evidence. I am sure the City of London police trains their officers in boundaries as part of its basic training?"

DC Halse could immediately sense that Sir Charles was not going to be complicit in assisting him.

"Yes, Commissioner, but with all due respect, this is not a crime scene. No crime had been committed here other than petty vandalism. However, the apron, which most likely was taken from our victim, was recovered here. Important evidence that links this scene with ours."

Warren took a few moments to consider Halse's response.

"Very well. Superintendent Arnold, please ensure DC Halse recovers the rag from Commercial Street with no issue."

"Yes, sir."

"As for this so-called message," Warren continued. "I do not think it wise for it to remain."

Halse was alarmed. "Again, with respect, Commissioner, would it not be prudent to take a photograph first?"

"No, Halse. I do not. We do not even know if the message is connected to the rag. It will be sunlight soon, and the risk of it being seen by locals could lead to public disorder. There is much tension in Whitechapel right now. Such references to Jews could ignite a riot. It should go without saying that no officer here would wish for a repeat of November last."

"Perhaps if you just remove the word 'Juwes,' sir?"

Warren was becoming impatient with this subordinate.

"Arnold, sponge, please!" barked Warren.

Superintendent Arnold handed the commissioner the sponge. The group watched in amazement as Commissioner Warren walked up to the wall and, without any hesitation, wiped the wall clean of the entire message.

"Now, DC Halse, there shall be no more discussion on the matter. I suggest you collect your rag at your earliest convenience and return to the City of London. The police of the metropolis has enough of its own business to consider."

Halse was stunned.

"You all heard the commissioner," bellowed Arnold. "There is nothing here of interest to us. Please return to your duties with immediate effect."

Within seconds, the scene was completely clear again. It was as if nothing happened there at all. DC Halse walked over to the now graffiti-free wall. He tapped it three times and shook his head in disbelief. He then proceeded to head back to Aldgate and the sanity of the City of London.

Why did the killer leave the apron here of all places? Where was he going? Was it connected to the writing? If it was his message, what did it mean? Why did the commissioner not wait for a photograph?

If the murderer was never caught, this moment might become one of the most significant of the case. DC Halse could only conclude that the pressure of the murders had given Commissioner Warren temporary leave of his senses.

Why else would he have done what he did?

* * *

30 September 1888

Leman St. Police Station, Whitechapel

Fred Abberline was in Inspector Reid's office. Edmund, like Superintendent Arnold, had gone home for a few hours to catch up on some much-needed rest after the events of last night. Fred was going over some of the witness statements from the scene of the Berner Street murder. The desk sergeant suddenly appeared at the doorway.

"Inspector, there are two men downstairs. They claim to have seen something of significance on Berner Street last night."

It was unusual for witnesses to come in so soon after a murder. Usually, they would take a day or two to consider whether what they saw was relevant and whether they wished to offer their testimony at all. Unusual, but not unheard of.

"Please bring them up, Sergeant."

Fred tidied up the desk and moved the pile of officer notebooks to the window shelf. He cleared the desk of any debris and pulled up two chairs on the other side of the desk before seating himself down again. He took a pencil and a piece of paper from the desk drawer.

"Inspector Abberline, I presume?" asked the taller of the two men.

Fred stood up to shake both men's hands. The smaller looked pretty nervous.

"Please, take a seat. I understand you gentlemen may have some information with regards to the murder on Berner Street?"

The men sat down as the taller one spoke again, "Well, Inspector, I do not. However, my friend believes he may well have. His name is Israel Schwartz, and he does not speak any English. He and his wife only recently moved here from Hungary, and he does not speak any of the language. He can only speak Hungarian and some Yiddish. I am here to help translate."

Abberline started to take some notes.

"You, sir, what is your name?"

The man paused a moment.

"David Cohen. However, I must stress that I do not wish to be involved in this in any official way. I am simply assisting a friend in providing a statement."

"Very well. It is noted. So perhaps Mr. Schwartz can begin by telling me where he presently lives?"

Mr. Cohen looked a little confused.

"Why must you know that, Inspector?"

"If Mr. Schwartz is providing us with a statement, we may wish to follow up with him at a later date. Therefore, we will need to know how to find him. So, his address?"

Cohen spoke to Schwartz in a language that Fred had never heard before. If this was Hungarian, then much praise to any man who could understand it. Schwartz gave a longer-than-expected response.

"He said that his wife was moving their lodgings yesterday, so he will give you the new address, which is 22 Back Church Lane, Ellen Street."

Fred wrote the address down.

"So perhaps if Mr. Schwartz can let me know what exactly he saw last night?"

Cohen again broke into the foreign language and addressed his friend. Schwartz took a moment and then replied at length. After a few moments of Cohen nodding his head, Schwartz finished.

"Okay, Inspector. He said he turned on to Berner Street around 12:45 a.m. He was coming from Commercial Road. He said he noticed a man ahead of him who was walking strangely. The man then stopped to speak with a woman in the yard."

"Can Mr. Schwartz describe that man?"

Cohen relayed the question to Schwartz.

He replied, "My friend believes the man was about five feet, five inches, around thirty years old, was intoxicated, had a brown moustache, a full face, broad shoulders, and was a Gentile."

"A Gentile?"

"Yes, a non-Jewish person."

"I'm aware of the word, Mr. Cohen. My surprise is, how did Mr. Schwartz reach that conclusion from behind?"

Cohen asked Schwartz, and Schwartz replied, "He said because he was of an English appearance."

Abberline put the description down in his notes. He opted not to include the Gentile reference.

"Mr. Cohen, please ask Mr. Schwartz what happened next."

As requested, Cohen passed on Abberline's question. Schwartz then started to mimic some actions as if being pulled. He then gave a movement of a man smoking a pipe. There were a few more sentences, of which Fred did recognise one word: *Lipski*. Then he stopped.

"Inspector, my friend said the man was trying to pull the woman into the street at first, but she would not move. So the man turned her around and threw her to the ground."

"Did the woman scream at all?" inquired Fred.

Cohen asked his friend.

Schwartz replied.

Cohen relayed the information back, "He said she did three times but not very loudly."

Abberline scribbled his notes down.

"Please continue, Mr. Cohen, there was more?"

"Yes. He said he thought it was a domestic incident and did not wish to get involved, so he crossed the street. The man shouted, 'Lipski' at my friend."

"How did he know the word was 'Lipski'? I mean, he does not speak any English. How does he know it was that word?"

Cohen paused for a second.

"He knows the word, Inspector. Every Jew living in Whitechapel knows the word regardless of their English language skills. Particularly of late with our community being under such constant suspicion."

Lipski was indeed a slur against Jews, and Fred knew this. He was involved with the case himself. Israel Lipski was an umbrella stick salesman and a Polish Jew. He was hung last year for the murder of a young pregnant woman by the name of Miriam Angel. The murder had shocked Whitechapel, and many Jews believed that Lipski was innocent and was not given a fair trial. As a result of the sentencing, his surname became widely used as a slur towards Jews.

Abberline continued his questioning. "I saw Mr. Schwartz act out smoking a pipe. What was that?"

Cohen paused again before speaking, "Did he? I missed that, Inspector." Cohen readdressed his friend in what Fred felt to be a slightly aggressive tone.

Schwartz replied to Cohen.

"He said there was another man who was smoking a pipe whom he passed."

"Another man? So how did Mr. Schwartz know if the 'Lipski' word was being addressed to him or the other man?"

Cohen turned to Schwartz and asked.

Schwartz shrugged his shoulders.

"He does not know for certain, Inspector, but again he believes the other man to be a Gentile too."

"But he does not know for certain. Can he describe the other man?"

Cohen relayed the question back, and Schwartz replied.

"He said the other man was taller. Probably closer to five feet, eleven inches. He had a fresh complexion, light-brown hair, a brown moustache, and wore a dark overcoat with an old, black, hard felt hat."

Fred wrote the information down.

"Okay, Mr. Cohen, can you ask Mr. Schwartz if he saw the first man attack the woman or see what happened to her after she was thrown to the ground?"

Cohen did as asked, and Schwartz responded.

"He said he did not see anything more with the woman. He felt the other man was following him, so he decided to run away. He believes the pipeman was running after him and that he managed to lose him by a railway arch."

Abberline frantically transcribed the information down.

"Okay, Mr. Cohen. Was there anything else?"

Cohen replied immediately, "No, Inspector."

"What we need now is an identification."

"What identification? Of whom?"

"The victim, of course. We will require Mr. Schwartz to come with me to the mortuary and identify that woman he saw last night was indeed the murder victim."

Cohen looked a little surprised by this development.

"So, Mr. Cohen, would you mind asking Mr. Schwartz?"

"Sorry, yes, of course."

Cohen spoke again to his friend, who replied with a simple nod of affirmation.

"Well, I will inform the desk sergeant of our intentions, and I will be back in a few minutes. Please wait here for a moment."

Fred took the sheet of paper he was writing on with him as he trudged out of the office. Once Abberline was out of earshot, Cohen addressed Schwartz in English.

"What was all that with the pipe, Avi?"

"I'm sorry, Joseph. I was caught up in character, and it just happened. I thought you would say the first man was smoking a pipe. It would have made him appear more English."

"Well, now we have a second man. Let's hope we did enough to convince him the killer was not a Jew. I should have known using an actor and a made-up language would be a bad idea."

"Again, I'm sorry, Joseph."

"We have to go to the mortuary now. All I ask now is you are convincing enough that she is the woman Schwartz saw. No more actions!"

"Understood."

"Now quiet. He will be back any second."

Fred returned to the office paperless, and took his hat and coat off the nearby stand.

"Shall we, gentlemen?"

Abberline extended his arm towards the door. The two men stood up, and all three left the office.

This is already the best lead for last night's murder, thought Fred. Israel Schwartz could well be the last person to have seen the victim alive other than the murderer himself.

What Israel Schwartz saw could prove to be a significant development in the case.

* * *

30 September 1888

First-Class Train Carriage

It was around 11:00 a.m. James had been on the train for less than an hour. The comfortable first-class compartment he was sitting in was all his. Still exhilarated by the events of just a few hours earlier,

James knew it was too soon for the Sunday papers to report on the murders. He could not wait to read all about it. It was somewhat of a genius masterstroke to commit two in one night. It would send the whores running, fearing that the next man they met could be him. Fear would grip their souls.

The first one had not gone to plan. James was surprised that the thrill of almost being caught was as enjoyable as it was. That slut was the riskiest. She almost made the club and alerted the Jews. Then the pony arrived. James did not think his heart could take much more, but the medicine helped him focus, and he escaped. It was not a satisfactory conclusion; he wanted to leave a more significant mark on the bitch.

To kill two whores in one night was hard work but a decision he felt very pleased with. The second one more than made up for the lost opportunity on the first one. She led him to a perfect spot cloaked in darkness and offered a great place to do his work. This one was his most satisfying yet.

He decided to leave two inverted V marks on her cheeks. The imbeciles would never know he was leaving his initial there for all to see. M was written right across her face. A little something was left in the bonnet too.

Once she was opened up, he was able to have some real fun. He extracted her kidney and wrapped it in part of her apron he ripped with his knife. It was a little easier to transport than the organ he took from the fat whore in Hanbury Street.

It was the same apron piece he left for them to find on the street with his little message on the wall in chalk. He thought he would be clever and give the police the impression that he was a local. He decided to write the message as if he was one of the many ill-mannered and poorly bred locals. It should be clear enough that he was taking responsibility for the first murder by linking it with the bloody apron of the second one.

The fools surely can't miss that, he pondered.

The Jews should not be getting credit for the work he did. He left even more funny clues in the graffiti.

"Bloody Jews!" he laughed.

The train was rattling at breakneck speed back towards Liverpool. James should be back on the exchange tomorrow. The world around him would be none the wiser that it was he who committed these deeds. James was excited to read the morning papers at breakfast tomorrow. The papers would no doubt be full of lots of delicious details about his extraordinary accomplishments.

In his bag was a large jar filled with gin and the whore's kidney. James was not yet sure what he was going to do with it. For now, he would need a safe place to hide it. He immediately considered placing it under the loose floorboard in his bedroom. He could get access to it whenever he was inspired to relive his actions. Florie never visited him these days anyway, and the children knew well to stay out of his bedroom. Maybe he could send it to the police next time he was in London as a small gift for their efforts.

James was beaming.

Slaughtering the infestation of whores was most rewarding. One by one, they would get to meet their Maker. They should be scared. The work was not over yet.

The work might never be over.

PART 8

Mary Jane Kelly

15 July 1880
Risca, South Wales

It must have been at least 3:00 a.m. when the banging on the front door came. Roused from a deep slumber, young Mary Thomas, just sixteen years old, found a couple of nearby blankets to wrap over her chemise. She did her best to give herself as much modesty that could be reasonably expected at this ungodly hour. With a strike of a match, she lit a candle on the bedside table. Mary ventured out of the bedroom towards the persistent banging on the door. Upon opening it, she saw before her two police constables with their hats under their arms.

Mary was feeling very uneasy.

"What's the meaning of this?"

"Miss, can we come in? We have an issue of serious importance to discuss."

The forlorn constables entered the cottage.

"You are . . . related to James Davies, madam?"

"He is my husband. Well, soon to be. We are engaged to be married. Why? What has happened?"

"It is with the deepest regret that we are here to inform you of his passing this very evening."

Mary was frozen.

"There was an unfortunate explosion in the mine. He and many other men were not able to survive this tragedy. The accident has taken the souls of all men who were working in that mine."

Was James dead? But only a few hours earlier, he was here, lamenting the fact he was working the night shift. Was he never to return? Mary could not fathom it. She remained in her frozen state.

The officer broke the silence.

"There is a London & South Wales Mining Company clerk who will be at the Cross Keys Hotel tomorrow. They will furnish you with details on what to expect over the coming days so that you are kept adequately informed."

"Rwy'n deall." Mary could barely move and had not noticed that she had answered in Welsh.

The truth was she did not understand what was happening at all.

"The doctors will require Mr. Davies's next of kin to sign the death certificate. As you were not yet man and wife, that will require one of his parents to do so. Would you be able to arrange that, or would you like for us to inform them?"

Mary took a moment to respond.

"Yes . . . I mean, no. I will let his mother know. She will come."

"We will leave you now. We are sorry for your loss."

The constables left the cottage. In the space of five minutes, her world was turned on its head. Everything was a haze. Mary felt disorientated. She was lost, bewildered, and stunned. She felt she must do something. She had no idea what. He was gone.

Mary was around seven years old when she moved to Merthyr Tydfil from Carmarthen with her family. Her father, John, tried his best to make a living as a labourer at the ironworks in Carmarthen and then as a miner in Merthyr, but work was not stable. Money was always a problem.

Mary first laid eyes on James when she saw him amongst the men with her father returning from work. He was just a boy doing a man's job. He was the prettiest thing she had seen, and she instantly became besotted. At every opportunity, she would find excuses to be close to him. James felt the same. He was two years older than her. When she was fourteen and he was sixteen, they started spending more and more time together. More and more time alone. It wasn't long before the passion between them overflowed. They became each other's first love. They both vowed to spend the rest of their lives with each other.

When Mary's father found out they were spending long periods alone together, he immediately confronted James at his home. This led to a massive fight in the street between Mary's father, James, and James's father. James found Mary the very next day and told her to go with him. He would take care of her. They did not need their parents. She was drunk on love and was angry at her father for trying to break their union. So she agreed.

James knew about Risca. Around six months earlier, they walked for the best part of a week from Merthyr. Luckily, there was work for him when they arrived. They found a small cottage at the edge of the old factory, and the owner agreed to let them lodge there.

For six months, their life had been perfect. Three months earlier, James gave Mary a ring handed down from his grandmother and asked her to marry him when they were both old enough to do so without permission. She was delighted.

Now he was gone. That dream, that, life had gone with him. Mary had a decision to make. Would she return to Merthyr and explain what had happened? Face the wrath of her father and James's parents? Or would she try to take control of her own life and move forward without the love of her life? It did not take long for Mary to reach her decision. Survival was all that mattered now. He would live on forever in her heart.

It was time to surrender the childish fallacies of youth and become a woman.

* * *

14 August 1885
Collier Place, London

Mary knew what was about to happen as she entered the main parlour. The two Maundrell sisters were standing on either side of the ornate fireplace, looking impeccable as ever.

"Marie Jeanette, my sister and I had such high hopes for you. This is truly disappointing," said Frederica.

Heleine remained silent.

"It is always the risk for a service like ours to recruit girls such as you from humble backgrounds. The overwhelming desire to revert to a more uncivilised existence is always there. Such as adopting unbecoming behaviours. Like a feral dog. You have proven that to be so."

Mary felt the inevitable coming. The sisters must be aware of the theft. She could not help herself. The clients had so much money. Unlike the clients back in Newport, they would not miss ten pounds here and there. Newport was different. Mary was caught by a client who reported her and her madam to the police for theft.

This incident took place four years earlier. Mary was just seventeen years old. The judge considered that in her sentencing. She only got two months, but Haggarty, the madam, got seven years. Mary had no desire to return to Newport. Small Welsh towns never forgot.

Mary always felt this way of life was temporary. After James died, she had to find a way to survive and fend for herself. She asked one of the neighbours in Risca to pretend she was James's mother and asked her to give the name for his death certificate as "Hannah Marie Thomas." Their names would be united in death if not in life. Her sister's name was Hannah. No one would make the connection.

As James was only at the mine for a few months, Mary was not entitled to any compensation and for the fact that they were not married. She could not face returning to Merthyr to tell both sets of parents what had happened. They probably found out from the newspaper reports at the time. The Davies family never got to give their son a proper funeral. They would not forgive her for that.

So she headed to nearby Newport instead. It was not long before she was recruited to Haggarty's brothel. Mary found herself in a similar position again now, repeating history, but in far more opulent and comfortable surroundings.

"We are aware from one of our clients that you have stolen money from him. Naturally, we have reimbursed him and offered him our deepest apologies. This type of behaviour, as you were warned, will not be tolerated here. You are, as of now, no longer welcome in this house. It would be best if you left immediately. You shall also leave behind your wardrobe of dresses as payment for the inconvenience and loss of trust you have brought upon our business."

"Madam, the dresses are mine!"

Frederica was becoming increasingly animated. "You should be thankful we do not throw you to the Boys to be outraged in any way they desire for what you have done."

The Boys were the men hired to protect the house from unsavoury types entering the property and ejecting anyone who crossed the line once inside—often more despicable than the men they were supposedly protecting the girls from. That was not a fate she desired.

"As you wish."

Mary turned and left the room. She walked down the long marble corridor and exited the front of the building. Now she had no place she could call home. No means of making money. No beautiful dresses.

After Mary finished her prison sentence in the autumn of '81, she made her way to Cardiff, where she had cousins. She learned that one, Henry, joined the Scots Guards. He got out from the life. Her other cousins William and Richard were quick to include Mary in their schemes. It was not too long before she was in front of a magistrate once again. This time, she was sentenced to six months for larceny in '83.

It was during her second time in prison that she had learned the existence of these types of houses. Mary had mentioned to another inmate, Irishwoman Jane Kelly, that she planned on heading to London upon her release. It was Jane that told her of these houses in fashionable Knightsbridge and Kensington. Around two years before, Mary arrived in the area.

Through speaking with local women, she found this place. Mary took a chance and knocked on the door. To her surprise, they let her in. They suggested that she have a French name as their house was known as the "Gay French House." She was already using her new alias inspired by her former inmate. Mary Thomas was now known in London, at least, as Mary Jane Kelly. The sisters decided to take it a step further. At the house, she would be called Marie Jeanette. The sisters gave her training in etiquette, speech, and hygiene before she was offered to clients. Such education gave Mary a sense of being beyond her class.

There were many clients—some more interesting than others. Most had money, which made them all attractive to Mary on a basic level. One client even took her with him to France on business. She got to see Paris. That was more than anyone else had achieved in her family.

Mary's overwhelming desire for money and security had once again been her undoing. She could not help herself. A most comfortable life had now been taken away from her, and it was her fault. She must start again. Where, she did not know.

Right now, she did know she needed a drink. That always did seem to make things a little bit easier.

* * *

8 April 1887

The Queen's Head, Whitechapel

Mary could not help but feel things hadn't turned out the way she hoped. From the Gay French House of Kensington to a doss house in Whitechapel. From fancy dresses and carriages to quick tiffs for the price of stale bread. Mary felt she could be excused for finding comfort in drinking.

"Can I get you another one?"

The voice was from a young man, who must not have been very much older than she.

"You may. I shall take a rum."

The young man called over the landlord.

"Beer for me and a rum for the lady please."

Mary noted that it was at least two years since anyone called her a lady. In recent years, she was treated no better than a piece of meat handed around the Ratcliffe Highway. She was just like every other girl who had the misfortune to find herself there.

She first arrived at Mrs. Buki's in Wapping. In the beginning, it seemed like a good place. Mrs. Buki went with her back to Kensington to demand her dresses back. Much to Mary's surprise, it was a successful trip. The money made on those was split equally with Mrs. Buki, but it did not last long. From there, she lodged at Mrs. Carthy's before being offered a chance of an everyday life with Joe Fleming in Bethnal Green. He was not fond of her drinking, and as such, she left him. She knew she gave him reasons to hit her, but it did not mean she cared for it. After one such night of drinking, she decided she had enough and headed to Whitechapel. Here she was.

"Name is Joe Barnett. I have seen you around the place but never had the courage to speak with you."

Mary was a little drunk already, but she found his sincerity endearing.

"Courage? You don't need courage, love. Just sixpence." Mary knew she would rarely get sixpence these days.

"Sorry, miss. You misunderstand. I am not speaking with you because I want the business. Well, it's not that I do not. It is just that I think you are very interesting. You have a very different way, you know, from any other girl around here."

"That's because, Joe Barnett, I am not like every other girl around here. I've been to Paris. I will have you know. I have seen places, met people. Yet through misfortunate, I find myself in this place."

"It's not so bad, miss. Yes, some would rob the clothes off your back given half a chance, but there are some good souls here too."

"You are a good soul, Joe Barnett? Is that what you are telling me?"

"I think so. I mean, I may not have much money, but I work hard. I drift between Billingsgate and the fruit markets whenever I can find the work. I believe, to survive in this life, you should work hard and pay your way."

"You know, Joe Barnett. I would be inclined to agree. I, too, work hard. Perhaps what I sell is different. I did not choose it. I was just left with no other choices."

"You still haven't told me your name, yet you keep repeating mine. I count three or four times now. See, that is one thing that makes you different."

Mary laughed. "I'm sorry, Joe Barnett. I am Mary. Mary Jane Kelly."

Joe put his hand out as if to shake her hand. Mary smiled and shook his hand in return.

"Now that we are officially acquainted, Ms. Kelly, I feel I must buy you another rum. May I?"

"You may, Joe Barnett."

***

3 October 1888

Scotland Yard, London

* * *

Inspector Donald Swanson was in his office at Scotland Yard, still compiling the witness reports from the double-event murder from the weekend, when there was a knock at his door.

"Enter!" he barked.

To Swanson's surprise, the visitor was none other than James Monro. He immediately felt the need to stand up, out of respect.

"Honestly, Donald, no need for that. Please remain seated."

Monro entered the room. He opted against taking a seat, as he slowly walked around the room, surveying the various files, folders, and papers strewn across the office.

"Tell me, Donald, how are you finding all this Whitechapel murders business?"

Now seated again, Swanson cleared his throat. "Well, sir, it is indeed a challenge, but I believe we have the best men on the job."

"That's good to hear, Donald. Tell me, are the City of London police playing nicely?"

"As nicely as can be expected, sir."

Monro looked at Swanson and smiled. "You are from Thurso if I am not mistaken?"

"You are not mistaken, Mr. Monro."

"Beautiful part of the world. My family were city dwellers, and as beautiful as Edinburgh is, it will never match some of the more scenic parts of our beautiful nature. Scotland will forever be in my thoughts, as I am sure it is in yours. As for cities, well, none are bigger than the one we are presently in. Would you not agree,

Inspector?"

"I would agree thoroughly, Mr. Monro. London is the best city in the world."

"You know, Donald. I would be inclined to agree. It really is. The newspapers are making far too much of this nonsense, if you ask me, with these Whitechapel murders. Common street whores who knowingly put themselves at such risk could not be expected to be given the same level of protection that should be afforded to every hardworking, decent human being in London. Police resources are limited and must be assigned to those most deserving. These women do not qualify as such. Anyway, I am no longer a member of the police. I work for the Home Office now. My humble opinions shall remain as such."

"Mr. Monro, I only speak for myself, but your presence here at the Yard is sorely missed. Your insights always add value, and I, for one, appreciate them."

"That is great to hear, Donald. I come today with some information which may or may not be of use to you. The Jew club on Berner Street where one of those whores was killed. As well as being home to every Socialist fresh off the boat from Eastern Europe, it is also one of the numerous meeting points for anarchists trying to dismantle democracy as we know it. They wish for our queen to be executed. These are people we do not wish to be part of our society. They will not stop at anything to achieve their aims. My advice, be mindful of the Socialist Jews. They cannot be trusted. In fact, be suspicious of all Jews. I find it just saves time."

"Thank you, sir. I appreciate the information."

"I'm glad my department can be of some small use during these testing times. I have every faith the good officers of the Met will apprehend this evil Jew in no time. I pay no currency to what newspapers say. I think Commissioner Warren is doing an adequate job with the limited resources. Anyway, I am distracting you from important work. I must leave you to it."

"Thank you, sir."

Monro headed towards the exit. "Oh, one more thing. The pipeman seen by that Schwartz fellow, he is one of mine. He need not be investigated any further."

"Very good, thank you, sir."

"No need to thank me, Donald. Are we not all just doing our job for the queen and country?"

"Indeed we are, sir. Good day."

Monro smiled at Swanson and left the room. Swanson sat back down into his chair. When someone as important as James Monro went out of his way to offer you advice, you had to listen. It made every sense that a radical or crazy Jew committed these murders. Swanson wondered what other clues he might have missed.

Back to the case files.

* * *

18 October 1888

Alderney Rd., London

* * *

The men stood around the kitchen table in George Lusk's home on the Mile End Road, staring at the items on the kitchen table.

"Honestly, gentlemen, it is nothing more than a morbid joke by an individual who has a sick sense of humour," claimed Lusk.

"Mr. Lusk, I no doubt your assumptions may well prove to be correct, but in light of recent events, we must remain cautious," said Mr. Reed.

Francis Reed was the assistant of Dr. Frederick Wiles. He was the only person at the surgery when the Whitechapel Vigilance Committee members arrived at the doorstep half an hour earlier. They requested the doctor to review a kidney that had arrived at the home of Mr. George Lusk, the committee's chairman, two days before. In the absence of the doctor, Mr. Reed offered his assistance instead.

Mr. Reed proceeded to take a closer look at the opened box on the table. After a moment of close examination, he offered an opinion.

"I believe this kidney to be of human origin."

The mood in the room was solemn.

"Surely it must be a pig's kidney? Where would such a man obtain a human kidney?" asked Lusk.

"There are ways and means. I would suggest I take this to Dr. Thomas Openshaw at the London Hospital to be fully certain. He will be able to give a formal medical assessment, I have no doubt."

George was still looking perplexed by the possibility that this organ was human.

"Of course, Mr. Reed, please take it. I have no desire to keep such a thing."

Reed carefully closed the box and wrapped it tightly in its original brown paper covering. He bade the men in the room goodnight before leaving, carefully carrying the item away with him.

Lusk sat down and picked up the letter that came with it from the table.

"This letter of gibberish accompanied it."

One of the members of the committee present was its treasurer, Joseph Aarons.

"What does it say, George?"

"The spelling is quite awful, but I shall read it if you so desire."

There was a general murmur of agreement from the five men crammed into this small room.

"Very well," said Lusk. "'From Hell. Mr. Lusk. Sor. I send you half the kidney I took from one woman. Prasarved it for you. Tother piece I fried and ate and it was very nice. I may send you the bloody knife that took it out if you only wait a while longer. Catch me when you can, Mr. Lusk.'"

The silence was palpable.

"Why do you think these were sent to you, George?" Aarons asked.

"I can only think the sender read my letter to the *Telegraph* a couple of weeks ago regarding the issue surrounding the reward. My address was printed along with the letter in the newspaper. The man or men behind this are disturbed individuals who garner enjoyment from such actions. It's a morbid joke and not much more than that."

Despite Lusk's defiance, it was clear that the rest of the room was concerned with these developments.

"Would it not be prudent to give the letter and the kidney to the police, George? After all, there is a chance it may well be genuine."

Lusk took a moment to digest the question.

"I shall take both to Abberline should the hospital confirm that the kidney is indeed human. The police will still need to trace the identity of the ill individual who engaged in this joke of the highest distaste."

Despite all his outward insistence that the kidney resulted from nothing more than a prank, George could not help but feel very uneasy privately. What if this was a piece of kidney from one of the Ripper victims? That meant he knew where he lived.

Perhaps vigilance needed to be closer to home.

* * *

8 November 1888

The Home Office, London

There was a knock at the door. The clerk entered the office of James Monro and closed the door behind him.

"Sorry to disturb you, sir, but the assistant commissioner of the Metropolitan Police, Dr. Robert Anderson, is here to see you."

"Send him in, do not leave the man waiting."

The clerk reopened the door and nodded at Anderson as the cue to enter. The white-bearded man entered the room, and the clerk closed the door behind him as he left.

"Always a pleasure, Robert, please take a seat."

"Thank you, James. I bring news."

The man from the Metropolitan Police seated himself opposite.

"The news is that Sir Charles Warren has resigned."

Monro laughed. "Again?"

"This time, I believe the home secretary will accept it."

Monro, still smiling, leaned back in his chair.

"I believe you could well be right, Robert. Let's say I have a suspicion that Mr. Matthews is far from satisfied with Charlie's work."

"Officially, the resignation is concerning Home Office control and influence in matters of the force. It will be submitted to this office first thing tomorrow morning."

There was a moment's silence.

"Who would have thought a general in the British Army would struggle so much with accepting authority from a civil servant? It was almost like this outcome was somehow engineered by such men?"

This time Anderson was smiling too.

"I could not possibly comment on whether such matters are true. I do wonder, however, who the home secretary will consider as his replacement. Any ideas?"

The two men were very comfortable in each other's presence.

"If I were a gambling man old friend, I would put my money on someone who Matthews believes is knowledgeable and would get respect from the rank and file. I know only of a few very select individuals."

Anderson now had a broader grin. "I can only think of one."

Monro smiled back. "Will that be all, Robert?"

Anderson got up from his chair. "That will be all, Commissioner."

The assistant commissioner then left the office, gently closing the door behind him as he exited.

Monro could not help but feel a sense of achievement. With Sir Charles now gone, the path was clear for him to finally get the role he was destined to have. It was nothing ever personal with Charlie. He was the result of a poor decision taken from higher up the food chain at the time. The fact that the man was a bumbling buffoon made the task to remove him that little bit easier.

"Goodbye, Charlie!"

* * *

9 November 1888

Thrawl St., London

Mary was starting to feel a little worse for the drink. A good few gins at the Horn of Plenty and the Britannia had begun to take their toll. She was still short of the money she owed McCarthy. She gave him bits and pieces when she had it, but the clients he gave her kept him from kicking her out onto the street. It was different when Joseph was around. Now she was on her own. McCarthy wasted no time in recruiting her to his growing collections of local ladies.

It was now just after midnight, and most of the pubs were closed. Mary knew it wouldn't be long before "Indian Harry" would be knocking at her door looking for rent or alternative payment. The clock was ticking.

It was a bitterly cold night, and it had been raining on and off. Mary was wandering along Thrawl Street in the hope of catching some last-minute opportunities. She bumped into George Hutchinson. Sweet man, but of no actual use to her. He never had any money. She knew all too well he had desires for her. When you had been dancing this dance as long as she had, experience allowed for awareness of various characters. Hutchinson was what she would call a "puppy." All doe-eyed and well-meaning but offered no value to anyone.

In a vain attempt out of hope, Mary asked George if he had sixpence. It could serve both of their requirements if he had. He said something about spending it all in Romford. There definitely would be no charity tonight; that was for sure. With that, she bade farewell and moved on. She needed to find some money.

George was poorer than her. After all, was Joe not the same? That fish-stinking imbecile lost his job and the little income that it provided. A good man, but he was unable to provide for her after that. If she was candid, she was pretty happy to be no longer living with the awful smell. Fish guts stench got into everything.

Mary knew all too well that if she started to allow refuge in their room to other women like her, he would not tolerate it. The plan worked as intended, and he soon left. Mary was back to looking after herself again. It was not her preferred choice by any means, but she was the only person she could truly rely upon. That meant reverting to the ways that got her this far in her life.

Whilst standing on the street, she suddenly felt from nowhere a tap on her shoulder.

"Remember me?"

The stranger was smartly dressed. He was wearing a nice collar and tie and a billycock hat. Far too well dressed for this street at this time of night.

The man leaned into Mary and whispered into her ear, "I'm the gentleman you decided to baptise in gin at the Ten Bells several weeks back."

His accent wasn't local. It was soft and well spoken, but not East or West End of London. Perhaps he was from the North?

At that moment, the memory dawned on her, and she let out a laugh.

She whispered back coyly, "Sir, I do, of course. I can only apologise. You had not caught me at my most demure."

"It's quite all right. I have money and beer and no one to share either with. You could be all right with what I have told you."

This type of customer is much more like it, Mary thought. He had money. He was smartly dressed and sporting a charming gold pocket watch in his waistcoat. She also spotted a lovely shiny silver horseshoe tie pin. With that, Mary cracked a smile, linked his arm, and started heading towards Commercial Street.

During the short walk towards Dorset Street, the man was altogether very quiet. Mary stumbled along the way, only for the man to stop her from falling. He then gripped her back, probably a little too tightly for her liking.

As they arrived at the entrance to Miller's Court, Mary thought it would be the right moment to discuss price and terms.

"Here we are. I have a private room, and as such, the price will be a florin."

Without even a hesitation of negotiation, he agreed. He leaned into her once again.

"A florin for what I have planned for you, my dear, is quite simply a steal."

Despite the strangeness in his eyes, Mary felt this could be quite a good evening indeed.

"Come, I will make you feel comfortable, dear."

With that, the pair embraced and kissed.

Mary thought this could be the answer to her immediate troubles. With her florin and whatever she could obtain by light-fingered means, it could well buy her more time with McCarthy.

Just as they entered the court, Mary abruptly stopped as she realised something.

"It seems I've lost my handkerchief!"

The man pulled a red one from his jacket and handed it to her.

"Here, please have mine."

With that gesture, Mary felt at ease and headed with him down the dark and narrow alleyway of Miller's Court, towards number 13.

As they reached the door, Mary addressed her client, "I lost the blooming key, but it's all right. I can open the door from the window."

Mary moved to the side of a small courtyard and put her hand through the broken glass and dirty rags to release the latch on the door from the inside. With that, the door unlocked.

"A woman of many hidden talents," Mary said proudly.

Mrs. Cox of number 5 walked past them in the alley.

"Night, Mary!" said Cox.

"Good night to you too, Mary! I'm going to sing now."

Mary Ann Cox smiled back.

Mary Jane Kelly entered the room ahead of the gentleman. Before following her in, the man took one last look up and down the alley. He slammed the door behind him as he went in.

"Jesus, love! Don't take the bleeding thing off its hinges!"

Mary headed towards the fireplace, where there were the smoulders of a previous fire petering out. She had some old newspaper on the small table and threw a few sheets onto the dying embers.

"There, we'll get ourselves nice and warmed up, shall we?"

The man stood in front of the door, staring at her.

"Before we begin, I will need to receive payment in advance," she clarified as she pulled the pin out from her hair and let it down.

After a moment of further staring, the man broke into a grin. "Why, of course."

He put down the small bag he was carrying, which Mary hadn't even noticed before. He reached inside his jacket and pulled out a suede drawstring bag. There was some lettering on the bag, but Mary could not make out exactly what it read. After a moment of rifling through the bag, the man pulled out a shiny fresh florin.

"A florin was the agreed price, was it not?"

He then placed the money on the table. Mary was optimistic that after tonight her problems would start to ease. This money man from nowhere was the perfect opportunity at just the right time. She was tired of this life. She was exhausted from running. She was exhausted from using her body to survive. She was tired of all the men. After tonight, things would be different. Maybe she could make a run for it to back Wales or even Ireland? Mary had held whimsical dreams of the Emerald Isle since her time with Jane Kelly in prison. She could start again fresh. It seemed that was all she was ever doing. Suddenly, without any prompting, Mary began to sing a ballad she knew. She had a pretty voice.

"Scenes of my childhood arise before my gaze. Bringing recollections of bygone happy days . . ."

The gentleman was surprised by this temporarily but soon became bewitched by her singing. As she continued to sing out the remaining verse, she started undressing in an orderly fashion. She took her shawl off first and folded it neatly on the only chair in the room. A bonnet was already there, but she did not wear it out. She followed that with her dresses and did the same routine. She then sat on the bed facing the malnourished fire in just her chemise, still singing, as she untied her boots. After they were unlaced, she placed them neatly beside the chair. She finished by jumping into the rickety old wooden bed just as the song came to its conclusion.

"Now, sir, time for you to collect your goods."

The man took off his overcoat and hat and placed them directly on top of Mary's clothes.

"Indeed it is. Indeed it is."

* * *

9 November 1888

Scotland Yard, London

George Hutchinson was sweating. He had never experienced a feeling like this. The gruesome imagery of what he saw was flashing across his senses every few moments. His heart was pounding. He had been sitting on the steps outside Scotland Yard for almost an hour now. It must easily be 4:00 a.m. His sense of time had stopped after he saw what was in that room.

A hansom cab arrived at the steps. The man George was waiting for appeared from the carriage. He got out onto the road, along with the constable who was sent to collect him. The constable made his way to the entrance of Scotland Yard whilst Inspector John Littlechild made his way over to Hutchinson, leaving the cab waiting.

"George, what the blazes is going on, man? Do you know what time it is?"

"I'm sorry, Mr. Littlechild. I didn't know where to go or who to see. I don't know what else to do."

"The constable said the matter was of urgent national importance. What is it? The Fenians?"

"No, sir. At least, I do not think so. It was him. I saw him."

"Saw who?"

"Evil himself, sir. I saw what he did. I have seen the horror of what he is capable of. The man is the devil incarnate."

"Calm down, George. Who did you see?"

"I saw *him*, Jack the Ripper!"

Inspector John Littlechild stood for a moment in stunned silence with George. He then physically moved George a few steps further out of earshot from the cab.

"Where? When?"

"I was hoping to see a girl I know on Dorset Street called Mary Kelly. She is a lady I sometimes see. I had been in Romford for the evening, and by the time I returned to Whitechapel, I had no money for my usual lodgings. I knew Mary was on her own in that room and, well, I don't know, hoped maybe she would offer me charity for the night, but she could not. I saw her on Thrawl Street and spoke with her. She needed money herself. As she finished speaking with me, I saw her speak with another man. He seemed friendly like they knew one another. I was suspicious of the man.

He did not look right for the area. I followed them back to Dorset Street and waited outside."

George took a breath.

"I remember you said how to watch those Fenians you wanted me to watch, and so I did the same. It must have been well over two hours or more when he came out. I followed him to see where he was going. I wanted to know where he came from. It was not far. He entered a doorway connected to a coffee house on Middlesex Street. I went back to see if Mary was okay. Her door was locked, so I looked through the window. I could see there was still light from the fire in the room. There were rags in the window. I pushed them to see inside. What I saw will never leave me, Inspector. He skinned her like she was an animal. He cut pieces of her off. Her face was gone. What kind of evil is this, Inspector?"

Littlechild paused a moment to absorb the information given to him.

"What happened next, George? This is very important. Did you go anywhere? Did you speak with anyone?"

"No, Mr. Littlechild. I ran all the way here. I did not stop. I could not think of anywhere else to go. My mind is in a haze. I banged on the door, and eventually, a sergeant answered. I told him I needed to speak with you as a matter of urgency. I said it was of national importance. He then sent a constable to knock for you."

"Okay, we must return to Whitechapel at once. I need to see the scene for myself."

"Please don't make me go back to that place, Mr. Littlechild."

"I'm afraid we must, George. I need you to find the courage to do so. Come, we shall take this cab."

George was reluctant. After a brief moment, Inspector Littlechild ushered him to enter the cab, and he got in.

"Dorset Street in Whitechapel at once, driver. Make haste!"

* * *

9 November 1888
Commercial St., Whitechapel

They were close.

"Inspector, you should stop the cab here on Commercial Street. I think the noise may draw attention if we go all the way to Dorset Street. We can walk from here."

Inspector Littlechild was impressed by George's sudden calmness after having been so shaken just thirty minutes earlier. The inspector noted that George's demeanour had steadily changed as they edged closer to Whitechapel. He had become reticent and withdrawn. Whatever he saw in the room had had the most profound effect on his character.

"Good thinking, George."

Littlechild pulled the trapdoor above his head to communicate with the driver.

"We wish to alight here, please, driver."

Once the horse came to a complete stop, Littlechild paid the driver through the hatch. The two men jumped out of the carriage, and the cab departed.

"Okay, George, you lead the way."

The two men walked up Commercial Street and took a left onto Dorset Street. It was dark and cold and no other soul was around. They were just a few steps down the street when George pointed across the road.

"She is down there, Miller's Court. Number 13. The door is on the right, and the window is in the courtyard. I shan't be going back there, Inspector. I will wait for you here."

"Very well, George. Do not leave!"

"I won't, Inspector. No man who saw that room will ever leave this place."

Littlechild was less impressed with George's drama. He crossed over the street. As he did so, he noticed the soles of his shoes were making a noise against the cobbles. He hoped they would not be detected by anyone else. As he entered the pitch-black passageway, the sense of dread suddenly enveloped him as he walked down the alley. He reached the door of room 13. He tried to open it, but as George had described, it was locked. He walked around to the courtyard at the side. Again, as George told, there was a broken window. There was no light in the room now, but he could make the shadowy shape of a body lying face-up on a bed. Even in the darkness, it did not look right. He put his hand through the crack of the glass to see if he could reach the door. To his surprise, he could. Very carefully, he unlatched the lock, and the door opened.

He walked around to the door and entered. The open door produced some rogue rays of light, but not enough to see much. He had some matches in his pocket and decided to strike one. He peered his head around the door.

"Jesus and all that is holy!" he muttered.

It was absolute carnage. The man who did this could not be of this earth. After a moment of grim reflection, professionalism overtook him. He moved the match towards the floor to ensure there were no pools of blood by his feet. There were none. Littlechild took a couple of steps inside the room and could see the rags that George pushed through the window on the floor.

Using his match, he checked for blood before walking the next few steps. It was clear. He blew the almost-burnt match out and struck up another. Littlechild then picked up the rags and put them back into the broken glass. Immediately the tiny shards of light from the window were gone. He walked backwards a few steps and backed out of the front door. He shook the match out. He then closed the door as quietly as he could. John knew, when the body would be discovered, the rags would now be back in the window. The scene was back to how it was before George came along.

That scene was every bit as horrifying as George described. Littlechild remained focused on the job at hand as he walked back up the passage. Hutchinson was still there. Littlechild crossed back over the street.

"Well, George, I can see why you did not wish to return to that place. I, too, shan't be wanting to return there anytime soon."

"He is not human, is he, Inspector?"

"Indeed, he is not, George. Now show me where this animal sleeps at night."

The two men headed back towards Commercial Street. Halfway down, they took a right turn into Wentworth Street, leading them to Middlesex Street. The dark was starting fade as daybreak was emerging. The walk was around five minutes. A few barrow boys were setting up for the day on the market.

"Over there, Inspector. The door beside the coffee shop, he went in there."

"What does he look like?"

"He had a dark overcoat, a billycock hat, a brownish-reddish moustache. Average height. He looked like a typical English clerk. He must have been around forty years old, I would say."

"You are certain he looked English?"

"Yes, Inspector, I believe so."

"Okay, George. Thank you. You did great work here tonight."

Littlechild reached for his purse from his inside jacket pocket.

"Here is a little something for your trouble and a bit more for your lodgings," he said as he handed him a handful of coins. "Stay at the usual place for the next few days. I will need to find you to discuss what we do next. Do not speak to anyone about this, George. I cannot stress that enough. It is vitally important you speak with no one until you see me next. Do you understand?"

"Yes, Mr. Littlechild."

"I shall take it from here, good night, George."

"Yes, Inspector, good night."

George looked exhausted as he headed back towards Wentworth Street.

Littlechild needed somewhere he could watch the door and not be seen as suspicious himself. He spotted a coster setting up on the corner of Middlesex Street and Wentworth Street. He would get a good view from that spot.

"Morning, sir."

"We're not open yet, guv'nor'"

"That's fine. I do not wish to buy anything."

"Then what do you want, sir?"

"I'm a detective with the Metropolitan Police, and I'm doing some important work with regards to watching Fenians."

"I would know nothing about that, squire."

"I would hope so. I ask that I stand with you for a while. I need to watch a door further down the street without arousing suspicion. I will pay you for the assistance, of course."

"You want to pay me for doing something you can do for free?"

"So we are agreed?"

"We are agreed, sir."

The inspector pulled out his purse and handed the coster sixpence. The market trader smiled as he shrugged his shoulders. He then carried on setting up for the day. Littlechild positioned himself and watched the door.

Now we wait.

* * *

***

9 November 1888

Miller's Court, Whitechapel

The time was around 10:45 a.m.

"Mary, open the door!"

Indian Harry banged on the door again. Still no response.

"Right, you want to do things the hard way, do you?"

Harry's real name was Thomas Bowyer, and he was an ex-Royal artilleryman who had spent fifteen years living in India. He was discharged just two years prior for being unfit. Now he found himself one of the more feared rent collectors and pimps in the employ of notorious local businessman John McCarthy. Most of the street was owned by McCarthy.

Harry walked around to the side of the room where the courtyard was. There were two windows panes. Both were broken, but Harry focused on the one which had some rags stuffed in it.

"Right, I'll just let myself in, shall I?"

Bowyer pushed the rags through, and suddenly the room filled with daylight. As he drew close to the window, he was not prepared for the sight that met him. Mary's body was lying on the bed, face towards the window. She was practically naked but cut up and slaughtered. Her face was horrifically disfigured, and parts of her body seemed to be everywhere. He stumbled back in sheer horror, and his face went pale white.

"What the Jesus?"

After a few seconds of disbelief, Bowyer gathered himself and sprinted out of the court towards the grocer's shop where he had been with McCarthy just a few minutes prior. As he dashed through the front door of the shop, his pace caused a ripple of commotion from the few customers present. He lifted the hatch on the counter and continued at speed out to the back room, where McCarthy had an office.

"What is it?" McCarthy asked.

"She's dead, John."

"Who is dead?"

"Mary Jane Kelly. Gutted like a fish in her bed, governor. I have never seen such a thing in all my life."

"What do you mean, man? What happened?"

"I knocked at the door to collect the rent, but I could not make anyone answer. I looked through the window, and then I saw her. So much blood, John."

"Bloody hell, Tom!"

McCarthy leapt from his chair, and the two men walked at extreme pace out of the shop and the short distance back to Miller's Court. Thomas was uneasy and nervous as they walked down the passage to the window in the courtyard. McCarthy peered through the broken glass. He too was not ready for the vision that welcomed him.

"All that is holy!"

McCarthy could only look for a brief moment.

"Was she with any of the punters we put her way?"

"Not one of ours. Whoever did this, she picked up off the street. I saw her myself after the last one we threw her."

"Okay. We are going to need the police for this, Tom. We need to go to Commercial Street and let them know what has happened here. We don't mention this to anyone right now but the police, okay?"

"Yes, John."

That was all McCarthy needed—more police attention. A girl murdered in one of the beds was not a great advert for a lodging house. Poor Mary. She was a good earner as well.

The two men were practically running up Commercial Street as they reached the station—pushing past pedestrians as they go. A walk that would usually take ten minutes took just half the time. They entered the building and made their way to the desk sergeant, who immediately recognised McCarthy.

"Well, Mr. McCarthy, what do we owe the pleasure today?"

"Is Abberline around?"

"He is not part of H Division anymore, sir."

"I know that, but he is assisting on the Ripper murders, right?"

"I believe so. Why do you ask?"

"It's important I speak with him."

"I can direct you to Inspector Beck, who is the inspector on duty."

"Very well, please fetch him."

The sergeant made his way up the steps to the detective's floor on the first floor. A few minutes later, the sergeant appeared with the inspector. Beck sauntered down the staircase. As he reached the men, McCarthy went to shake his hand, which Beck ignored.

"What do you want, McCarthy?" John took his hand away.

"There had been a murder in one of my rooms. It looks like it might be the work of Jack the Ripper."

Beck smiled before taking a moment to realise McCarthy was serious.

"You are not joking?"

"Do I appear as if I am joking, Inspector?"

"I will get my hat and coat."

The inspector raced back up the stairs to get his hat and coat. He returned in what seemed like a flash. As he galloped back down the stairs, he shouted at McCarthy.

"Where is this?"

"Miller's Court, Dorset Street."

Inspector Beck then addressed the desk sergeant, "Send for Superintendent Arnold to meet us there immediately, Sergeant."

"Yes, sir."

The three men immediately left the station. Inspector Beck was nervously excited about what he was due to discover.

Was this really another victim of the Ripper?

PART 9

Five Sided Triangle

9 November 1888
Middlesex St., Whitechapel

Littlechild was starting to feel the fatigue, but he knew he had to stay focused. After all, was this not what he was trained to do? Special Branch would not be as it was for the work he and others had done for Monro over the years. They were the best officers the Met had, and he, in effect, was running the whole department with Monro now at the Home Office. He must lead by example.

It was now around midday, and suddenly the suspect appeared from the doorway, looking refreshed and respectable. The world around him was blissfully unaware that this man, who seemed to be unassuming and nonthreatening, had been the very man striking fear into the heart of the empire. This disappointingly average man was nothing to fear at all.

Littlechild immediately sprang into action as the suspect headed south down Middlesex Street to Aldgate station. As thought by Littlechild, he was looking to leave the area. He followed him from a safe distance into the station. He pretended to read some literature on the notice board as the man bought a ticket from the booking office.

Once the man paid for his ticket and headed for the platforms,

Littlechild raced to the kiosk window.

"That man, which direction is he heading?"

"Sorry?"

"I am with the Special Branch of the Metropolitan Police, and I believe that man to be a Fenian. Now tell me exactly where he is heading."

"Right, I see. The man bought a single fare westbound to Euston Square, sir."

"Very good. I shall require the same."

"Of course, no charge, Officer."

The attendant promptly handed Littlechild a ticket.

"The next train?"

"Platform 3, in approximately three minutes."

"Your service is appreciated."

Littlechild then practically sprinted towards the platform to get his suspect back in his line of sight. As he paced down the stairwell to the platform, he once again had a visual of the suspect. He kept his distance. He noticed a discarded newspaper on one of the benches nearby and picked it up. He pretended to thumb through it from a safe distance as not to be spotted.

After a few minutes, the train could be heard clattering down the track towards the station platform. The steam of the engine was seen before the train arrived. The carriages ground to a shuddering halt, and a sudden release of pressure from the engine exhaled as it stopped. Both the suspect and Littlechild boarded the train. The train was busy. Littlechild realised that today was also the day of the

Lord Mayor's Show. The inspector decided to walk down his carriage to get a little closer to the man he was following.

The train clunked and shook its way through station after station before finally reaching Euston Square, where both men disembarked. Littlechild used his years of expertise to ensure the suspect was entirely unaware that he was being followed. Distance and discretion. The target made his way calmly towards the exit of the station. Littlechild followed.

Where is he going?

Littlechild quickly realised the suspect was making his way to Euston Station. They both walked through Euston Square to Euston Grove. The walk was just a few minutes. The men entered the station from the grand entrance on Drummond Street, passing through the imposing roman forum style "Euston Arch." Littlechild slowed down. Having been at this station many times before, he felt confident he could keep a healthy distance. The exit was on the left side, and the entrance was on the right side. Upon entering the station, the target made his way to the booking office. Littlechild discreetly made his way to the seating area in front of the statue of Robert Stephenson that dominated the hall.

He sat down and still, with the paper in his hand, pretended to read it whilst he waited patiently for the target to finish his transaction. As the suspect concluded his business, Littlechild went to the same window and addressed the attendant behind the glass.

"I am Chief Inspector John Littlechild with the Special Branch of the Metropolitan Police."

He took his warrant card out from his inside pocket and passed it to the attendant to review. The man reviewed the document and handed it back.

"How can we assist the good men of the police, sir?"

"The man who was here just before me. Where is he going?"

"That gentleman purchased a first-class carriage ticket to Liverpool Lime Street, sir."

"I shall require the same."

"That ticket is twenty shillings, sir."

"This is urgent police business. Your superiors can reclaim the cost from Scotland Yard. Ask for me. I do not have time to waste. Please issue me the ticket immediately."

The attendant took a moment to consider whether he should honour the officer's request. A shrug of the shoulders and a written entry into a logbook later and the ticket was now Littlechild's.

"The train departs from platform 1 at 1:15 p.m."

"How long is the journey time?"

"It is an express train, so a little over five hours."

"Very good. Thank you."

Littlechild could still just about see the suspect making his way to the platform. He sped up his walking pace in a bid to close the gap. As he approached the platform, he could see the target showing his ticket to the guard at the platform gate. The suspect then moved his way down the platform towards the first-class carriage.

The policeman showed the guard his ticket as he reached the barrier. The guard clipped his ticket and handed it back to

Littlechild with a courteous nod. The detective was now too making his way to the first-class carriage.

Chief Inspector Littlechild could feel a sense of excitement bubbling. By the end of this day, he would be returning to London with the identity of Jack the Ripper. The Special Branch would once again demonstrate its essential purpose, this time beyond identifying risks to the state through dismantling Irish terrorism. Now the department was dismantling terror itself. No doubt Monro and Anderson would appreciate and value the work he had done.

They would be the first people who should know after he did.

* * *

9 November 1888

Miller's Court, Whitechapel

Abberline arrived at the scene of Miller's Court, where he was met with a solemn nod by one of the constables from H Division guarding the entrance. It was only 1:00 p.m., but the narrow passage was dark even then. At the door was Superintendent Arnold.

"Afternoon, Fred. Hope you have not just had your dinner."

The biggest surprise, noted Inspector Abberline as he entered the tiny room, was the smell. He was not expecting that. It was not pleasant. Then he spotted the body. The room was incredibly dark, but the full sight of the victim was probably better left in the shadows. The vision was almost unreal. She had been dehumanised beyond any form of recognition. Arnold entered the room not long after Fred.

"We were waiting hours for the bloodhounds, but the bloody things never showed. The Yard is all over the place today. I got McCarthy to break the door down."

"So, this is one of John's houses?"

"The man is a cretin, and I would love nothing more than to pin this on him, but there is little doubt this is the work of the Ripper."

"You call him that now do you, sir? I never had you down as a man who would be influenced by such sensational journalism. Who found the body?"

"One of McCarthy's men, a Thomas Bowyer. He was round collecting overdue rent. And no, I am not influenced by such newspaper tomfoolery. It happens to be a better description than just being a murderer. You only have to see the poor mare lying there."

"Has the room been photographed?"

"It has."

Abberline immediately noticed clothes piled neatly on a chair and boots by the fire.

"Did we fold those clothes?"

"No, they were like that when we entered the room."

"Is it not peculiar she meets with such a gruesome end, yet her clothes and shoes are left in such an orderly fashion? Perhaps the killer did it after? Or perhaps she was intimately comfortable with the killer? What do we know of the victim?"

"McCarthy named her as a Mary Jane Kelly. She was living here with her husband. One of the neighbours told us they separated around a week ago. He moved to a new lodging house nearby. He was Joseph Barnett. I've sent some men to fetch him and take him to the mortuary for formal identification. How he can, I do not know, but we must try. Her body will be moved shortly."

Fred moved around the room slowly and gravitated towards the grate of the fire. He noticed something unusual in the ashes. With a pencil, he trawled through the remnants and found a small piece of cloth and some metal wire.

"What is it, Fred?"

"I'm not sure. Perhaps it is some clothing? Why would she or the killer be burning clothes? I doubt very much she would burn her own clothes judging by her circumstances. The killer must have done it. I presume he did so for heat, which I can only imagine because the room was freezing. If that is the case, then I estimate he murdered her at night. Does the coroner have an estimated time of death?"

"Thomas Bond of A Division did the initial examination and Bagster Phillips a little later. Both men seem to think she was murdered in the early hours too. They have both since gone to the mortuary to await the body for closer examination in the light. An ambulance will be here shortly."

"Any witnesses at this stage?"

"Just a neighbour thus far, Mary Ann Cox, who resides a little further down the court at number 5. She said she last saw Mary Kelly entering the room at around 11:45 p.m. with a man carrying beer. He was stout, wearing a billycock hat. He had a blotchy face and a heavy carroty moustache. It's the first time we have had a description like this. The deceased then engaged in singing until around 1:00 a.m., as the witness claimed she heard her."

Fred took one last look around the room and did his best to try and see beyond the blood and gore that was at every turn. It was practically impossible.

"Interesting description. Yet no beer in the room, it would seem."

Arnold nodded in agreement.

"Well, there is little else I can do here, Superintendent. May I also speak with any witnesses that come forward? Perhaps be part of the interview of Barnett?"

"Absolutely, Fred. Make your way to Leman Street, and I shall meet you there in a while with Barnett."

Fred could not wait to leave the room. In his haste to do so, he failed to spot the dried-out *F* and *M* cloaked in shadows on the other side of the corpse. The smell of death was not something he wanted to continue inhaling.

There were at least five murders that could be connected to this killer. The police were still no closer to stopping this monster. As well as the uncomfortable stench, there was an even more awkward realisation that he was getting worse. It was five weeks since the double event, but this return to murdering was by far his most daring and gruesome one yet.

He was mocking them now, and Fred knew it.

* * *

9 November 1888

First-Class Train Carriage

Littlechild had been on the train for just over an hour. He sat lost in thought as the train hurtled through the countryside. Alone in his first-class compartment, he contemplated his next move. The Inspector made his decision. He got up from his seat with his newspaper under his arm, opened the door, and exited to the train's corridor. The target was just two compartments up. Littlechild wanted to speak with Jack the Ripper himself.

He cleared his throat as he approached the compartment door. What if the target suspected him? What if he still had the knife? This was not the safest thing he had ever done, but he must find out for himself what kind of man he was dealing with.

In a swift motion, he pulled open the compartment door and entered.

"Sorry for the disturbance, old chap. I have to move from my compartment as the gentleman I am sharing with is transporting fish. I cannot bear the smell for much longer. May I come in?"

James looked up at the man entering his compartment, face emotionless.

"You are free to do so," replied James.

He was rather enjoying the privacy of his own compartment, but it would be impolite to turn away a fellow first-class traveller.

"That's kind of you, sir."

Littlechild could feel the sweat on his palms as he closed over the compartment door behind him. He then took a seat almost directly opposite the target. James had already returned his focus to his newspaper. Littlechild decided he would pretend to do the same.

After a few minutes of thumbing through the pages, with the odd look up to observe his target, Littlechild decided he would break the ice.

"I see the police are still having trouble locating this Ripper fellow?"

James slowly raised his eyes from his newspaper and gave Littlechild an intense stare. The new arrival had just introduced his favourite subject. He closed his copy of *The Daily Telegraph* and put it down beside him.

"I know," replied James. "It seems the police are showing levels of incompetence that would not be tolerated in the world of business."

Littlechild could sense the lack of respect for the force.

"Perhaps. It could be incompetence. Or it could be that the killer is a clever individual, too smart to leave behind obvious clues."

James smiled. "Perhaps it is both."

Littlechild knew what smugness looked like on the face of criminals. He saw it once again here.

"Such brutality against innocent women shows his cowardly side too, would you not agree?"

James's smile faded immediately.

"What makes you think any of those women were innocent? Yes, the injuries he inflicted were quite shocking, but stating the women were innocent seems quite wrong. They were all drunk whores, from what I understand."

Littlechild was taken aback but did his best not to reveal so on his face. This unassuming businessman had a pure hatred for his victims. No sense of guilt or remorse at all.

"Still, despite their circumstances, they did not deserve to die in the manner they did, I feel."

James was now getting a little impatient with his guest. He clearly did not understand the excellent work he had done for that community. He was ridding them of vermin, only for more to reappear. His mission to eliminate all whores in Whitechapel might never be completed. Fools like this would never understand.

James did his best to remain polite.

"One thing is for certain, he has created a level of fear on the streets of London that I have not seen in my lifetime. If it helps keep those unfortunates from engaging in their activities, even for a little while, perhaps that is not the worst thing. Fear is sometimes a good thing."

Littlechild did not want to push too hard on the subject of the Ripper. He did not want to raise suspicion, which could, in turn, put his safety at risk. He wondered where he stored the knife.

"You could be right, sir. I would not know about such matters.

All I do know is I want to keep my wife and daughters safe from harm. They will not be coming to London anytime soon, I can assure you!"

James smiled again. "Then I am sure they will be quite safe, sir."

James picked up his newspaper, reopened it, and started to flick through the pages again.

Littlechild now had a good understanding of this person. This man was not wild. The fact he had such coldness towards his victims and how they died did show something of the insane. No ordinary man could bring themselves to commit such horrors, but aside from that, he was entirely ordinary.

The two men sat in silence and continue to read their respective newspapers.

To the naked eye, no one would ever suspect this blotchy-faced businessman as being London's most notorious murderer.

Littlechild needed to know everything there was to know about this ordinary monster. When they arrived in Liverpool, he would pick through every facet of his life.

When he returned to London, the world might not know everything there was to know about Jack the Ripper, but Inspector Littlechild most certainly would.

* * *

12 November 1888

The Home Office, London

* * *

Chief Inspector John Littlechild arrived at the office of James Monro. He was met by the clerk responsible for looking after Mr. Monro's general correspondence and administrative duties.

"Can I help you, sir?"

"Yes, I'm Chief Inspector Littlechild of Special Branch. I wish to speak with Mr. Monro as a matter of urgency."

"I'm afraid that is not possible. Mr. Monro is presently engaged in a meeting with the assistant commissioner of the Metropolitan Police."

"Excellent, Dr. Anderson is here too. Would you mind disturbing them? They will both wish to speak with me on this matter."

The clerk looked at Littlechild for a few seconds before getting up from his desk.

"Very well, I shall ask him if he can entertain your request."

The well-dressed civil servant knocked twice on the door before entering Mr. Monro's office.

"What is it, Rigby?"

"My sincerest apologies for the rude interruption, but I have a gentleman outside who wishes to speak with you and Dr. Anderson as a matter of some urgency. He said he is from Special Branch. Chief Inspector Littlechild?"

Both Monro and Anderson replied in unison, "Send him in!"

"Of course."

The clerk exited the office, and Inspector John Littlechild entered. The clerk closed the heavy oak door behind him as he left.

"Hello, John, whatever is the matter?" asked Monro.

"Well, Mr. Monro, I have some important intelligence I wish to share with you and Dr. Anderson."

Littlechild took a seat beside the assistant commissioner.

"Well, spit it out, Littlechild!" barked Anderson.

"I know the identity of the Whitechapel murderer, the man otherwise known as Jack the Ripper."

The silence was thick.

Littlechild continued, "This may not be the outcome either of you had expected, but the truth is truth. He is truly a rather unremarkable man. His name is James Maybrick, a cotton merchant trader out of Liverpool. You would not look twice at this man if you saw him on the street. It is quite unfathomable why such a man could do such a thing."

Monro leaned back in his chair, ready to probe further.

"How do you know this Maybrick is the Whitechapel murderer?"

"Well, sir, like your good self, I have a wide range of informants across the city. This particular one has assisted me previously on Fenian matters. Friday just past, in the early hours of Saturday, he came looking for me at Scotland Yard. One of the constables was sent to fetch me. I arrived at the Yard to see this man who was as white as snow and in a state of shock. He then informed me that he had just seen the body of the victim in Miller's Court. He had been 'friendly' with her previously, and I believe he was hoping to be 'friendly' with her again that night. However, he had no money, and her being a whore, well, the 'friendship' could not be transacted, shall we say?"

Littlechild took a deep breath before continuing.

"He then witnessed her talking with a man who raised his suspicion. He looked a little too affluent for the area, so my man decided to keep watch. Around two hours later, the man left Kelly's room and headed back to his private lodgings. My man was immediately suspicious and decided to follow him. This was to a coffee shop on Middlesex Street, just a five-minute walk from the victim's abode. He then went to check on his lady friend. What he saw through the window of her room when he got there shook him to his very core. He then ran all the way to Scotland Yard from Whitechapel."

Monro sat forward again.

"How do you know your man is not the murderer? Maybe he came looking for you as he knew he needed an alibi for an act that he committed. Who better as an ally than an upstanding member of Her Majesty's police? Did you consider that, John?"

"I did, sir. I have known George for some years now, and I have never seen him so petrified. I truly believe him. What's more, he led me to the exact location where he last saw the murderer. I waited and watched the house all morning, and I did not leave that spot. Around midday, a man who perfectly matched the description George gave appeared from the doorway. He headed towards the underground, where he then connected to a Liverpool-bound train from Euston."

Anderson smiled. "You got on the train, didn't you, John?"

"Absolutely, sir! You do not wait for the opportunity to request your attendance. You attend to the opportunity. I boarded the train and kept a close eye on him all the way to Liverpool. He did nothing special on the journey. As I say, a rather unremarkable individual. When we arrived in Lime Street just over five hours later, he took a cab from the station to an area of Liverpool, which I later learned was called Aigburth. Naturally, I followed in my cab."

At this point, Littlechild took out his notepad from the inside of his jacket pocket and referred to his notes.

"He resides in a property called Battlecrease House. Quite a pretty house. I must say it appears cotton pays rather well. I knocked on a neighbour's door and pretended I was from Liverpool police investigating a gang of sophisticated thieves we believed were now operating in the area. I was alerting people to be vigilant and to keep an eye on anything suspicious. They were more than happy to furnish me with all sorts of information, which was most illuminating."

Monro was visibly proud of his protégé.

"This is what I mean, Robert. The force needs more Littlechilds and fewer Warrens. This is real detective work that gets results. Not bloody mindless soldiers in shiny new boots!"

Anderson offered a wry smile and a slight shrug of the shoulders in response.

"My apologies, please continue, John."

"Yes, sir. So, such information I was able to obtain was, he is married to an American woman who is over twenty years his junior."

Both Monro and Anderson raised their eyebrows.

"He is a keen horseman, who has his own horses on the property and is a member of the Wirral Hunt. He spent several years working in America. Perhaps that is where he met his wife? His brother is a famous music man who goes by the name of Stephen Adams."

"Would I know any of this artist's work?" Anderson asked.

"I would not know, sir. I must admit, music is not a passion I hold. As for James Maybrick, I was able to ascertain that he conducts much business in London and regularly visits the city. I returned to London on Saturday and visited the coffee shop at 6 Middlesex Street, where he had lodgings. The owner is Ms. Miriam Nathan. I told her I was there on Fenian business. She said the lodger told her his name was Mr. Smith, a travelling salesman. He had paid for three months lodgings in advance. He came and went as he pleased and often went out for long periods at night when he was in residence. That agreement had just come to an end. I asked to see his room. It was in a very tidy condition, to my surprise. There was nothing there. I took yesterday to recover from the lost sleep of the past few days. I then came directly here. I have not spoken with anyone else on this matter."

Monro addressed Anderson, "Your department once again has shown it cannot be effective in protecting the general public from outside forces. It is why the city must always have intelligence at the heart of what it does. The Special Branch and other such functions act as a safety net against these threats. Our work should never be compromised."

"As you know, James, I would be inclined to agree with you wholeheartedly on this matter. However, the commissioner has very different views. On this more pressing issue, what do you suggest we do next?" asked Anderson.

"What do we gain by bringing him in?"

After moments of silence, Littlechild replied, "A terror will be removed from the streets of Whitechapel, and the unfortunates will feel safe again?"

Dr. Anderson had his own views.

"These wretches of human life have lived under the protection of the Metropolitan Police for far too long. Degradation attracts degradation. I see no reason to enforce their sense of safety. It merely endorses their ability to continue their vices with abandon."

"I believe Robert makes a very interesting point, John. The praise for catching this deranged lunatic will be fleeting. It will do nothing to solve the ongoing issue of vice in the East End. This information could be used in a more meaningful way."

"What are you thinking, Mr. Monro?" asked Littlechild.

"It has suited our ambition of keeping anarchists and Socialists under control by focusing our combined efforts of promoting the idea of the killer being a Jew. I see no real reason to change that strategy. Their ability to recruit and fund their cause is being severely hampered by suspicion of their creed. Providing we ensure he does not return to Whitechapel, we can continue in our aims."

Monro had more to add.

"I would also speculate that should it be known this murderer was a member of the higher class. It could well have the opposite impact on our aims. I can only imagine how that can be used as a recruitment aid. Warren handed them a victory at Trafalgar Square. I strongly suggest we do not hand them a victory in Whitechapel!"

Both Anderson and Littlechild nodded in agreement.

"Our work is unseen by the public and largely misunderstood. All of us in the room pledged to protect the best interests of Her Majesty the Queen. This is one such time. Between us and only us do we keep this information. We continue promoting the idea of a Jew amongst our relative departments. If that does not work for whatever reason, then promote the idea of a Fenian. The truth is best kept hidden."

Monro continued, "John, please arrange surveillance on Mr. Maybrick, and if he makes any attempt to return to London, we shall decide our next move then. For now, I would like for you to explore ways in which we can eliminate this threat discreetly without any link to Whitechapel. Also, get your man George to visit Abberline and give a witness statement that the man he saw was a Jewish spiv. This should keep the Socialists occupied."

"Robert, continue influencing Swanson, as you have already been doing so admirably. His loyalty to you is impressive. I, too, will continue with the messages I have been maintaining."

Monro took a large inhale of breath.

"Gentleman, if we get this right, we can navigate through these choppy waters. We will strangle the threat of revolution and ensure the papers no longer have reason to continue undermining the great work of the Metropolitan Police."

The three men all looked at each other to affirm the pact.

"It is time for us to do what we do best," concluded Monro.

*　*　*

24 November 1888

Battlecrease House, Liverpool

The last of the couples were saying their goodnights to James and Florence. The ball at Battlecrease House had been a success. Many from the exchange—including the influential George Bridge and his wife, Eleanor—even graced them with their presence. Other guests included the Brierley brothers. James noted one, in particular, was paying more attention to Florence than was perhaps polite at such an event. It was a collection of the city's biggest movers and shakers in cotton. Illustrious names such as Rogers, Samuelson, Cook, and Stern had also been in attendance.

James was pleased with his wife. Florie did an excellent job tonight, and he was delighted with her overall performance. The house staff too delivered a wonderful evening.

"Thank you ever so much for coming, Mo," said James to his friend of many years, Morden Rigg. "It is always a pleasure to host you and your wife," he added.

"Nonsense, James, the pleasure is always ours. It was a captivating evening. Well done to you both."

Florence delicately smiled at the couple. "Y'all are always so kind and very gracious."

As the couple left for their carriage in the front drive, James realised they were the last of the guests. Now it was just James and Florence in the hallway. She looked demure in the finest scarlet muslin with lace and silk.

"I must say, Florence, you do look exquisite tonight."

"Thank you, Mr. Maybrick. I shall be retiring now. Good night."

James was smiling. Florence sauntered towards the stairs and glided her way up to the first floor. James watched her all the way before he moved to the drawing room to pour himself a neat whisky.

"What's the phrase? Whisky makes you frisky?"

Perhaps his amorous nature was connected to his increasing sense of invincibility. It had been a fortnight since his last piece of work in Whitechapel, and as usual, the police were none the wiser. His tolerance towards arsenic was also getting stronger. The cold sensations in his hands and feet seemed to be dissipating. His nerves were steady.

He downed his drink in one large gulp.

"Time for Mrs. Maybrick to receive a call."

**

20 December 1888

Battlecrease House, Liverpool

**

The gentle sobbing was the only noise in the room. James got up from on top of his wife and pulled his trousers up from his ankles. Florence was still clothed, but her dress was torn and ripped. She remained still on her bed, other than for the soft shaking of her crying. It was almost a month since they'd hosted the ball at Battlecrease. James and Florie were getting along well after the event. Then over a matter of weeks, James started becoming more aggressive and paranoid. Today he unleashed all the steam that had been rising within him upon Florence.

"I warned you, Florie. You will learn to show more respect for your husband."

James continued to tidy himself up and flattened his hair with the palm of his hands. Florence was motionless. Her left eye was swollen. James had given her a vicious punch to the face. Usually, when he struck, he did so about her body, hidden from view away from the world. However, his loss of control at the moment had left his mark publicly. Such attacks also did not usually end in such brutal intercourse. James was getting more violent.

"You will do well to remember your place, Florence. I own you, and I can do whatever I wish. I would suggest you start learning how to be more of a dutiful wife. It will save you from such punishments in future."

James almost went for his knife from under the floorboard in his bedroom. He was close to making Florie another one of his victims. For reasons he did not understand, he did not. The horrors of the last job still flooded his senses. Maybe love prevented him.

He was confused.

One thing he was not confused about was Florie's public display of disrespect. This could not go unpunished. James was aware she had been going to dances in the city. She was observed by his best friend George Davidson at one such gathering. She was seen dancing with that scrote, Alfred Brierley.

Not content with hosting one whore master, she now had eyes on another. One thing the whore wouldn't be able to do was to benefit from James's money. He would ensure a new will was drafted in the morning so the bitch would not receive a penny.

Perhaps her new whore master would cover her costs and debts. James was tired of doing so, the ungrateful bitch.

* * *

10 January 1889

Regent Street Club, London

Michael had now been waiting for approximately twenty minutes for his intimate friend David to appear. As yet, there was still no sign. His patience was becoming a little thin. He had always resented lateness, especially as he was always punctual. To meet the basics of social courtesies should not be handled with such difficulty by others.

After receiving another whisky from one of the waiters, Michael's attention was drawn to a well-dressed gentleman approaching his table.

"Mr. Stephen Adams?"

"I am he," replied Michael.

"Well, you are, of course, Mr. Michael Maybrick, but go by the stage name Stephen Adams, is this not correct?"

Chief Inspector Littlechild dusted himself down and sat himself opposite. The two men sat briefly in awkward silence.

"Sorry, who are you? I am waiting for a friend."

"Ah, yes, David! He will not be joining you, I'm afraid. He arranged this meeting at my request. I told him that I was a cousin of yours looking to surprise you after many years away. Being the earnest type, and of course one of your biggest admirers, I'm sure he only had your best interests at heart. I would suggest it would be best for all to maintain that narrative."

"I will ask again. Who the hell are you, and what do you want?"

"Mr. Maybrick, I represent Her Majesty's government. I serve the crown. You can call me John. You must focus on the information I will bestow upon you between now and when I leave this establishment. Your life and the lives of others will be changed forever. What I am about to discuss with you is the most sensitive nature and requires the utmost restraint. Are we understood?"

Michael nodded in solemn acceptance.

"Very well. I shall begin. Are you familiar with the man known as the Whitechapel murderer, sir?"

"Of course. It is all that has been written in the London press over the past few months. Wait, you cannot think for one moment I am him?"

Littlechild laughed.

"Oh my, Mr. Maybrick, no, we do not. We do not feel you would have the stomach for such atrocities. You are a man of the arts, after all, with a more 'sensitive' nature, shall we say? No, but we do know who he is. That's why I am here. You know of him too."

"What do you mean?"

"Please note, Mr. Maybrick, in this room right now are several men that are ready and able to escort you from this building, quite brutally as well, I might add, upon my command. Any exuberant reactions to what I am going to tell you will result in such action being taken. This is not a position you wish to find yourself in, I can assure you!"

Littlechild paused for a moment.

"The man the press has christened Jack the Ripper is, in fact . . . your brother James Maybrick."

Michael was paralysed. After a second of stunned silence, he recoiled in his seat, then suddenly jolted bolt upright.

"This is absolute poppycock—totally absurd, man!"

"May I remind you again, Mr. Maybrick, this discussion requires less dramatics and more calm."

Michael fell back into his seat, visibly shocked.

The government man leaned in and spoke in a lowered tone, "Mr. Maybrick, the man who lives and breathes today is not the same man you could lovingly call a dear brother. The monster who has been killing unfortunates in Whitechapel is not a man with whom anyone could have any affection. Your brother James—the businessman, the family man—died the same night Polly Ann Nichols was found dead in the street. From that moment on, he ceased to exist. What remains in his place is pure evil. The sooner you accept that conclusion, the sooner we can discuss what we need to do next."

Michael was struggling.

"How do you know? How can you possibly know James is guilty of these horrendous acts?"

"We know with absolute certainty, sir. I am a man of many friends. I have eyes and ears across London and beyond. One of my contacts spotted your brother speaking with the most recent victim, Mary Jane Kelly. He was watched accompanying her back to her private lodgings on Dorset Street. My man was highly suspicious. A wealthy-looking man like this walking around Whitechapel at that time of night was inviting trouble. Or at the very least, he was looking for it. So my man waited in the bitter cold. Around two hours later, your brother emerged from the dwelling. My man then followed him through the back alleys to his private lodgings. He then returned to the scene of the crime to check on the victim. He saw first-hand the results of your brother's grotesque destruction of that poor woman's body. Not a sight any man could easily stomach, I can assure you. Our enquiries extended from there. We are under no doubt that the Whitechapel murderer and your brother James Maybrick are the same."

Michael was still confused. "If you are so certain with the evidence you have, then why has he not been arrested?"

Littlechild leaned back and smiled. "That is a very pertinent question, Mr. Maybrick. Right now, just four people on this mortal coil know the real identity of the Ripper. You are one of them. It can stay that way. My colleagues and I feel that should the murders cease, this whole debacle will fade into the annals of history as just another mystery. There is value in the public suspecting the killer was a crazy Communist Jew. A respectable English businessman murdering unfortunates at will—imagine? There has been enough unrest and rebellion in this city of late. We do not wish for more. This is England. That is why we need your assistance."

"Sorry, my assistance? My assistance to do what exactly?"

"To ensure Jack the Ripper disappears permanently, of course."

The secret policeman delivered his point with little emotion whilst picking some rogue fluff off his trousers.

Michael needed clarity. "Let me try and understand this. You want me to conspire in the murder of my brother?"

"No, Mr. Maybrick, you do misunderstand me. There will be no conspiracy. We want you to do it. We are not assassins. We expect you to do your duty for your country. To be perfectly blunt, for your own self-preservation. If the name Maybrick is to be forever associated with the name of Jack the Ripper, whatever legacy you would have hoped to have achieved through your musical canon will be rendered void and meaningless. How can anyone listen to one note composed by a man whose brother committed such horrendous murders? If you assist us in achieving our aims, we can protect your name. We can protect your legacy. We can ensure that your remaining life is one of comfort. I am much more in favour of the carrot instead of the stick."

Littlechild paused for a few seconds.

"For the avoidance of any doubt, there is always a stick. If you do not comply, we can ensure the world also knew about your true sexual orientation. I can only imagine what that would do to your musical career."

"You absolute fucking bastard!"

"Now, now! You are at the big boys' table, and you shall have a little more respect. Who would ever want to be associated with the Maybrick name between your perversions and your brother's murderous ways? Quite a family, aren't we? You see now why you must do what needs to be done?"

There was a long pause. This time the gravity of what was being asked hung in the air like an evil fog.

"We are aware that for many years now, he has been nurturing addictions to certain toxic chemicals. Perhaps if he were to consume a fatal dose from such a thing, would it come as such a shock? Be assured, if James kills again, or if we find out that you have discussed any of this with anyone, we shall point the Metropolitan Police and London newspapers in the right direction. He needs to be eliminated before he strikes again. I shall be in touch."

The mysterious man then stood up and walked over to Michael, who remained seated. John put his hand on Michael's shoulder.

"Think of it instead as doing God's work. What's the Bible

verse? He will wipe every tear from their eyes, and there shall be no more death."

He patted Michael before proceeding to walk off.

Michael locked his stare at Littlechild's back as he calmly strolled out of the room. How could James do this? Did he do this? How did they know such intimate details? Who exactly were these people? What the hell was happening?

Michael knew his future was now alarmingly uncertain.

Except for one fact.

There would be at least one more death.

*　*　*

15 January 1889
Knowsley Buildings, Liverpool

There was a knock at the office door. It was Thomas Lowry, the nineteen-year-old clerk hired by James to handle the business's day-to-day admin and clerical duties. He had been with James for several years now.

"I have a Mr. Valentine Blake to see you, sir."

"Please send him in, Lowry."

As Mr. Blake entered the room, James wiped his clammy hands on his trousers as he stood up. He reached his hand out from across his desk to shake his guest's hand.

"Very pleased to meet with you, Mr. Blake. Please do take a seat."

"The pleasure is mine Mr. Maybrick."

"So, Mr. Blake, how can I be of assistance to you?"

"Mr. Maybrick, my business partner and I have been working on a chemical process that can make a more abundant and easier to harvest plant equal to cotton. We believe this will radically change the industry. The raw material is ramie grass, grown in abundance across Asia. We are looking for prominent cotton merchants in Europe and the United States to help us market this revolutionary new product. Your experience and knowledge across both sides of the Atlantic would be hugely useful."

"Revolutionary, you claim? Mr. Blake, I am presented with such ideas more frequently than perhaps you may realise with the utmost respect. They all say the same thing, but cotton remains king. There are excellent reasons for that, I can assure you."

Blake shuffled in his seat.

"I find that often the introduction of such new materials into the market can depend on the chemicals and processes adopted before it becomes a bale. I will need to know more about those things first," explained James.

"I am sure you can appreciate, Mr. Maybrick, this process and the chemicals used are of a highly commercially sensitive nature."

"I do not wish to obtain your trade secrets. It is a question of price, and the chemicals may be obtained more easily in Liverpool."

Blake considered his position for a moment.

"Very well, Mr. Maybrick. The process requires grinding the grass down into a pulp. A special chemical mix that includes arsenic is then added to the pulp. This mixture draws out the natural colour pigment of the grass, which is drained off. It also strengthens and expands the grass into a fluff like consistency not dissimilar to raw cotton itself. It is then left to dry. From there, the material is handled as if it is cotton."

"You use arsenic in this process? That is unusual," replied James.

"It is not as unusual as you may think, Mr. Maybrick. Many manufacturers are introducing arsenic colour dyes, for example. I believe the colour green in most ladies' dresses is the result of using an arsenic-based dye. It is a great chemical substance. Austrian peasants have been consuming grains of arsenic for generations. The levels of toxic chemicals humans can tolerate are often startling."

Maybrick smiled. "One man's poison is another man's meat, and there is a so-called poison which is like meat and liquor to me whenever I feel weak and depressed. It makes me stronger in mind and body at once."

Maybrick took a breath.

"I do not tell everybody, and I would not tell you, only you mentioned arsenic. It is arsenic. I take it when I can get it, but the doctors won't put any in my medicine, except now and then a trifle that only tantalises me."

Blake said nothing.

"Since you use arsenic, can you let me have some? I find difficulty getting it here."

Blake considered this unusual request. "Well, Mr. Maybrick, I do have some I have been using for experiments, but as these are now perfected, I have no further use of the remaining grains. You are welcome to all I have left."

"How much exactly do you have, and what would it be worth? I would happily pay in advance."

"Mr. Maybrick, I do not hold a licence to sell drugs, and therefore that would be illegal. However, I would suggest a quid pro quo arrangement if you are open to such an idea. I shall return to Liverpool in one month from now with all I have remaining as a present. It is well over one hundred grains. If you could do your very best with the ramie grass product, it would be most appreciated."

"I believe we have an agreement, Mr. Blake."

The two men stood up, shook each other's hands, and smiled.

"I shall see you next month, Mr. Maybrick. Oh, please be careful. You will soon have enough arsenic to poison a regiment!"

"Do not fear, Mr. Blake. I am not a man to take such reckless risks."

"Thank you for your time, Mr. Maybrick."

Blake exited the office, and James sat back down in his chair. He licked his lips in anticipation of what was coming. That level of arsenic would be the most he had ever seen. It would be enough to keep him strong for many, many months. He could build his strength back up and return to Whitechapel to continue his work.

Jack would soon be back.

* * *

21 March 1889
Flatman's Hotel, London

Florie rose up from the rather luxurious chaise lounge in the hotel room to receive her visitor.

"My dearest John, I am so pleased to see you!" she said as she opened the door and gave her friend a huge embrace.

"Oh, Flo, what is happening?"

Florence had written to her childhood friend John Baillie Knight a few days earlier, announcing her arrival in London in advance. She asked him to call upon her at this hotel at this time.

"Your letter indicated that you are in some trouble?"

They both took a seat in the sitting room suite connected to the hotel room.

"I fear this is so. James thinks I am here to visit the countess and assist her in finding her a suitable surgeon for her illness. The truth is, I am in London as I am preparing a separation from him."

"You are doing what? Why?"

Florence inhaled a deep breath.

"You have no idea the pain he has inflicted upon me in our marriage and continues to do so. He keeps another woman in Liverpool, whom he has not given up despite being aware of my knowledge. He also has been violent towards me on many occasions. I cannot cope with such intolerable cruelty."

Baillie Knight was shocked. "My dear Flo, I had no idea. This is truly awful behaviour." John sat in deep thought for a few seconds before continuing. "I understand your position. It would be best if you protect yourself. Would you please visit my solicitors Markby, Stewart, and Company tomorrow? They would be most expert in handling such matters. I would then strongly advise when you leave London, you should join your mother in Paris. You must not return to that place!"

Florence started to cry. She could not bear to tell him the whole truth. Her real reason for booking this hotel was to see Alfred Brierley in private, away from Liverpool. He would arrive tomorrow.

"I feel so alone, John."

John got up and sat beside his friend. He held her tightly as she cried wildly into the shoulder of his coat.

"There, there, Florie. It will all be okay. You will overcome this."

After a few moments of uncontrolled tears, Florence started to regain her composure.

"I knew you would understand. You are indeed one of my dearest and closest friends."

John smiled as Florence took a handkerchief from her dress pocket to wipe away her tears.

"Come, Florence. Let us go to dinner and look towards the future. We shall wallow no more. Tonight, we shake off the morbs!"

Florence laughed. "Thank you, John. Please give me a few minutes to prepare."

"Take as long as you need."

Florence ventured into the adjourning bedroom to get ready. John remained seated in his chair. For all of James's faults, John could not help but be concerned with what was happening. He did not believe Florence truly understood the profound nature of what she was proposing.

Tonight was not the night to make that clear to her.

* * *

23 March 1889

Flatman's Hotel, London

Alfred Brierley was an opportunist. He had spent most of his adult life avoiding marriage but now had recently found himself engaged. However, he did not declare this fact to Florence. He found her very attractive, and there was no doubt there was sexual chemistry between them.

The reality of their entanglement was about to batter them both. Brierley was concerned Florie might be looking at this liaison as something more than it was perhaps to him. He needed to nip it in the bud.

Florence and Alfred were sitting at the table in the adjourning suite of the hotel room, eating breakfast. They had spent the previous evening engaged in a passion-filled night that seemed never to end. Their bodies were exhausted but equally satisfied.

"Florie, my sweet . . . about last night."

Florence stopped eating and took a napkin from the table. She used it to wipe the corners of her lips delicately.

"What about it, Alfie?"

"To be with you like that was far more enjoyable and pleasurable than I could have ever imagined. It was most truly a special night. I shall never forget it."

Florence could sense there was a "but" coming her way.

"This, whatever we may call it, cannot exist beyond this room today. You are a mother and a wife, and I am due to be engaged to someone else. As magical and wondrous we feel right now, there are too many people who will suffer due to this being more than it should be. Do you understand?"

"Well, I understand that for the first time in years, I have woken up feeling happy and content. I do not see that as suffering."

"The discovery of us would lead to much chaos, Florie. I would rather blow my brains out than put you or anyone else through that shame."

Florence had a sudden sense of disgust at the reality of what had happened here. She immediately felt an overwhelming sense of guilt.

"You are right. We must end this intimacy at once. There is too much to lose for all parties."

They sat looking at each other in silence for a few seconds before Brierley smiled.

"It was amazing though."

"That it was," replied Florence, now smiling too, before taking a long sip of her tea.

* * *

* * *

29 March 1889

Aintree Racecourse, Liverpool

The Grand National was Liverpool's most significant annual social event. All who was anyone would ensure their face was seen trackside. So much so even the Prince of Wales had attended this year. However, James was entirely distracted from the excitement of the royal party. Through his binoculars, he spied Florence down by the track. He could not believe his eyes. The whore and her whore master were brazenly walking back arm in arm along the concourse. They had no idea that James was watching them from the stand. The anger that filled James at that moment flushed through every fibre of his being. He had taken a whole grain of arsenic that morning from his recent acquisition from Valentine Blake. It gave him intense strength. As he boarded the omnibus at Knowsley Buildings earlier, he noted those present were himself, Florence, their friend Christina Samuelson, and that rake Alfred Brierley.

"The bitch!" James said aloud.

None of the other guests nearby caught his anger. He continued to watch the couple walk along before they stopped to exchange some words. Brierley then left her on her own. After a few more minutes, James watched as Florence proceeded to follow.

Brierley was soon back with the rest of the cotton exchange

group, many of whom have come on other omnibuses across the city. James was doing all he could to remain calm. He decided he wanted to speak with the whore master himself.

"Alfred, join me for a moment, would you?"

Brierley was not expecting such a request.

"Of course, James."

Alfred stood alongside James as Maybrick continued to survey the course with his binoculars.

"Do you know how long it takes to break a filly, Alfred?" James then pulled the binoculars down to look at Brierley's face.

"I must confess, matters to do with horses is not something I would have very much knowledge. I would wager money on any horse with an interesting name in the hope it can run fast."

James's face was ashen. "Oh, I don't know, Brierley. I think we all have more knowledge of these things than perhaps we even realise. The answer is around six weeks."

"That's useful to know."

"Do you know how one breaks a filly?"

"Again, I do not."

"Well, it very much depends on breeding and temperament of the foal. They need to respect the rider. That can take time and patience. In the end, they become subservient, as they should be. The horse becomes accustomed to the body of the rider. Sometimes a new rider can upset the balance. Some new riders can suffer a bite or injury from a filly not properly broken in. They must always proceed with caution."

Florence, at that moment, arrived back at the party and immediately spotted James speaking with Alfred. Her face dropped.

James stared intently at Brierley, who was that little bit taller. James's face was blotchy and red. His eyes were soulless and black. He did not blink once. There was tension here that Alfred did not enjoy.

"Thank you for the advice, Mr. Maybrick. I shall keep that in mind."

James said nothing and stared at Brierley, slinking off to speak with his brother nearby with a forced smile. James's eyes then meet with Florence's. He held that same intense stare with his wife for what felt like an eternity to Florence.

James then suddenly turned his focus towards the course and raised his binoculars as if nothing had happened.

Florence knew at that moment, James knew. There would be consequences.

* * *

29 March 1889

Battlecrease House, Liverpool

Florence immediately ran up the stairs as soon as they arrived back at Battlecrease. James chased after her. He had told the cab to wait in the drive. Florie managed to get to her room and tried to lock the door behind her, but she was too slow. James managed to get his foot wedged in the door and flung it open, sending her flying back onto her posterior.

James entered the room and towered over her. In one quick motion, he leaned down and, with a swift punch, hit her clean in the face as she sat on the floor. Now she was lying on her side and crying uncontrollably. James got up from his kneeling position.

"You thought I did not know about you and your whore master? I turned a blind eye. I assumed you would get whatever you needed out of your system. Instead, you decide to humiliate me in public." James was bursting with rage and was now shouting. "You stupid bitch! Such a scandal will be all over town tomorrow!"

Maybrick then motioned to punch her again with his fist raised but instead held it in the air. He took a deep breath and dropped his fist down. His rage was simmering.

"You do not know what you are dealing with, Florence. You will leave this house tonight. You will take your whoring body out of this place. I cannot bear to even look at you!"

James then pulled her up by the front of her dress, ripping it in the process. Florence was now standing up again, and fear immediately halted her tears.

"You will get out now!"

He then pulled her to the door and threw her out into the hallway. James shouted for the housemaid.

"Bessie!"

Within seconds she appeared at the top of the stairs.

"You will send her away immediately. I do not want her in this house for one minute more."

"Mr. Mayb—"

"Do as I say!"

Bessie took Florence, who was now shaking and sobbing. She picked up the fur cape abandoned on the floor and wrapped it around Florence's shoulders as she gently guided her down the staircase. They reached the bottom of the stairs when James came flying behind them and pulled the cape off Florence's shoulders.

"You can take this off right now! I bought it for you to wear in London, what a joke that is! You will not leave this house with it!"

Bessie did her best to calm him down. "Master, please do not go on like this. The neighbours will hear you."

"Leave me alone. You don't know anything about it!"

Bessie continued her best to reason with him, "Don't send the mistress away tonight. Where can she go? Let her stay till morning."

James then directed attention back to Florence. "By heavens, Florie, if you cross this doorstep, you shall never enter it again."

Suddenly, James started to breathe slow and heavy. It was like he had just been hit by a train. He then laid himself down across an oak settle, closing his eyes and becoming rigid.

Bessie decided that now was a good time to send the cab away. She then took Florence back up the stairs towards her bedroom.

"You are fine now, Mrs. Maybrick. The master has calmed down. I shall set him up for the night downstairs. You go to bed, and I am sure things will be much different in the morning."

Florence did not say a word. She was in a state of shock. After Bessie laid Florence down on her bed, she headed back downstairs.

James had not moved from where he was lying and looked very stiff.

"Master, you will be more comfortable in the parlour room, sir."

She gently raised his arm and wrapped it around her shoulder as she lifted him from the settle. He was now practically asleep and making some incoherent murmuring noises. They slowly walked towards the dining room. There was a chaise lounge nearby, and Bessie managed to get him to lie down on it. After a few moments, he was snoring and fast asleep.

This was the worst Bessie had seen Mr. Maybrick. It was like his anger was becoming worse by the day. She was convinced those powders and pills he kept on taking day and night were most certainly not making him better. It would appear quite the opposite.

These were tense times at Battlecrease.

* * *

30 March 1889

Battlecrease House, Liverpool

James appeared calm, but Florie knew that underneath the I, he was anything but calm. He sat in silence as Dr. Hopper, the family physician, did his best to act as peacekeeper. He was a little older than James, and what were once thick, luscious locks of black hair had turned to salt and pepper. He had a beard to match.

"Mr. Maybrick, I understand that for a man of your stature, the pressures of the daily world can become quite burdensome. Your wife must be beside you in those challenges. Support you, as it were. She can only do that with comfort and ease, with your patience and understanding. To damage her physically as you did last night will not serve your ambitions well."

James was not impressed. Florence also did not present as someone with much care of the situation either. Dr. Hopper could sense words were falling on deaf ears.

"If not perhaps for each other, then perhaps you both should consider how a separation would impact your children? There is nothing good to be gained from such a disintegration of a marriage."

James remained silent.

"Florence, perhaps you could outline your expectations on how you can perhaps come to an arrangement that works for both parties?" the doctor suggested.

Florence focused on the doctor as best as she could through the damage inflicted on her swollen left eye by her husband. With Mrs. Briggs's help, Florence went to see Dr. Hopper that morning about her injuries and asked his advice for the best course of action for arranging a separation.

Although she had visited John Bailie Knight's solicitors, who drafted a letter for her, she at the last moment opted to return to Liverpool and abandoned all notions of separation. Until the present morning.

"Firstly, I would say that Jim needs to learn to control those fists of his. They tend to find their way to my eye sockets of late."

Sir Jim remained emotionless.

"I would also add that I will not be sharing a bed with him ever again. I do not wish for any more children. He can do what he wants, but he will no longer be doing it to me."

James smiled. "Did she tell you, Doctor, about her indiscretions? I very much doubt so. She is very good at persuading men to bend to her charms. For example, various moneylenders have stood her for loans she cannot afford to pay. She tends to go beyond her means."

Dr. Hopper seemed encouraged by communication, even if it was not the most productive.

"Well, Mrs. Maybrick, may I suggest that should Mr. Maybrick handle the matters of a financial nature, would that go some way in assuring you that his motives are well placed?"

Florence ran her tongue over her teeth. "If Jim is willing to handle those outstanding issues, I would be willing to reconsider my position."

Dr. Hopper looked visibly relieved. "Mr. Maybrick, is this agreeable?"

James sat in silence for a moment. "Fine. I shall take care of the debts. Sometimes, Arthur, I wonder if there is no limit to my patience with this woman. Any man with her as a wife would be pushed to the edge of sanity, I can assure you."

Hopper gave an uncomfortable smile. "If that is settled, I must return to my surgery."

The two men stood up. Florence remained seated. The men

shook hands as James escorted the physician to the entrance hall. After a brief exchange of pleasant goodbyes, the doctor left.

James rushed straight back into the sitting room, grabbed Florence by the throat, and lifted her six inches from her seat.

"Go crying to anyone like that again, and I swear as God is my witness, Florence, I will slit your throat without a second's notice, you fucking whore! Do you understand?"

Florence's face was going red as she tried with all her might to pull his hand from her throat but to little avail. She nodded in agreement as rapidly as she could as the oxygen drained from her lungs. He then threw her back into her chair as he let go of her neck. Florie immediately gasped in desperation to get air back into her lungs.

She could not believe he could be any crueller than he had been of late, but he kept finding new depths. Jim had lost all sense of control.

James leaned into her about an inch away from her face and whispered, "You have no idea what I am capable of, Florence. You will do well to consider that."

The blackness in his eyes pierced her soul. The monster who called himself her husband then calmly regained his composure and whistled a jolly tune as he left the room.

Who was this man? He was no longer James.

* * *

6 April 1889

Mikado Café, Liverpool

Brierley was waiting patiently at a table near the window. He took the liberty of ordering a pot of coffee in advance. Just as the server was arriving with the coffee and cups, in walked Florence. She immediately spotted him and went over. Alfred politely stood as Florence took her seat.

"My dear Florence, whatever is the matter?"

"I'm so sorry for calling you away like this. I do not have anyone else I can talk to so candidly within this city. I need to speak with someone."

Alfred poured a coffee for Florence before then pouring one for himself.

"Indeed. We are good friends. Friends can speak freely with each other."

"We are more than just friends, Alfie."

Brierley shuffled uncomfortably in his chair.

"We had agreed that this thing, whatever name it has, cannot simply continue when we returned to Liverpool, Florence. Our 'friendship' is already the talk of the exchange. Such a public rendezvous as this does nothing to quell those rumours. Whilst I am sympathetic to your desire for a friend, I cannot be anything more. You must understand that."

Florence looked away with a sulk, not dissimilar to a child being told that they could not play with their favourite toy.

"Florence, you are very dear to me, but there is much at stake here for both of us."

She returned her focus to Alfred. "Perhaps if circumstances were different?"

Alfred smiled. "Perhaps."

Florence took a delicate sip of her coffee. "He is getting worse, you know? He has blackened my eye, ripped my dress, and only yesterday pulled me around the room by my hair. The man is losing control of himself, and it is me who bears the brunt."

Alfred's face dropped. "My god, Florie, I had no idea he was such a brute to you. Are you okay?"

Florence once again averted her gaze to the window. "I don't know who this man I married is anymore. He has been taking these pills and powders, which I believe are making his behaviour much worse. Things such as arsenic, which he calls his medicine. I am at the end of my rope with it all."

Alfred took a sigh. "The man is an imbecile. He would rather slowly kill himself with toxic substances than tend to the needs of his beautiful wife. If he does not learn to change his ways soon, the chemicals will make the choices for him. You may need to start considering how mourning wear would suit your complexion."

Florence looked startled by the prospect. "The thought had not crossed my mind. What if such a thing should happen? What becomes of the children and me?"

"You would hope the man has some moral decency about him to ensure there is a comfortable trust fund for the upkeep and well-being of his wife and children upon his passing."

"For the children, perhaps. He has already made it clear at Christmas that he ensured no provisions for me in his will. I would be desolate should he die suddenly."

Alfred again twitched in his chair uneasily. "Perhaps you should only deal in certainties right now. If something happened to Maybrick and that was the case, I am sure people will come to your aid. I, for one."

Florence smiled. "Like a medieval knight on a white horse? A fairy-tale ending?"

Brierley smiled back. "I am far from the chivalrous knight, but I would not abandon you so easily as your husband has. As I say, your best option right now is to manage what is in front of you today. Things, in the end, will find their natural conclusions."

Florence paused a moment.

"Different circumstances can mean different outcomes?"

Alfred took another sip of his drink. "Exactly."

Florence took a long and thoughtful sip of her coffee.

PART 10

End of May

8 April 1889
Regent Street Club, London

Michael Maybrick was sitting in his favourite leather chair, reading the paper and enjoying a slow whisky. The club was quiet this afternoon, but that was not a problem for Michael. He wanted peace. That was until he was disturbed by a familiar face. It was the secret policeman.

"Good to see you so relaxed, Mr. Maybrick," he said as he took a seat opposite.

"Good heavens, man, what are you doing here?"

Chief Inspector Littlechild settled into his chair.

"I am somewhat concerned you may not have taken our last conversation seriously. It's been over three months—yet your brother remains amongst us, and you seemingly are most content sipping whisky here."

"Have there been any more Ripper murders?"

"That is true. Let us not kid ourselves, however. That so far is by luck rather than by any design on your part. Do I need to refresh your memory of our previous conversation?"

Michael folded the paper neatly and placed it on the table in front of him.

"The conversation where you told me I must murder my brother, you mean?"

The inspector smiled. "Let's keep the hysterical language to a minimum, shall we?"

Michael took a deep sigh. "You must understand what you have asked of me is not a simple task."

"The simplicity of a task does not reflect its significance. It simply has to be done. What is the biggest challenge you face?"

"Aside from the morality of such a thing, I do not even know how one procures such toxic chemicals."

"I had a suspicion that might well be the case. I have taken the liberty of obtaining such powder James enjoys. Empty the contents into any food or drink of his. The powder will do the rest. It will be a slow and painful death that will last for several days. This will make it look all the more self-inflicted."

Littlechild pulled a small brown envelope from inside his jacket pocket and placed it inside the newspaper on the table.

"He is staying with me next week," announced Michael.

"Perhaps you should try then. I need not tell you that you do not let him out of your sight. The consequences of him committing any more acts in Whitechapel will be eternally profound for both him and you!"

"You have already made that very clear."

"Good. I find clarity helps focus the mind. My colleagues and I expect everything to be concluded by the end of May—which is quite apt, do you not think?"

"Forgive me if I do not share your appreciation for the wordplay."

The government man got up from his chair in preparation to leave.

"You need not appreciate anything I say, Mr. Maybrick, but I would strongly advise you to learn to do so, and fast. Time is slipping away from you, and I am the only one who can help."

As Littlechild walked away from the table, with his back turned, he said again, "End of May!"

Michael slumped back in his chair and stared at the newspaper on the table.

* * *

14 April 1889

Wellington Mansions, London

It was early Sunday morning when the doorbell rang. Laura, the housekeeper, answered the door. It was Dr. Charles Fuller, a friend of Michael's.

"Hello, Laura. Is Michael home?"

"Greetings, Dr. Fuller, he is. Please do come in."

The physician entered the hallway of the magnificent Georgian apartment. The high ceilings and marble floors were evident of a more decadent bygone age. Dr. Fuller always felt the place suited Michael's character. Michael's success was visible in every ornate detail of this beautiful apartment. He was more than just a musician. He was a celebrity now.

The housekeeper took Fuller's hat and coat whilst he held on to his Gladstone bag.

"Master Michael is presently having breakfast in the dining room. He requested for you to join him."

The physician offered a smile in response. "Very well. I know the way."

Dr. Fuller walked the long hallway before reaching the heavy oak door at the end. He gave it a knock.

"Come!" boomed the voice behind the door.

Dr. Fuller entered and saw Michael sitting at the very end of a rather long dining table. Almost too big.

"Charlie! So glad you could come. Please sit."

Michael took a napkin and cleaned the corners of his mouth. The doctor took a seat at the opposite end of the table.

"Of course, Mickey, it sounded urgent."

"Well, as you obviously can gather, it is not me who needs your assistance. It is my brother James who is staying with me presently."

"I see," replied the physician.

"He has been up all night with shivers and shakes. He has been complaining of numbness. He keeps saying he is petrified of being paralysed."

"Is he on any medications at present?"

Michael took a second before responding, "No. Not that I am aware of."

"Well, indeed, it does sound rather odd. Where is he now?"

"He is in bed in the guest suite. Laura will take you to him. I would appreciate it if you could let me know your diagnosis before you leave?"

The doctor did not say anything but offered a solemn nod in agreement instead. Michael then pushed a bell button on the wall beside where he was seated. Within seconds the housekeeper appeared.

"Laura, please can you escort Dr. Fuller to the guest suite, please?"

"Of course, Mr. Maybrick. Please, Doctor, follow me."

Dr. Fuller got up from his seat and followed the housekeeper out of the dining room. They headed back towards the front door before stopping at a door on the left.

"I shall leave you now."

He knocked loudly three times.

A barely audible voice could be heard, "Yes? Who is it?"

"I am Dr. Fuller, a friend of your brother. He said you are feeling unwell, sir?"

The voice was now louder and much clearer, "Oh yes, please do come in, Doctor!"

Dr. Fuller opened the door and entered the room. It was dark. The curtains were still drawn. In bed lay James. The physician made his way to the chair beside the bed and put his bag upon it.

"Hello, Mr. Maybrick. Your brother tells me you have been suffering from chills. Is this correct?"

The previous tone of meekness returned to James's voice.

"It is. I have not been able to sleep one wink. I get chills followed by numbness. The stiffness in my arms and legs have been so bad. I fear being paralysed."

Dr. Fuller removed his stethoscope from his bag.

"Okay, Mr. Maybrick, I am going to take a couple of measurements. I will need you to roll down the blanket so I can access your chest."

James pulled the blanket down and undid the first few buttons on his pyjama top. Dr. Fuller then put in the earpieces of the device before placing the chest piece on the now-bare sternum area of James. The doctor moved the piece around until he could hear a clear beat and held it in position for about twenty seconds.

"Heartbeat is slightly more elevated than usual, but nothing I would be too concerned with."

James looked at the doctor with his eyebrows raised. The doctor put the stethoscope back into his bag and removed a small, thin brass case.

"I wish now to check your body temperature."

Fuller removed the thermometer from its case.

"Please open your mouth, Mr. Maybrick. I will place this thermometer under your tongue. Please then close your lips to hold it in position for a few moments."

Fuller did precisely that, and James obliged. After a few seconds, he removed the thermometer and examined the reading.

"Your temperature is normal."

"How can that even be?"

Fuller put the thermometer back into its case and then back into his bag.

"There are no obvious symptoms at this time of anything major. There is every possible chance it was some form of passing fever, but you are fine now."

"I feel far from fine."

"How is your digestion? Your lavatory habits usual?"

"I have not been able to pass a stool for quite a few days now. My urine is quite a dark brown."

"I see. My view would be a gastrointestinal irritation. It would be best if you drank more fluids. I will prescribe you a nerve tonic and some liver pills."

"That's it?"

"Unless there are other symptoms I can't see, I believe this to be the best course of action."

James pulled up the blankets and turned himself over like a petulant child.

"Goodbye, Doctor."

Dr. Fuller was a little puzzled by the childlike reaction.

"You live local, Mr. Maybrick?"

Still, with his back turned, Maybrick did not attempt to face the doctor.

"No. Liverpool."

"Well, if you happen to be in London again soon, and your symptoms do not subside, you can call on me at my surgery on Albany Street. I will be more than happy to take another examination."

"Fine."

Fuller shook his head in mild amusement as he closed his bag. "Good day, Mr. Maybrick."

James did not respond.

The doctor left the room and closed the door behind him. He then proceeded down the hall back to the dining room. He found Michael looking out of a window.

"The examination is complete."

Michael turned around. "What's the diagnosis?"

"My honest answer?"

"Please, Charlie."

"I do not believe your brother is suffering from any ailments of the body."

"I see. So he is perfectly well?"

"I see nothing wrong with him. I have prescribed him some nerve tonic and liver pills."

"Well, thank you again for coming at such short notice. You are a good friend."

"No need to thank me at all."

Michael pressed the bell button.

"Well, apologise to Gertie on my behalf for taking you away from her on a Sunday. You shall have royal box tickets at my next Palladium show as a small token of thanks."

Laura arrived at the door.

"Well, if you insist, Mickey! She will be delighted to hear that.

Enjoy the rest of your day."

"Bye, Charlie."

Laura closed the door behind her as she led Dr. Fuller out of the apartment. Michael once again looked out of the window. He thought the small amount of powder he put in James's brandy last night would be enough to set the wheels in motion. James's reaction was giving him hope. Instead, it was just another bout of hypochondria.

Michael would need to administer more of the powder. Where and how, he did not know.

He did know it needed to be done by the end of May.

* * *

20 April 1889

Albany Street, London

James was waiting in the reception area of Dr. Fuller's surgery. He had only met with the doctor on Sunday past, but he was feeling much better now. He was intrigued by Michael's physician. Perhaps he could offer more insight than the other doctors. When they had last met, he was not so sure, but he was feeling remarkably better as the week went on. Spontaneously, he decided to take the first train down from Liverpool that morning to avail himself of Dr. Fuller's offer of another consultation. James did not warn anyone of his visit.

The young clerk who welcomed James reappeared from the

doctor's office.

"Dr. Fuller will see you now, Mr. Maybrick."

"Very good," replied James as he stood up and made his way into the surprisingly spacious and ornate room. Being a London doctor to the rich and famous seemingly paid well.

"Well, I must confess, Mr. Maybrick, I was not expecting to see you again so soon," the physician announced whilst standing up to greet his guest. "You do look much better."

James and the doctor both sat down.

"That is in large part thanks to you, Doctor. My brother has always spoken very highly of your abilities. After your visit last week, I was not so convinced. However, as the week went on, I started to feel much better."

"That is always good to know. However, it is unusual that a patient who recovers insists on a meeting again so soon."

James took a deep sigh.

"I have been feeling unwell for a long time. I am speaking years. The aches, pains, numbness, and stiffness had been getting worse and worse. Last Saturday night was one of the worst attacks I had suffered, yet you could see no wrong. I am intrigued how such a thing could even happen?"

Dr. Fuller leaned forward, resting his elbows on his desk. "Are you familiar at all with the emerging area of psychology, Mr. Maybrick?"

"No, Doctor, I cannot say I would know anything about that."

"As a physician, I like to keep involved with all manners of areas that affect the human body. There is an interesting Austrian who has been speaking on such issues for several years now. This particular specialism focuses on one's brain."

"Really, in what way?"

"The basic principles stem from what we feel and the things that we do. Some suggest these things were formed as part of our personality at birth. Some suggest such traits are developed and acquired over time due to circumstances and environment. Some suggest it could be a combination of both of these things. Nature and nurture, if you will."

"Intriguing. I like to ride horses, so that could have been something I was born with?"

"Maybe not horses specifically, but most certainly a desire to experience high speeds."

"Interesting. This is from studying the brain, you say?"

"Indeed. The brain is probably the human body's most powerful yet least understood organ. It is quite remarkable. It has the power to make us sometimes do things, feel things, or see things that are not there. At present, we cannot remedy ailments of the brain with medicine. We are still learning. I only mention this, Mr. Maybrick, as I believe some of the issues you have physically been experiencing may feel incredibly real to you. Still, a physician such as I cannot identify any physical cause. I must then have to ask what must be at the root of the pain you are feeling. I am wondering if they could be manifested from the brain."

"Manifestations? Hold on for one moment. Are you suggesting

the illnesses I have been experiencing are not real? My brain is somehow making me feel that they are real?"

"I believe we must consider all possibilities."

"Would that not make me insane? Are you seriously suggesting I am an insane man? That I am mad?"

"I do not think you are insane, Mr. Maybrick. You are not locked in an insane mind. Things are just not fully functioning as they should. What I believe I am saying is that through rest, more time with your family, less everyday stresses, perhaps your brain will not produce as many manifestations of the symptoms you have been experiencing lately."

"You do not believe my symptoms to be real at all?"

"Mr. Maybrick, I genuinely cannot find any obvious physical reason for their existence."

"My mind is playing tricks on me?"

"In a manner of speaking, yes."

"I must be frank. I had never considered such a thing. Very curious."

"I would strongly suggest you avoid any high-stress situations that could ignite these symptoms. Abstain from high-intensity activities. Go home, be with your family. Take time to enjoy springtime. Enjoy the things you have, Mr. Maybrick. I am certain at the very least you will feel better."

"What about medications?"

Dr. Fuller gave James a lingering look before taking out his prescription book. He picked up a nearby fountain pen and started to write.

"As I said, Mr. Maybrick, there are no medications for ailments such as yours. Rest and relaxation are your best remedies right now. I will exchange your liver pills for lozenges, as I believe they will have a more calming effect." Fuller handed James the prescription.

"Thank you, Doctor."

Maybrick folded the paper and put it inside his jacket pocket.

"No need to thank me at all, Mr. Maybrick. Please just follow my advice."

The two men stood up and reached over the desk to shake each other's hands.

"I will most certainly try."

* * *

24 April 1889

Clay & Abraham Chemist, Liverpool

Clay & Abraham Chemists proudly boasted themselves as chemists to Queen Victoria and adorned the large and dominant royal crest above their shop window. It was probably the most famous chemist in Liverpool. This was the type of chemist James believed was best suited to his needs.

The bell rang as he entered the shop.

"Hello, Mr. Maybrick. Are we looking for a pick-me-up today?"

James was reminded that this was one of the numerous chemists he would come across the city to give him his daily fix. He was obviously more of a regular than he perhaps realised. Since his visit to Dr. Fuller, he had decided to stop his other "medicines." He also threw away his hunting knife the very evening he returned home to Battlecrease from London. That now sat at the bottom of the stream that ran by the house.

Despite the earlier promise of feeling better, he found he was starting to get aches and pains again over the last few days. He decided to register the prescription given to him by Dr. Fuller.

"Hello, Mr. Clay. No, not today."

"How can I assist you, Mr. Maybrick?"

"I was feeling well up until a couple of days ago. I have a prescription given to me by a doctor in London. May I collect it here?"

James handed the chemist the folded piece of paper from inside his jacket pocket.

"Of course. This will not take long for me to make up if you are okay to wait for a few moments?"

"That's fine."

Clay then went about his shop to locate the items on the docket. He quickly found the lozenges and tonic.

"How are Mrs. Maybrick and the children?" The chemist then started to wrap and pack the items.

"They are all very well, thank you. And you, your family?" James tried his utmost to appear interested.

"Thank you for asking. We are all in excellent health. Being a chemist, and a royal one at that, it would most likely not be a great advertisement should we be otherwise."

"Indeed not." James suddenly realised just how pompous this chemist was.

"There you go, Mr. Maybrick. That will be sixpence, please, sir."

James removed the suede bag from inside his jacket pocket. He pulled a sixpence from the purse and placed it on the counter.

Clay swiped it. "I hope you feel better soon, Mr. Maybrick."

"So do I, Mr. Clay. So do I."

James then exited the shop and went out onto the street. The air was mild, but his skin was icy-cold. He was almost shivering.

James could not believe this was just in his mind. It all felt painfully real.

***

25 April 1889

Battlecrease House, Liverpool

Bessie answered the front door. A smartly dressed man in his thirties with luggage stood there.

"My name is Edwin Maybrick, brother to James. I believe he resides here."

"Yes, sir, he does indeed. Please come in."

James appeared from the parlour and raced towards his younger brother.

"My dearest Edwin!" James firmly gripped Edwin's hand as he shook it.

"Hello, Jim," replied the young brother.

Bessie struggled to bring the visitor's luggage from the step and inside the front door.

"Come here, let me look at you. America suits you as it suited me. You look well," announced James.

Edwin could not repay the same compliment. James did not look at all well.

"It's true the place suits my spirit. What about you? How are you? You look quite pale. Are you ill?"

"Oh, Eddie, if I was to tell you of every ache, pain, and ailment I am enduring these days, I would keep you occupied for many hours. Do not worry about me. I am delighted to have you here. That alone has raised my spirits!"

Florence then appeared from the dining room but stopped dead in her tracks when she noticed the guest in the hall. Her face was red and flushed.

"Florence," Edwin offered in a low tone.

Florence took a second to compose herself.

"Edwin. Jim, dinner will be served in the dining room in one hour. Why don't you and Edwin have a drink in the parlour whilst I fetch the children to meet their uncle."

"Yes. Let's have that drink, Eddie. We have much to catch up on. The children will be excited to meet their uncle from America."

The two men headed to the parlour as Florence approached Bessie, still having difficulty with the luggage.

"Bessie, did Edwin arrive alone?"

"Yes, mistress."

"I shall fetch someone to help you with those bags. Would you please put them in the guest suite? I shall wager that Mr. Maybrick Jr. will be staying with us for a little while."

Florence turned back around and headed towards the kitchen.

This was one house guest she could do without.

* * *

27 April 1889

Battlecrease House, Liverpool

It was another big day in the Liverpool social calendar. It was the Wirral Hunt steeplechases. It had been a month since the Grand National and the subsequent gossip that ensued. Today was an opportunity for James to recement his place with the elite members of local society. Show the likes of George Bridge he was still a force to be reckoned with at the Cotton Exchange.

However, all was not right. It took him the best part of an hour to get dressed. There was a knock at the bedroom door.

"Jim, are you okay in there?"

It was Florence. Perhaps she cared after all.

"I am fine, bunny. I shall be down shortly."

"We shall see you in the dining room for breakfast."

His hands were shaking, and his legs were stiff.

After a few moments, he gathered enough energy to start making his way towards the door. His walk was difficult and slow.

"Come on, James, get yourself together, man!"

He had not taken any of his other medicines for a week after visiting Dr. Fuller in London.

As James took a few more steps, he could feel his legs moving a little easier. He held on to the wall as he moved. He reached the top of the staircase and started to take a step down slowly. In doing so, his right leg stiffened suddenly, and he slipped. He managed to cling to the banister as he slid down three steps. He stopped to regather himself. Thankfully, nobody saw.

James took some deep breaths and waited for a few moments. After a short while, he tried bending his right leg at the knee. The leg was still incredibly tense. However, by repeating this exercise a dozen times, he could feel the joint loosening again.

James reattempted his descent. This time it was easier. His legs were more fluid than before. As he reached the ground floor, he released a huge sigh and dusted himself down. He then walked as briskly as he could towards the dining room.

Today was not the day to show any weakness.

***

27 April 1889

Battlecrease House, Liverpool

It was early evening, and Florence and Edwin were in the parlour. It was the first time they had a chance to be alone since his arrival at the house.

"I cannot help but sense you are trying to avoid me, Florence."

"Well, Edwin, do I not have good reason to?"

"Whatever is it you think I will do?"

"I have not the faintest idea, Edwin. All I know is that I asked you to stop writing, yet you insisted on sending your letters. I have thirteen in all from you."

"You kept them? I thought you would burn them. I must admit, this enthuses me."

"Well, it is prudent to dampen that enthusiasm. Jim is your brother. I am your sister-in-law. This is not appropriate behaviour."

"Yet you kept the letters?"

"I could not risk them being seen in the ashes of the fire. It's safer where I have them."

"I did mean what I wrote, Florence. You can come back to America with me. We can be together."

"Have you taken complete leave of your senses, Edwin? Are you hearing the words you are saying?"

"My heart endorses every word I have said and written."

"Yes, but your mind needs to regain control. What you suggest is insanity! Do you honestly think I would leave my children behind? That is what would happen. That would be the very least of it. The scandal alone could ruin your career and business. Do you also think James would accept this arrangement without so much as a fight? You will be excommunicated by all your family and abandoned by all your friends. It is absolute madness, and I will speak no more of it. Neither should you!"

"Perhaps if circumstances were different? If Jim was not here?"

"Well, Jim is here. I am his wife, and my duty is to him. He is your brother, and your duty must be to him as well. This game you are playing, Edwin, ends today."

Edwin took a long sip of his whisky. "As you wish."

There was a knock on the parlour door. It was Nurse Yapp.

"Apologies for the disturbance, mistress, sir."

"What is it, Yapp?" barked Edwin.

"It is Master James, sir. He is at the front door. He does not appear to be at all well."

Both Florence and Edwin put down their drinks and raced to the front of the house. As they entered the hallway, they could see James was soaking wet and paler than he ever had been, leaning unsteadily against the front door pane. The pair rushed to him.

"My darling Jim, you are soaked through, my love. Whatever happened?"

Edwin took his brother and put his arm around his shoulder as he carried him into the house.

"My dearest bunny, I knew you cared," James spluttered as he limped towards the staircase with Edwin.

"He is as stiff as iron and just as heavy," Edwin announced as he struggled to carry James along.

"I just overdid it with the wine. I am fine."

"I'm sure it has nothing to do with that medicine I saw you take earlier at the office then?" asked Edwin.

"What medicine?" enquired Florence.

"That damned strychnine or whatever it is. He took quite a dose in front of me."

The two men slowly manoeuvred their way up the stairs, step by step. Florence remained in the hall.

"It makes me strong," muttered James.

"Well, it clearly is failing, dear brother."

"Yapp, once the master is settled in bed, please bring him some mustard and water," instructed Florence.

"Yes, mistress."

Florence was genuinely concerned. James had always regularly complained of health issues, but mostly they were trivial. This run of illness he was currently experiencing seemed to be getting worse and quite rapidly. Florence could not help but feel an overwhelming sense of guilt for betraying her husband. He would need his wife by his side more than ever, being the wife she should be. Edwin must also start being the brother he should be.

Jim was going to need them both.

* * *

28 April 1889

Battlecrease House, Liverpool

Florence stood outside James's bedroom with Dr. Humphreys, another family physician of the Maybricks.

"How long has he been complaining of his health?" he asked.

Florence scratched her head.

"I thought he simply had a bad brandy at the races yesterday. Well, he had been ill on and off for a long time. It just seems of late he is ill more than he is well. I fear it may be to do with that other medicine he takes."

"What other medicine?"

"He does not like to speak of it, but I know he has been taking that white powder for years. I believe it is strychnine. He claims it helps with the malaria he contracted several years ago when he lived in America. I have my concerns."

Dr. Humphreys raised his eyebrows in surprise.

"I have not heard of strychnine being prescribed for malaria. It must be a remedy the Americans use. I shall examine him now."

It was mid-morning. James was lying in his bed, unable to move his limbs. The bouts of dizziness and clumsiness had cleared from yesterday, but the stiffness had returned aggressively. Yesterday was not the day he had hoped it would be all around. There was a knock at his bedroom door.

"Come," shouted James.

Florence entered the room with Dr. Humphreys.

"Jim, my sweet, Dr. Humphreys is here to examine you."

"Good morning, Mr. Maybrick," greeted the physician.

"Is it a good morning? I would not know," was the glib reply.

"I shall leave you be with the doctor, Jim. I shall be outside if you need me."

"Thank you, bunny."

Florence left the room.

"So, Mr. Maybrick, what exactly is the matter today?"

"Well, is it not obvious? Are you not the doctor? I cannot move any of my limbs."

"I will need to take some readings."

The doctor took out a thermometer and a stethoscope. He quickly took Maybrick's temperature under his tongue before putting on the stethoscope and checking his heartbeat.

"Your heartbeat is slightly elevated, but your temperature is normal. I will now press on various points of your arms and legs. Please confirm whether you can feel the pressure."

"I can feel that."

The doctor moved to a different point on his leg.

"Yes, that too."

Dr. Humphreys then pushed down on his left forearm.

"Again, I can feel that."

"Well, that concludes the examination, Mr. Maybrick. I cannot find anything that is obviously wrong. Are there any other symptoms I should be aware of?"

"The symptoms worsened yesterday after a strong cup of tea. I have also had a constant headache for over a year now."

"I see. Tell me, Mr. Maybrick, are you aware of the effects of nux vomica and strychnine on the body?"

"I think I know a great deal of medicine. I cannot stand strychnine and nux vomica at all."

"Well, Mr. Maybrick, I would be advising you only eat meat once a day and take some beef tea thickened with Revalenta."

Dr. Humphreys put his equipment back into his Gladstone bag.
"That's it?"

"If your symptoms persist into tomorrow, I will come by again."

"Very well. Thank you, Doctor."

"You are welcome, Mr. Maybrick. I shall leave you now."

Dr. Humphreys picked up his bag and exited the bedroom. He found Mrs. Maybrick in the hallway, patiently waiting.

"How is he?" she asked the doctor as soon as the door was closed.

The doctor moved close to Florence and spoke in what was almost a whisper, "If he is using strychnine to medicate himself, then you are right to be concerned. It is indeed a very dangerous and toxic substance if used in excess."

Florence put her hand to her mouth. "My! What would happen if he was doing such a thing?"

"Quite simply, it would kill him."

The doctor let that statement hang in the air for a moment.

He continued, "If he should ever die suddenly, call me, and I can say you have had some conversation about it."

"Thank you, Dr. Humphreys. I shall walk with you out."

As the pair walked down the staircase, Florence could not help but think that Jim might be unintentionally killing himself, believing it to make himself better.

He needed his doting wife now, more than ever. Poor Jim.

* * *

2 May 1889

Battlecrease House, Liverpool

Florence was worried. She returned to James's room to see him curled up in bed and shivering under the covers. All Florie could see was the vibrating shakes of his body. She had never witnessed James in such an awful state. The convulsions and delirium were ruining him. He should never have gone to the office. It was far too soon.

James returned much earlier than usual. His condition worsened rapidly. After he had his lunch at Knowsley Buildings, freshly prepared for him by Florence, he took a turn. Edwin personally delivered the food to his office and reported that James was fine at that point.

Dr. Humphreys came by and prescribed various tonics. He instructed Florence and the staff not to give him any other food or drink.

Florence had been sitting in his room, vigilantly watching over him until he eventually found some calm and fell asleep.

He had awoken suddenly and saw Florence seated on the chair across the room.

"Florence, please come close. I must confess all. I fear I do not have much longer."

Florence moved near to James by kneeling beside his bed. His face was glazed with sweat and his skin almost translucent. He coughed hard.

"What is it, my dear husband?"

James took a second to catch his breath. "I am Jack," he spat out.

Florence gave a faint smile. "You are James, my darling. The delirium has taken hold of your senses. Who is Jack?"

James coughed again. "May the good Lord have mercy on my soul."

"Sssh, my sweet. You will recover."

James gave her a forced and uncomfortable smile. "My dear, dear Florie, you have no idea what I am. I murdered those whores in London. I . . . am . . . Jack!"

James engaged in another round of coughing as Florence looked at her husband, puzzled and confused.

"But, James, this is nonsense. Why ever would you say such a thing?" She stood up and shook her head in disbelief. "I am going to fetch the nurse. You are hallucinating."

Florence then left James on his own.

"Death will become me. I pray for swift mercy. No heart," muttered James. He then curled up under the covers and started to shake.

Florence returned to see James violently shivering under the covers. Delirium could play cruel tricks on a person's mind.

* * *

3 May 1889

Knowsley Buildings, Liverpool

* * *

James felt exhausted. Despite spending the majority of the previous day in bed, he had still not recovered fully. That morning, he felt strong enough to leave the house, despite the protest from Florence.

There was no one in the office. It was late Friday afternoon. It was deftly quiet.

Earlier, he had met with Dr. Humphreys at the house and who again could not find anything wrong. At the physician's suggestion, James went for a Turkish bath. He mustered up the very little energy he had left and got dressed and headed into the city. There was some temporary relief from the aches and pains, but he could now feel them coming back at pace.

James took the ledger he was writing in a few moments before and wrapped it in brown paper, ready to bring it with him back to Battlecrease. He then sat alone in his office, contemplating all he had done, both good and bad. He had never been one for remorse, but he did feel an impending sense of something he could not describe. It was the only feeling he had.

Despite all his business success, the damage he had done to those poor women of Whitechapel was something he would have to carry with him. Their souls would most likely usher him down to the very pits of hell to eternal fire and damnation. It was what he deserved.

The words of Dr. Fuller had stayed with him since his visit last month. Perhaps he was born this way? Maybe at heart, he was a gentleman? Who knew what could have been?

Since his confession to her yesterday, Florie had not said any more of it. Perhaps she thought he was in a state of fever. Maybe she would realise it was not delirium, and she would be the one to put him out of his misery.

It would not take much. The pain of living was worse than the peace of death.

He knew he was not brave enough to do it himself. The great Jack the Ripper was just a plain and simple coward. No monster of the dark.

He was just a weak and frail man who had lost all he ever had and was now heading directly to hell.

* * *

5 May 1889

Battlecrease House, Liverpool

It was early evening, and James was alone in his room when Edwin entered. James had been bed-bound for some days now. His condition was getting progressively worse. Edwin was carrying a glass tumbler of alcohol.

"You awake, brother?" he asked.

"Eddie, yes, come."

Edwin closed the door behind him softly as he entered the room. He took a seat beside the bed. James's eyes were dark red, and his face was ashen.

"I fear the end is close, Eddie," spluttered James.

"Do not speak such nonsense, James. You will be fine."

James was breathing heavily and finding it hard to get his words out.

"I do not believe this will pass. It will not be long now."

"That's enough of this talk. You must continue to fight, dear brother."

"I have spent my entire life fighting for something. I am tired of fighting. I am ready to meet my fate."

Edwin took the glass in his hand moved it towards his brother's mouth.

"Here, drink this."

"What is it?"

"It is brandy and soda. I know it is against doctor's orders, but they do not know everything. You will feel better about it, I am sure."

Edwin gently held the glass tumbler to James's lips as he delicately sipped the alcoholic liquid.

"It tastes strange."

"Your taste is damaged through illness, brother. I assure you, it is brandy. You are strong, James. You will recover, and you will be that man you were again. You must keep fighting."

James was starting to doze off.

"Fight. I must fight," James tiredly said as he drifted back to sleep.

Edwin got up from his chair, readying to leave.

"Sleep well, brother."

* * *

* * *

8 May 1889

Battlecrease House, Liverpool

It was around 9:00 p.m. Nurse Yapp was peering through the curtains of one of the children's bedrooms out onto the drive of the house. Michael Maybrick was talking with his younger brother Edwin. She watched Edwin hand Michael the same envelope she had handed him earlier in the day.

"I wanted you to see this before coming into the house," claimed Edwin.

"What is it?" asked Michael.

"Yapp, the children's nurse, intercepted it. It is a letter written by Florence to what appears to be a lover."

Michael looked at the envelope and, despite some smudging, read the name aloud on it.

"Alfred Brierley?"

He then turned the envelope over and removed the letter. He took a few moments to read the contents to himself.

"It is essentially her confessing to their affair," Michael concluded.

"It would appear so."

"Assist me with my bags into the hallway. This house needs discipline and promptly."

The two men carried the bags through the front door where the housemaid was waiting.

"Bessie, isn't it?" asked Michael.

"Yes, sir."

"Round up all the staff immediately to meet with me in the dining room."

"Yes, Mr. Maybrick.'

"I shall check on James," asserted Edwin as he made his way up the staircase to the bedrooms.

Michael proceeded to head to the dining room. Within minutes, all members of the staff were assembled in the dining room. Michael wasted no time in addressing them.

"Due to the illness of my dear brother, I am informing you all that with immediate effect, I am taking control of all matters in this house. Is that understood?"

"Yes, sir," came a unified response.

"I must approve anything the mistress asks of you. It would be best if you kept me informed of her movements and actions. Again, is that understood?"

"Yes, sir."

"Good."

"You may now all return to your duties. Except for Nurse Yapp."

The room cleared with just the nurse and Michael remaining.

"Master Michael?"

"I know you have your ear to the ground in this house. My brother Edwin shared the letter you intercepted today from the mistress. Would you please furnish me with all the information you have? Do not leave any detail out, no matter how unpalatable it may be."

Yapp did not hesitate to pass on what she knew.

"Yes, sir. I believe the mistress has been poisoning Master James."

Michael was expecting the story of an affair, but Yapp was now talking about poisoning.

"What makes you come to that conclusion?"

"Several reasons, sir. I saw the flypapers."

"Flypapers? What do you mean by flypapers?"

"They contain poison, sir. She was soaking them in water. I believe in doing so, you can extract the arsenic from them."

"I see."

"Also, please forgive me for telling you this. I believe she has been untrue to Master James."

"Again, what do you know about this?"

"I was cleaning her room, sir, and came across her collection of letters. They were from three different men, none of which are her husband."

"Were there names on these letters?"

"Yes, sir. The most recent is from Alfred Brierley. I believe the letter today was for his eyes. He is another cotton merchant, a man who we have hosted in this house on numerous occasions."

"I cannot say that I am shocked. I am just surprised at her sheer audacity."

"As I said, sir, there are letters from two other men also."

"Their names, Yapp?"

"The largest number of letters, around thirteen in total, are from your brother Edwin, and five are from a Mr. Williams."

Michael wiped his face in discomfort with this latest revelation.

"I shall be speaking with Edwin on the matter. I must impress upon you the need for discretion. Have you ever witnessed her being unfaithful to my brother James?"

"I have not, sir."

"Well, Yapp, I believe I can trust that you will keep me fully informed of every detail of her mistress's movements and activities?"

"Indeed, Master Michael, you can trust me implicitly, sir. I pray Master James recovers soon."

"That will be all for now, Yapp. Please ask Edwin to come."

"Yes, sir."

Nurse Yapp left the dining room. Michael shook his head as he waited for his brother by the dining room window. After a few moments, Edwin appeared.

"You called for me?"

Michael did not look at his brother directly and continued staring out of the window.

"Close the door."

Edwin shut the door.

"What did Yapp say about the letter?" asked Edwin.

"Your interest in letters does not end at this, does it, Edwin?"

"What do you mean?"

Michael was now facing Edwin, face flushed.

"You know very well what I mean! Love letters? To your brother's wife?"

"Ah, those letters."

Michael took a seat at the table. Edwin followed.

"Are you a complete imbecile man? I sometimes wonder between you and James how I came to be related to either of you. She is your sister-in-law!"

"I cannot explain. Something is infatuating about her—*was* infatuating." Edwin started to hold the back of his neck for self-comfort.

"Need I explain to you the full gravity of the situation should this become public knowledge?" continued Michael.

"No, you do not."

"Edwin, you are an absolute fool!"

The young brother now had the appearance of a scolded child.

"I know, it was a childish and dangerous thing to do."

"Thirteen times? Yes, very much so."

"I'm sorry."

"Your apology has no value here. It serves no purpose. We must unite and focus on the enemy in front of us now."

"What do you mean, enemy?"

"Yapp has strong evidence to suggest your dearest Florence has been poisoning James."

"Good God. That cannot be true."

"I rather suspect you wish it was not, but the evidence she

provided is pretty damning. Which means she must have a motive. I believe she is trying to kill him to get his money and run off with this Brierley fellow. Unless she was planning to run off with you?"

"No, she was not. I am only aware of this Brierley today."

"Well, we must protect James now. We will need him to sign a new will that hands the company to you and the house and other valuables to me. She must not see a penny in the event of his death. Do you understand?"

"I understand."

"Now you know which side you are on. I will need your assistance over the next while."

"Whatever you require, Michael."

"Good. Let's start by making sure her visits to him are few and far between. Make no mistake. We are very much at war now."

"Yes, Michael."

***

10 May 1889

Battlecrease House, Liverpool

Michael was sitting in the dining room alone, nursing his third whisky. His mind was tired. It had been an eventful day. It was just after midnight.

Dr. Carter had been drafted in earlier to give a second opinion to Dr. Humphreys. However, James was too ill to be examined. Both doctors agreed to provide him with a double dose of bismuth and some brandy in the hope it would bring him around a little. It did not. Michael was rubbing his temple when there was a gentle knock on the door.

"Come!"

It was the nurse drafted in from Liverpool's Nurses' Institution, Nurse Gore.

"What is it?"

"I'm sorry to disturb you so late, sir, but you said to report anything suspicious."

The nurse instantly had Michael's attention.

"What have you observed?"

"It is the mistress, sir. She took the bottle of Valentine's meat juice your brother Edwin left for Master James and returned it to his bedside table moments later. I felt obliged to make you aware."

"You did the correct thing, Nurse Gore. Where is this bottle now?"

The nurse came closer and placed the bottle on the table in front of Michael.

"James did not consume any of this after the mistress returned the bottle?"

"No, he did not. I came to you immediately, sir. This occurred just moments ago."

"Thank you, Nurse Gore. Please continue the great work, and if you should witness anything else, please do not hesitate to make me aware."

The nurse gave a respectful nod before leaving the room. Little did Nurse Gore know, Michael himself had laced the bottle with arsenic. He had masterfully removed the adhesive label with a scalpel that secured the lid to the bottle. Michael then added a tablespoon of the special white powder the secret policeman had given him. He then reglued the lid label back to the bottle. He might as well have a career in forgery should his musical career end. Michael had then given Edwin the bottle to bring to James's room.

However, this latest development was intriguing. What was Florence doing? Whatever it was, it did not look good for her.

He would have no guilt in seeing her pay for the death of his brother.

* * *

10 May 1889

Battlecrease House, Liverpool

It was early evening. Florence softly entered James's bedroom. The nurse on duty was applying a cold, wet cloth to his forehead.

"Nurse Wilson, may I? I have some tea for him."

"Yes, mistress, of course."

The nurse left the press on his forehead and then moved over to the other side of the bed. Florence put the beef tea down on the bedside table.

"Oh, my dearest Jim!" Florie said as she grabbed his hand.

He quickly came around and saw his wife standing there. "Bunny, bunny!"

Florence smiled at her husband. "Yes, my sweet?"

"How could you do it? I did not think it of you. How could you do it? How could you do it?"

The nurse looked up at Florence, who looked back at the nurse. All Florence could do was offer an uncomfortable smile. She looked back down at her husband.

"You silly old darling, do not trouble your head about things."

James moved his head a few times, mumbling incoherently before falling back asleep.

"He is delirious and getting worse," said Florence to Nurse Wilson.

"Indeed, mistress."

"I shall leave him to sleep."

Florence gave a nervous smile towards Nurse Wilson as she left the room.

What did the master mean?

Nurse Wilson could not help but feel uncomfortable by what she heard from the dying man.

* * *

10 May 1889
Battlecrease House, Liverpool

Michael was in the drawing room reading a newspaper when Bessie, the housemaid, entered.

"Sorry to disturb you, sir. Mr. Thomas Lowry and Mr. George

Smith are here to see you."

Michael put the paper down and got up from his seat.

"Very good. Thank you, Bessie."

Michael followed Bessie into the hallway where Thomas Lowry, James's young clerk, and George Smith, James's bookkeeper, were waiting.

"Gentlemen," greeted Michael.

George Smith cleared his throat. "Mr. Maybrick. Can I say, we are both very saddened to hear that your brother is so gravely ill."

"Yes. Thank you. I trust you have the paperwork? May I see it?"

"Certainly."

Smith opened the bag he was carrying and handed Michael, a couple of sheets of paper. Michael proceeded to take a few moments to read the documents.

"Very good. Everything is in order. I shall get him to sign the papers now. If you would mind just waiting here?"

"Of course, Mr. Maybrick."

Michael then turned his attention to the housemaid, who was patiently waiting in the background.

"Bessie, please fetch Edwin and tell him to meet me in the master's bedroom immediately."

Michael walked up the staircase to the first floor.

The two employees stood in the hallway, waiting. After a moment or two, Edwin arrived via the kitchen. He greeted the men with a brief nod as he ascended the stairs at pace.

A couple of awkward minutes passed before suddenly a

booming voice could be heard shouting. It was clearly James.

"Damn you! Why can you not just leave me to die in peace?"

The two men in the hall looked at each other uncomfortably. A few moments more passed before Michael and Edwin descended the stairs.

"There you go, gentlemen. The document is signed. We thank you again for assistance at this time."

"Very good, Mr. Maybrick," confirmed Smith. "We shall now leave you in peace."

Bessie appeared and opened the front door for the two men to leave.

Once they departed, no words were said. Michael breathed out a huge sigh.

Edwin raised his eyebrows in agreement.

* * *

11 May 1889
Battlecrease House, Liverpool

Around 4:00 a.m., the children were awoken by Mrs. Hughes and Mrs. Briggs and taken to see their father for the last time. Florence was curled up in her bed, suffering from "swooning." James's health had deteriorated, but Florence was unable to communicate. She was carried in to see her husband in the morning but remained unresponsive. She was quickly returned to her room.

Around midday, Dr. Carter arrived back at the house to give

Michael the result of the tests carried out on the bottle of meat juice he had given him. It had indeed contained arsenic—no shock to Michael, of course. The physician confirmed that he and Dr. Humphreys would not pass a verdict of natural causes should James die.

It was now early evening, and George Davidson, James's oldest and most loyal friend was called. He was sitting with James in his room.

The house was quiet. Death was close. All in the house could sense its presence. The stillness that lay over the place was deafening. Nobody dared speak of it, but the entire house could feel it.

James was no longer conscious or reacting to any stimulus. George leaned in close to hear his breathing. The gaps between each breath were long and drawn out.

Nurse Gore continued to mop his brow. "I do not think it will be long now."

George held his friend's hand tightly. It was ice-cold.

After a few moments, James exhaled a long, rattling breath. His eyes opened, and his pupils were instantly empty of all life.

The nurse went to check for a pulse on James's wrist. There was none.

"He has now passed," she confirmed.

George stood up from his seat, leaned over, and held his friend in his arms. He could not help but sob at the demise of his best friend. After a couple of moments, he regained his composure and gently laid him back down on his bed. He then delicately raised the bedsheet and put it over James's head.

He did not utter a word. He simply picked up his hat and left the room. Michael and Edwin arrived together, just as he was leaving.

"He is gone," George confirmed as he walked past them.

The two brothers stood at the door, staring at the covered body on the bed.

"May your soul rest in heavenly peace, dear brother," said Edwin.

"Death shall be no more," whispered Michael.

PART 11

Trials and Tribulations

12 May 1889
Prince William St., Liverpool

It was early Sunday afternoon, and Florence was locked in her bedroom. Michael had given strict instructions that she was not to leave the room. Edwin had removed her house keys from her earlier in the day.

Now the two brothers found themselves on the other side of Liverpool. The house they stood before was relatively modest in comparison to Battlecrease. Michael was unimpressed. Moments after James died, Edwin alerted Michael of the existence of Sarah Ann Robertson. Another skeleton in the closet to deal with for Michael. With a murder trial most likely imminent, he could not risk James's character being assassinated by those looking to defend Florence. Sarah Ann was a risk and needed to be out of Liverpool today.

"Are you sure this is the house, Eddie?"

"It is. I have checked on her once or twice at James's request."

Michael banged loudly on the front door. After a few moments, the door opened slightly ajar to reveal a pretty middle-aged woman timidly peering around it.

"Sarah-Ann?"

"Yes. Who might you be?" the woman asked in a strange mixed accent.

"My name is Michael Maybrick, and this is my brother Edwin, whom I believe you already know. May we come in?"

"Hello, Edwin. I am not sure. Where is James?"

"This is the reason we are here. Please, can we come in?"

Sarah-Ann took a few seconds before agreeing to allow the two men to enter. She led them to the front parlour room.

"Please take a seat" she said as she ushered them to a nearby sofa.

All the three took a seat.

Michael cleared his throat. "I will not prolong the issue any further. James is dead."

Sarah stared at Michael for a few moments before breaking her confused trance. "What do you mean he is dead?"

"He has been poisoned and is now deceased."

"Poisoned? By whom? I need to see him!"

"You will be doing no such thing. You will be taking your belongings and leaving Liverpool—today."

"He is my husband!"

"No, he is not and never was, you stupid woman! He was married to another who was most likely the one who also killed him. There is nothing for you here. You must leave the city immediately."

Sarah-Ann then started to sob hard.

"For goodness's sake! Eddie, do something, will you?"

Edwin was not prepared for a woman to emotionally break down in front of him. "Like what?"

"Give her a handkerchief or something."

Edwin reached inside his jacket pocket, took out a pristine white cotton handkerchief, and promptly offered it to Sarah-Ann. She took it and started to slow her breathing down whilst wiping her eyes.

Michael took a deep breath and decided to continue in a more comforting tone.

"I do not know the full history of your relationship with James, nor do I wish to. Edwin has been a loyal brother to James. I did not even know of you until the last couple of days. Regardless of that history, he has been married for the past nine years. They have two children."

"They have children?" Sarah-Ann looked bewildered by this news.

"Yes, a boy and a girl."

"He never said. He knew how much children meant to me." Sarah-Ann stopped sobbing.

Michael continued, "There is nothing here for you. I will, of course, give some money to cover your travel and a little more, but you must leave right now."

"What of all my belongings? Jewellery? Dresses? I shall need time to pack."

"They all stay. You leave with the clothes on your back right now, at this very moment. I must return to London for urgent business, so I will accompany you to the station and put you on a train myself."

"This is all so sudden. I mean, I don't know!"

Michael stood up. "Come, we leave now. Give Edwin your keys."

Sarah-Ann took a few moments to look around the room and compose herself. She too then stood up.

"So be it. The keys are in the door, Edwin."

"Eddie, just lock up for now, and we shall decide what to do with this place when I return from London."

"Yes, Michael."

Michael and Sarah-Ann exited the parlour. Edwin heard the front door close. He too took a long look around the room.

"James, what were you thinking?"

* * *

13 May 1889

Scotland Yard, London

James Monro was becoming increasingly annoyed with Home Secretary Henry Matthews, who appointed him as Sir Charles Warren's successor as commissioner of the metropolis. The interference and meddling were becoming rather tiresome. He had now been in the role for six months and was already starting to sense it might have been a poisoned chalice.

There was a familiar knock at the door. The double tap followed by a double tap was always Robert's trademark.

"Come, Robert!" shouted Monro.

The assistant commissioner entered Monro's office. He was not alone. Chief Inspector John Littlechild was with him.

"We have some news we wish to share," announced Anderson.

"Well, come in and be seated, gentlemen."

The two men each took a chair opposite Monro.

"He is dead, sir," declared Littlechild

"Who is dead?" Monro enquired.

"The man the papers called Jack the Ripper, sir."

"That silly man from Liverpool?"

"Yes, sir."

"Was it the poison?"

"It would appear so. However, an unexpected but potentially fortuitous event has also unfolded. It appears his American wife was unfaithful. The brother is accusing her of his demise."

"The brother we persuaded to assist?"

"The very same."

"This is going somewhat away from the original plan. Although I do see the benefit of him using the situation to his advantage. Perhaps he has more about him than we first realised."

"My sources tell me that tomorrow she will be arrested for his murder. I have some press influence up there. I can ensure her character is questioned thoroughly and publicly."

"When the case arises, I will ensure we have a judge who would take a rather dim view to such a wicked woman! She should have been a better wife. She will deserve what comes her way," added

Anderson.

Monro leaned forward in his seat. "Well, gentlemen, I would see this as a satisfactory conclusion to the whole affair. We need to ensure Jack the Ripper remains a mystery to the general public. They will never get to learn of the great work this intelligence unit has done to keep London safe."

"Indeed, we shall mention no more of this whole episode," concluded Anderson.

Littlechild gave a nod of agreement, but he knew there were still one or two loose ends to tie up before this matter was fully concluded.

That would be left up to him to execute.

* * *

14 May 1889
Battlecrease House, Liverpool

Florence had been laid up in bed for the past couple of days, drifting in and out of consciousness. She had a notion of being made aware that James had died. Florence also vaguely remembered Edwin coming in to take her keys at one point.

She, too, remembered Michael also came into the room to instruct the nurse that she was no longer mistress of the house and was to be detained in this room.

Who the hell did he think he was?

Florence also asked to see her children at one point, only to be told that they were removed from the house.

It was early morning. Florence had not eaten for a day or so. Suddenly her bedroom door opened without warning and entered Dr. Humphreys. He did not say a word. He checked her pulse briefly and left the room as quickly as he had entered it.

A few minutes later, what sounded like a herd of elephants thundered up the stairs and stopped just outside her door. The door flew open, and a crowd of men entered one by one. One of them stood at the foot of the bed and addressed her.

"Mrs. Maybrick, I am superintendent of the police, and I am about to say something to you. After I have said what I intend to say, if you reply, be careful how you reply. Whatever you say may be used as evidence against you. Mrs. Maybrick, you are in custody on suspicion of causing the death of your late husband, James Maybrick."

Florence was speechless. Then the crowd of men left the room, except for one police constable.

"Madam, there will be an officer outside your door day and night. You cannot leave this room until further notice. I shall be the first to keep guard. Please convey all your needs to the nurse."

With that, he too left the room.

What just happened? Florence was stunned. Why had Edwin and Michael allowed this to happen? They both knew all too well James was poisoning himself for years with his powders, yet here she was being accused of his murder. She asked the nurse to send a cablegram to her lawyers in New York. However, she was quickly informed that the inspector would deny it being sent.

Denied representation, denied her freedom, and denied a chance to challenge all that was happening to her, Florence knew she needed to regain her focus and energy as quickly as she could. Things were unravelling at pace, and she needed to be ready to face all coming her way.

Florence very quickly realised she was entirely alone.

There were no white knights coming to her aid.

* * *

16 May 1889

Battlecrease House, Liverpool

Florence was curled up in her bed. The house was eerily soundless. Suddenly there was a flurry of hushed voices and hurrying footsteps outside the bedroom.

"Nurse, is anything the matter?"

"The funeral starts in an hour."

"Whose funeral?"

"Your husband's. If it were not for you, he would have been buried on Tuesday."

Florence stared intently at the nurse for a moment before attempting to get up from her bed, readying herself to get dressed. The nurse, alarmed, rushed over to block Florence's path.

"Stand back! I will see my husband before he is taken away."

The nurse refused to move. Florence shoved her to one side and made her way to the policeman standing guard at the other side of the bedroom door. With her trembling hand, she opened it. Slightly perplexed, the officer turned and faced Mrs. Maybrick.

"I demand to see my husband. The law does not permit a person to be treated as guilty until she is proven so."

The policeman took a moment to process the request.

"Follow me," he said.

The nurse was now supporting Florence and assisting her to reach her husband's bedroom. The policeman gently opened the door. As they entered, Florence could see the casket upon the bed. It was already closed and covered in white flowers. Florence collapsed to her knees.

"Leave me alone with the dead."

"I'm sorry, madam, I simply cannot," replied the constable.

Then an avalanche of tears gushed from her eyes. Florence was sobbing violently. After a few minutes, a wave of calmness overtook her, and she rose to her feet. Without the aid or support of the nurse or policeman, Florie walked gingerly back to her bedroom in silence. She took a seat near the window and sat in silent contemplation.

After a while, the silence was broken by the harsh tones of the nurse.

"If you wish to see the last of the husband you have poisoned, you had better stand up. The funeral has started."

Florence stumbled to her feet and clung rigidly to the window ledge as she watched the coffin of her dead husband being carried from the house to a horse-drawn hearse.

Once the hearse was out of sight, Florence immediately fainted and collapsed to the floor.

* * *

17 May 1889

Battlecrease House, Liverpool

Michael was drawn to the commotion occurring in the hallway. He got up from his chair in the morning room and made his way to the source of the noise. He could recognise that crass American drawl from a mile away. They were being blessed with the presence of Baroness von Roques. Bessie, the housekeeper, was doing her best to keep her outside of the house, but she was more persistent than the housekeeper anticipated.

"I simply cannot allow anyone to enter this house who does not have permission to do so," Bessie pleaded.

"You silly girl, you will step aside right now."

"Let her in, Bessie," confirmed Michael as he entered the hall.

The housekeeper moved to one side and allowed Florence's mother to enter the house.

"Baroness."

"Where is Florence, Michael?"

"She is in her bedroom. You may go to her if you wish."

"I did not seek your permission, Mr. Maybrick. You are, after all, merely a guest in this house. Perhaps that is something you should consider."

The baroness pushed past Michael as she moved up the staircase at pace. She noted the policeman seated outside Florence's bedroom.

"You there, I demand you let me see my daughter immediately."

"I am under strict instruction to keep the prisoner isolated."

"Prisoner? How dare you? This is her house, and I am her mother. Move out of my way."

The baroness ignored the policeman and entered Florence's bedroom, where a nurse was tending to her daughter. Florence turned to see her mother in the doorway.

"Mama!" she exclaimed.

The baroness raced to her daughter's bedside.

"Mon bel enfant. Qu'ont-ils fait?"

The nurse was not impressed by the baroness using French.

"You must speak in English."

"Indeed," confirmed the policeman. "I warn you, madam, that I shall write down all that you say."

The officer then produced his pencil and pad, ready to make notes. The baroness did not break her focus from Florence to acknowledge either statement.

"Mother, they all believe me to be guilty, but I swear to you, I am innocent."

"My darling Florence, I will do all I can to help you. Have you made contact with our lawyers in New York?"

"They refused to send my cablegram. I asked Dr. Humphreys to engage with a local lawyer I know to be friendly. He eventually was permitted to see me. Please see Mr. Cleaver in the city. He will furnish you will all the information."

The baroness stood upright and straightened her back.

"I shall go and see Mr. Cleaver now, my darling. As for the rest of you in this room I suggest you handle my daughter with absolute care and respect. If you fail to do so, you will get to discover how we in America handle such things very quickly. Michael Maybrick is no match for me, I can assure you!"

The baroness leaned down and kissed her daughter's forehead delicately. She then fired a scowl at the nurse and policeman before leaving the room. The policeman cleared his throat and put the pencil and pad back inside his pocket. He closed the door behind him as he went. The nurse continued her duties as if nothing had happened.

Florence was inspired and motivated by the arrival of her mother. She truly was a force of nature. She was glad to have such an influence fighting in her corner.

Florie knew she needed all the support she could get.

*　*　*

18 May 1889

Battlecrease House, Liverpool

Florence stirred from her slumber to find both Dr. Humphreys and Dr. Hopper standing over her.

"Mrs. Maybrick, we must check on your condition. Please can you sit up in the bed," instructed Dr. Hopper.

Still battling with sleep, Florence did as instructed. The two men quickly examined her by checking her temperature and her pulse. After a couple of moments, both men looked at each other and nodded in agreement. They then left. Florence was still rubbing her eyes to properly awaken when she heard the thud of many footsteps coming up the stairs.

Several men entered the room, including Florence's legal representation and the two doctors. The policeman who had arrested her was also present at the foot of the bed. It was he who started to speak.

"This person is Mrs. Maybrick, charged with causing the death of the late James Maybrick. She is charged with causing his death by administering poison to him. I understand that her consent is given to a remand, and therefore I need not introduce nor give evidence."

One of the men she did not recognise also spoke, "You ask for a remand for eight days?"

Florence's lawyer Arnold Cleaver replied, "I appear for the prisoner."

Then the oldest gentleman in the room, whom she also did not know, spoke, "Very well, I consent to a remand. That is all."

Then the men promptly left the room just as quickly as they entered it. Within moments it was just the nurse and Florence who remained.

"You must get up now and get dressed," said the nurse.

"What is happening?"

"They are taking you to prison."

Florence had a suspicion that was happening, but nobody seemed to want to offer any details. Not even her own legal team. The nurse helped Florence put on a simple dress.

"Will I be able to see the children before I leave?"

"I am afraid that will not be possible."

The nurse tightened the strings at the back of Florence's dress. A little too tightly. They were putting shoes on Florence's feet when there was a knock at the door.

"They are ready to take you now."

Florence was starting to feel quite flustered. "I need my handbag. Please help me find it."

The nurse gave a wry smile. "You shan't be needing that where you are going."

The nurse then opened the bedroom door to allow the two police officers to take Florence away.

As they both took her down the stairs, she could see her mother held back on the landing by another policeman.

"My dearest Florence!"

Florence started to cry, "Mama!"

"Be strong, my child! I will come for you."

Within moments, Florence was bundled into the back of a carriage, and the horse started to canter off. She looked back towards the house, not knowing if this was the last time she would ever see Battlecrease again.

Or indeed that life.

* * *

18 May 1889

Walton Gaol, Liverpool

When Florence awoke, she realised everything was different. Gone had the comfortable bed, the luxurious bedding, and soft pillows. Instead, she found herself in a dimly lit cell on a rock-hard bed. Beside her was a chair with a china cup containing milk and a small plate with stale bread. The cell was devoid of anything more. This was the life Florence was facing now.

She started to recall the events since leaving Battlecrease. After a two-hour drive, they had arrived at Walton Goal in the outskirts of Liverpool.

Florence remembered how she shuddered as she looked at the tall, gloomy building upon arriving. She could hear a bell ringing. Suddenly the big iron gates swung open and allowed her and the escorting policemen to enter the grounds. The governor met Florie at the main door.

"You will be taken from here to the women's part of the prison."

At that moment, a female warder started to lead her away. The policemen who brought her into the prison then left. The two women crossed a small courtyard and stopped at a large door. The warder unlocked the door and ushered Florence through it.

After a short walk down a narrow passage, they reached a room marked, "Reception.' A bench ran along each side of a plain wooden table in the centre of the room.

There was another female warder on the other side of the table.

"You must submit all of the valuables in your possession."

Florence took a brief look at both women, hoping either would show an ounce of sympathy for her between them. Neither offered any. She proceeded to remove her jewellery.

"A watch. Two diamond rings. A brooch," the second warder barked as he simultaneously wrote down the items in her ledger book.

After a few moments, the second warder indicated Florence must stand on the nearby weighing machine. Again, a note was added to the ledger.

After the formalities concluded, Florence was guided by her first warder out of the reception and through the building.

"You will be taken to a cell especially set apart for sick prisoners."

After a short walk, the warder opened the wooden door to this tiny room and told her to go in. After tentatively passing through the door, Florence could hear it slam shut behind her. Then the unmistakable sound of the lock clicking. She once was again alone. She fell to the nearby bed and started crying.

"Oh my god, help me, help!"

Nobody came. After a while, she fainted.

Apart from her mother and legal team, not one person had

offered the sound of a friendly voice. The Maybricks had decided she was guilty. Alfred was nowhere to be seen.

After all that had happened in her life so far, it was now she felt truly alone.

* * *

31 July 1889

St. George's Hall, Liverpool

Sitting alone in the deepest bowels of the law courts prison, Florence Maybrick contemplated what was to come her way over the coming days. She had been incarcerated in one form or another since her husband died. Now, she was about to face the full force of the British judicial system. It had been over two months of waiting.

A lady could be forgiven for feeling her fate might be somewhat already preordained. The affair she had had with Alfred Brierly had been daily news. She was branded a murdering whore by strangers and acquaintances alike. Spat at and hissed at—Florie had been overwhelmed by it all.

How did it come to this? A young American woman from a socially affluent Deep South family, now facing God knew what. The last few months had been a whirlwind of emotion, pain, and drama—with no end in sight. What would become of her?

Two warders arrived—a man and a woman. The man knocked on the bars of the holding cell.

"Mrs. Maybrick, it's time."

From his extensive set of keys, he picked the one that unlocked her cell. For a brief moment, the door was open. A slight sense of freedom. Florence knew all too well it was temporary. He proceeded to lock the cell behind her and resume his lead.

As they all walked through the dark, cold, narrow stone corridors towards the staircase beyond the walls, Florie felt a sense of unease about what was to come. She could not shake the gnawing feeling in the very pit of her stomach. She constantly felt on the verge of being sick.

Her counsel had already instructed her that the court would not allow her to take the stand. The evidence and testimony of others would ultimately judge her.

"This surely cannot be the true course of justice if the accused does not even get to have a voice?" she said to Arnold Cleaver, her lawyer.

However, as was explained to her, the rules of engagement were set before a word was said in court. Florence must now put her faith and belief in those representing her. She must hope the evidence available was enough. Enough to prove that she did not kill her husband. Against the backdrop of local gossip and national scandal, she must pray for understanding. The understanding of a foreign legal system to ignore the bloodthirsty hysteria. Would the jury and Judge Stephen objectively review the evidence presented to release her? The feeling of unease became even more heightened.

As she glided up the wooden staircase to take her place in the dock, she could hear the mutterings and whispers of all those present in the room. The babbling murmurs started to die down. She could feel all the eyes focusing on her in her black mourning wear. She did her very best to appear dignified and calm. She felt far from either. Briefly surveying the crowded court, she saw nothing but disgust and hatred from all corners.

Again, that sickening feeling of the inevitable washed over her. She was the freak show entertainment—a figure of titillation and amusement for others. Nobody seemed to care about what was just in this room. Another show to see. Just another lamb to the slaughter.

Florence stood motionless in the dock as the courtroom cackle began to soften. She had spent over two months in prison, awaiting the opportunity to start defending herself. Time dripped by exceptionally slowly. The strain on her mentally had begun to take its toll. Insomnia and stress were not good bedfellows for one's peace of mind.

Florence had hoped the trial would be moved from Liverpool to London, where she felt she would have had a fairer hearing. Lack of funds made that option unviable.

A clerk in the courtroom started proceedings by standing up from his seat and addressing her directly.

"Florence Elizabeth Maybrick. You have been charged of feloniously and wilfully murdering your husband, James Maybrick. How do you plead?"

Florence cut a gaunt figure as she replied through a mournful tone, "Not guilty."

Judge Stephen, a man in his twilight years, asked that all witnesses leave the courtroom. Florence noted one exception was allowed to stay—Michael Maybrick.

The prosecution QC, Mr. Addison, started to explain the basis of their case. Florie noted how they were focused heavily on her affair with Alfred Brierley. She was not surprised by this tactic.

"They lived together as man and wife at Flatman's Hotel. They slept together, went out together, and on the Sunday about one o'clock, they unexpectedly left together, he paying the bill."

That statement by the prosecutor gave Florence a sense of deep regret. Regret for betraying her husband, regret for bringing Alfie into this whole mess, and regret clinging to childish ideals of happiness. She should have just accepted her lot.

Addison continued his opening statement covering all aspects of her supposed means of murder combined with her apparent motive. Alfie had ended their relationship. What exactly was she to gain?

The speech concluded by running through the chain of events, as they saw it at least. In finishing his monologue, it appeared to Florence that Addison was deliberately trying to confuse the jury regarding the meat juice found with arsenic and the meat juice that James consumed. Was this a deliberate tactic?

The first witness called was Michael Maybrick. Florence felt an overwhelming sense of disgust towards her brother-in-law as he took to the witness box to confirm his name and occupation. He never did like her much.

Florence's defence lawyer was the formidable and widely respected QC Sir Charles Russell. Michael quickly attempted to induce the jury into believing that she was not caring for James's welfare effectively.

"I arrived at the house on the eighth of May. I was very much shocked to see the state he was in, being only semiconscious. Shortly afterwards, I saw Mrs. Maybrick in the morning room, and I said to her I was not satisfied with my brother's treatment."

As Russell rightly demonstrated, Florence procured the arrival of a professional nurse and called upon both Dr. Humphreys and Dr. Carter to attend to her husband.

Michael then dared to claim she was tampering with his medicines and changing the labels on bottles.

"She explained that there was so much sediment in the smaller bottle that it was impossible to dissolve it and she was putting it into the larger bottle so that the medicine might be more easily shaken."

Was that not an acceptable reason to change bottles? However, promoting the idea of tampering suited Michael's sinister version more fittingly.

Russel moved then to establish Michael's bias towards Florence and her assumed guilt, keenly aided and abetted by that duplicitous wench Alice Yapp. Michael also confirmed he made his feelings known to the household staff. Florence hoped the jury would note that Michael had it in for her the moment he arrived at the house.

The topic moved to the letter Florence sent Michael earlier in the year, where she made it clear she was concerned about the powders James was consuming.

So much for being a heartless wife!

Of course, he claimed he destroyed the letter, and his memory of the content was somewhat vague. The man was truly a snake.

Florence was emotionally drained by proceedings already, and that was just the first witness.

Next to give testimony was the family doctor, Dr. Hopper. He confirmed the Grand National incident and subsequent reconciliation. He also asserted James as a hypochondriac who would often self-medicate with powders not prescribed by him. Indeed, this fact alone had to hold some value with the jury. James was intent on overdosing himself.

The rest of the day went in a blur. Various testimonies came and went. The meddling sisters gave their version of events. The weak-minded Edwin denied James ever took powders. Thomas Wokes, the chemist, was confirming her purchase of flypapers that contained arsenic.

Then came another local chemist, Cristopher Hanson. Florence had altogether forgotten her visit to his shop to purchase more flypapers. Although Florence knew they were for cosmetics, the second batch of flypapers also contained arsenic. That was two purchases of arsenic flypapers from two separate chemists. Florence knew this did not look good.

She had been extracting the arsenic to use with lotions to give her a more youthful complexion on her skin. She knew the jury would struggle with such notions.

The session concluded with members of James's office staff. Lowry and Smith confirmed the numerous bottles found in his office—twenty-eight in total! They also described the lunch that was prepared for him in late April. Why should the prosecution have such obsession with food given to James two weeks before he died? It confused Florence. Perhaps it would confuse the jury also? Maybe that was the point?

The judge adjourned the court. The two warders escorted Florence back down to the holding cell. She did not know what to make of the day. It was a whirlwind of emotion. As she headed back down the narrow passageway, she could not help but feel that she was more alone now than ever. People she thought were friends and family, all conspiring to see her pay for the death of her husband.

Was this what they called justice? Thus far, it did not feel that way to Florence.

* * *

7 August 1889

St. George's Hall, Liverpool

This was it. Quite literally Judgement Day. Florence had spent the past week listening to testimony after testimony after testimony.

She did not think she could reach lower depths of emotional exhaustion after the first day, yet as each day passed, she was introduced to new lows.

The revelations that Florie had to contend with seemed to be endless.

On day 2, she learnt that Nurse Yapp sent a telegram to Michael, urging him to come to Battlecrease House, where she promptly told him she believed Florence was poisoning James. Yapp also read her private mail to Alfie. Instead of sending it as instructed, she handed it to Edwin, who turned it over to Michael. A nest of conspirators.

The last few days were focused mainly on testimony from various doctors, describing the many symptoms of arsenic poisoning and technical aspects of what medicines and potions could contain such concentrations. It was all very hard for Florence to keep up with.

There were testimonies from the police who arrested her. Also were the nurses who recruited to assist in the care of her husband. Florence's case was not strengthened by their testimonies.

Then yesterday, Judge Stephen spent the entire session summing up the proceedings. Florence felt he seemed to ramble on about unnecessary things at times, but perhaps this was usual in British courts. She would not know. Then, remarkably towards the end of his extremely long summary, he referenced the testimony of Dr. McNamara from the Dublin Hospital.

"Had Mr. Maybrick been saturated, as in exceeded the amount of arsenic he could bear, then there would be common results. These being extreme redness of the eyelids and other effects that come with the stomach and bowels. In the case of Mr. Maybrick, it was not the vomiting that resulted from arsenical poisoning. In Dr. McNamara's professional opinion, this was not a case of arsenical poisoning."

Those few sentences seemingly exonerated Florence right there and then. If James did not die of arsenic poisoning, then surely it was irrelevant how much arsenic was found in Florence's possession? That was not how he died. However, she knew better than to remain over-optimistic. The trial had not concluded yet.

It was now mid-morning. The courthouse cell remained as soulless as it had done since Florence had been held here waiting for each day's proceedings to begin. She considered that regardless, today would be her last day in this place. The rest of her life would now be decided one way or another. The two warders appeared at the cell door. No words were exchanged today. There was an unspoken understanding of the gravity of the day.

The male warder opened the cell door, and Florence once again followed him through the depths of the courthouse to the steps that led her up to the waiting courtroom and to her fate.

The judge made it clear that overnight he had reviewed all the medical evidence. He started to focus on the testimony of Dr. Stevenson, which contradicted the testimony of Dr. McNamara.

"Taking the symptoms and the post-mortem appearances into account, I have no doubt that he died from arsenic. That is Dr.

Stevenson's evidence."

What was happening? Florence was confused. Did it seem Judge Stephen was now promoting the idea that despite the lack of consensus amongst the doctors of arsenic poisoning, on probability, he most likely was poisoned? How could he be allowed to show such bias against her? She was right to remain cautious.

The judge then raised the point of how continued dosing could have led to the demise of James. Before she knew it, he was back referencing the lunch James had in his office two weeks before his death, where traces of arsenic was later found on the jug. This again? Edwin transported the food to James.

Could he have not have laced the food with arsenic?

The judge continued to ramble on once again for what seemed an eternity to Florence. Eventually, he reached the part all present in the room had been waiting for in patience.

"Gentlemen, I have dealt with all matters which have occurred to me in my consideration of the case. I do not wish to spin out the last words to you. I accordingly will ask you to consider your verdict."

The jury rose to their feet and, one by one, filed out to a nearby room to deliberate. After the jury cleared, the judge stood up and left the room too. The clerk then rose to announce that the court was adjourned. The warders appeared. Florence knew the protocol.

When she came back, her entire life would be decided in a split moment.

The nerves had taken hold of her now.

***

***

7 August 1889

St. George's Hall, Liverpool

It did not take long. Perhaps just half an hour or so before a warder returned to the courthouse cell. Florence was in discussion with her solicitor when the announcement came.

"The jury has reached a verdict."

Time seemed to accelerate at breakneck speed. Florence's heart was thumping hard. Before she knew it, she was back standing in the dock. Instantly, she felt it was not going to be good news. No person would make eye contact with her. The tension was unbearable. An uncomfortable silence gripped the room.

Then the clerk of arraigns arose and addressed the foreman of the jury, who then also rose.

"Have you agreed upon the verdict, gentlemen?"

"We have."

"And do you find the prisoner guilty of the murder of James Maybrick or not guilty?"

"Guilty."

Florence immediately fell backwards onto her chair as if punched in the chest.

The clerk confirmed the verdict directly to Florence.

"Florence Elizabeth Maybrick, you have been found guilty of wilful murder. Have you anything to say why the court should not pronounce sentence upon you according to the law?"

Florence stood up, and with the last ounce of energy she could muster, she addressed the court.

"My lord, everything has been against me. I am not guilty of this crime."

Judge Stephen then placed a black cap over his wig.

"Prisoner at the bar, I am no longer able to treat you as being innocent of the dreadful crime laid to your charge. You have been convicted by a jury of this city, after a lengthy and most painful investigation, followed by a defence which was in every respect worthy of the man. The jury has convicted you, and the law leaves me no discretion, and I must pass the sentence of the law."

The judge took a long inhale of breath.

"The court doth order you to be taken from hence to the place from whence you came, and from thence to the place of execution, and that you be hanged by the neck until you are dead, and that your body be afterwards buried within the precincts of the prison in which you shall be confined after your conviction. And may the Lord have mercy upon your soul!"

The room flooded with boisterous murmurs of shock.

That was it. Florence's fate was sealed. She would now be hung for the death of her husband. Florence could feel no more. All sense of emotion or feeling had instantly been purged from her soul.

Her life, as she knew it, ended at that moment.

* * *

*　*　*

3 September 1889

Flower and Dean St., London

George Hutchinson poured the very last drops of gin from the bottle he had been nursing into a tatty ceramic cup. Sitting on his flea-ridden bed and surrounded by dirt in this grimy doss house, he knew he would need more gin.

There was a knock at his door. He got himself up and opened it. Before him stood a face he had not seen for almost a year.

"Inspector Littlechild. What are you doing here? How did you find me?"

The well-turned-out policeman entered the room.

"It is my job to find people, George."

George closed the door behind Littlechild, who took a quick look of disgust at the room he found himself in.

"Why are you here? I have not heard from you since you told me to give that statement about the Jew to the police," said Hutchinson.

"You are drinking rather heavily these days, George, I hear. Perhaps I am concerned for your health."

"You have never expressed an interest before. Maybe you are worried I am loose with my tongue when drunk? Why did you make me lie, Mr. Littlechild?"

The two men remained standing.

The policeman gave a brief pause before replying, "The truth is far less important. The truth is irrelevant. You did a good thing for your country."

George picked up the cup he left on the side table and downed the last few drops. He then turned his attention back to his visitor.

"Why does it not feel like that? Mary Jane's killer is not brought to justice."

"He is dead. That I am certain. There will be no more Jack the Ripper."

Hutchinson stood a little more upright. "Well, that is something. Will you tell me who he was?"

"That I cannot. I will say that he died a slow and painful death."

George gave a small smile. "That does please me somewhat."

Littlechild put his hand on George's shoulder. "George, London had not been kind to you of late. I have a gift I hope you will accept."

George looked up at Littlechild. "What is it?"

Littlechild smiled. "Free passage to Australia. Your name is listed as an able seaman on the *Ormuz* leaving London Docks tomorrow at 9:00 a.m. Ask for Marshy. Tell him John sent you. You will be required to do basic labouring tasks in return for your passage. It would be best if you regarded it as an opportunity for you. Australia is an exciting new world. You can create a whole new life for yourself." The secret policeman removed his hand from George's shoulder.

"Leave London? For good?" asked Hutchinson.

Littlechild gave another look around the room. "With all due to respect, seeing how you live, do you have much else to stay for George?"

George sat back down on the bed. "I suppose not. It would be good not to see the same streets over and over. They keep reminding me of Mary and all that happened. I should thank you, Mr. Littlechild."

The chief inspector made his way to the door and opened it. He turned back to his host as he opened the door.

"Don't thank me, George. Be ready to board that boat two hours before sailing. This is the last we shall ever see of each other regardless. I hope you take this opportunity. Look after yourself."

Littlechild left and closed the door gently behind him.

"Australia it is then."

PART 12

Setting Suns

8 June 1892

Three Nuns Hotel, London

Nearly four years had passed since the last victim of Jack was murdered. There had been one or two similar attacks since, but the horrific carnage of Mary Jane Kelly seemed to be the last of his handiwork and by far the most gruesome. A sense of unfinished business wrapped Fred Abberline like a rigid straitjacket he could not shake off. He was never going to shake it off.

Today was the day he officially said goodbye to the police at his retirement dinner—his place of work for over twenty years. He had received his final promotion as chief inspector just two years earlier, but he felt it was a hollow celebration. Such a lavish farewell did not make him comfortable either. Everyone came out to wish him the best. There were even people outside who could not gain access to wish the popular detective a good send-off.

It was a beautiful sunny day, and you could be forgiven for thinking all was good in the world. It was not. Jack evaded capture, and Fred was officially standing down. He could hunt Jack no more.

Fred's former boss Superintendent Thomas Arnold gave a well-considered speech, and he appreciated the sentiment. Arnold finished his presentation and urged the guests to raise a toast.

"Enjoy a drink to remember Fred's great service to the people of Whitechapel and London!"

After the formalities concluded, Fred felt a little more relaxed. He was never one for such attention.

A musky odour of stale beer mixed with fresh furniture polish hung in the air. He did his best to quickly navigate his way through the mass of well-wishers in the lounge bar. The room was a heaving crowd of many people looking to give their best to the retiring officer. As he pushed through the crowd, he took a few slaps on the back and shook the odd hand along the way. Fred soon spotted Mary Jane Kelly's landlord, John McCarthy, who immediately made his way towards him.

"Well, well, well, Mr. Abberline, the police do know how to lay on a nice farewell, don't they?"

McCarthy offered a smile as he shook Abberline's hand.

"Lovely hotel this. I've had the pleasure of dining here on a few occasions myself. It is a worthy venue for your send-off."

"I must confess, John, I was not expecting to see so many people like yourself from Whitechapel in attendance."

McCarthy took a swig of beer.

"Come now, Chief Inspector, we may be of Whitechapel, but we recognise a good mutton shunter from a bad one. You were well liked. We all knew how hard you tried to catch the Ripper, but it wasn't to be. The fact he remains a mystery is no one's fault."

Both men took a moment in silence.

"I'm here with the boy," said McCarthy. "He's over there somewhere, probably trying to make a copper giggle. He has aspirations in entertainment, he does. I encourage it myself. Whitechapel is not a place where aspirations have much chance of hope, as you well know."

Abberline cocked his head slightly.

"For someone who does not feel that Whitechapel offers much hope, John, you seem to have done quite fortuitously on a personal level."

A wry smile crossed McCarthy's face. "Well, that's just business though. I see opportunities, and I take them. That doesn't mean events, Chief Inspector, do not sadden me. I am still human. A man still needs to make a few shillings, don't he?"

The two men surveyed the room with its hive of activity. Police officers in their uniforms shared conversations and laughed with local tradesmen. A community ravaged by tragedy and poverty but still looking for the light in each other. Fred felt there if he were better with words, he would find something poetic about the scene.

Without warning, McCarthy broke the silence in a hushed tone.

"I still think about that day, Fred. It haunts me, it does."

Abberline, without missing a beat, knew what McCarthy was talking about. The two men avoided eye contact.

"So do I, John. It haunts me too."

After around ten seconds of silence and quiet reflection, McCarthy raised his spirits suddenly.

"Anyway, Inspector, I guess you will be getting some of that famous Eastbourne sea air into your lungs, will you?"

Abberline also tried to brush off the veil of morbidity. "That's right. I shall be returning to my hometown, where I hope to spend my remaining days eating fish and drinking beer on the pier before watching the sunset over the sea."

"That sounds like heaven to me, Mr. Abberline. It really does. Well, we, the residents of Whitechapel, offer you our greatest thanks for all you have done down the years. It is time to break off those shackles of the force and enjoy the rest of your days in peace, sir."

The notorious local businessman offered his hand again, which Chief Inspector Abberline wasted no time in accepting.

"You take care of yourself too, John, and try to stay out of trouble!"

McCarthy smiled and doffed his cap in response. He then started to make his way through the thronging crowd.

Fred decided he should also make his way through the sea of people towards the bar. In doing so, he found Superintendent Thomas Arnold waiting with two freshly poured beers in his hands. Upon seeing Abberline, he handed him one.

"You deserve a drink after talking to that ratbag McCarthy." Arnold in his Essex drawl left no room for sentiment.

"I don't think he's all that bad, Tom. He is just like many others in Whitechapel. Survival is all that matters."

"There are those who survive, and there are those who profit from the damned. Anyway, we are not here to talk about him. We are here to send you off back to the seaside. So get that beer into you. There will be a barrel load more on its way!"

Fred took a large gulp of beer and, whilst doing so looked around and caught a glimpse of McCarthy and his son leaving the room. For whatever others might think of John McCarthy and his family, Abberline felt Whitechapel needed people like him to maintain a certain level of control when the police were unable to. Fred was also one of the few people who knew that John paid for Mary Jane's headstone without any family. Such announcements of charity would not be good for business.

Whitechapel itself might not offer much hope, but the little it had in community spirit did. As the saying goes, "Say well is good, do well is better."

The area needed more of those that did well and less of those who only said well. That was how a man's character should be judged. Perhaps then, hope could indeed spring eternal.

Abberline knew he would forever be connected to this area despite the brutality of violence and battle for survival. In many ways, he would miss it. It would always be the biggest disappointment of his time on this earth that he could not offer the people of Whitechapel the peace of catching Jack the Ripper.

He would never have that peace either.

* * *

25 January 1904
Aylesbury Prison, Bucks

* * *

Florence stood outside the large iron gates of Aylesbury Prison. Dawn was breaking, and the air was cold. Florence did not mind it. The air she was now inhaling was on the side of freedom. Fifteen long years she was incarcerated in the prison system for the murder of her husband. Now she could once again walk amongst the free. She was almost entirely free herself.

The prison's matron was assigned to accompany Florence to Truro. She had opted to spend the remaining six months of her sentence at the Home of the Community of the Epiphany, a religious retreat where she could find peace with God and nature equally.

"Florence, are you ready to take the cab?"

A horse and carriage arrived to escort the women to Aylesbury Station, where they would start their long trek from Buckinghamshire to Cornwall.

Florence took one last long look at the prison walls.

"I shall never be more ready, matron."

The two women climbed into the carriage with the assistance of the driver. After a few moments, the driver took the horse's reigns, and the carriage started to move. The sudden movement surprised Florence. She had not been in a carriage for many years. One would suspect many things would once again be unfamiliar to her until, eventually, they became familiar.

As the carriage rattled its way down the road on the rough cobbles, Florence's mind wandered back to how she came to be spared the noose. She was kept separated from the other prisoners at Walton Gaol after Judge Stephens passed sentence. The cell could only be described as a waiting room for death. Florence's stay there was around three weeks.

Each day she could feel the gallows edging closer and closer and the noose getting tighter and tighter. Her legal team had petitioned the Home Office for a commutation of her sentence. It looked for all intents and purposes that it would not come. Then, on the eve of her scheduled day of execution, word came from the governor himself.

"It is well, it is good news!"

Florence remembered instantly fainting. She awoke in the hospital block of the prison. Death would have to wait for her a bit longer.

Florence always remained thankful her fate was not death despite what the next decade and a half would bring at Woking Convict Prison and then Aylesbury Prison. Her time in the system was demanding and laborious. The thoughts of eventual freedom sustained the long periods of solitary confinement, strict discipline, and hard labour. It had profoundly changed her.

Florence left the prison system a husk of the woman she had once been. She entered it as a vibrant young lady in her twenties and left it as an institutionalised woman in her forties. Prison had altered entirely the fibre of her being forever. Florence prayed she now got the opportunity to reunite with her children.

The fifteen years lost were not hers alone.

***

***

22 October 1941

Gaylordsville, Connecticut

The night sky was drawing in. The chilly wind was starting to whistle through this small cottage in the middle of the Connecticut countryside. Florence was wrapped in a heavy knitted blanket in front of a crackling fire. She was exhausted. Frail, wrinkled, and all alone. Almost eight decades on this earth and this was what she had become. Alone, broke, and tired in a tiny run-down shack.

The many cats she offered refuge to kept her in some company. Although the company of the human kind, she had been content to live without for many years now. The first half of her life was chaotic and confusing. Something could be said for the peace and tranquillity of nothingness now.

It had been over thirty-five years since Florence left Aylesbury Prison. After six months seeing out her remaining sentence at a convent, she reassumed her American citizenship and returned to the United States.

After being encouraged to write a book about her lost fifteen years, she spent a brief period lecturing on prison reform across America. However, she was never comfortable with such publicity. Florence tried her best to leave the old life of Maybrick, Liverpool, and imprisonment behind her, but it was not easy. Eventually, she found her way to this tiny town in Connecticut that had no idea of her past. Florence was able to live in peace, albeit poor and with no access to a sustainable income. Her time in prison had prepared her well for such a meagre and reclusive existence.

Florence could feel that tonight something was different. It felt as if all the remaining energy she had in reserve was starting to drain and ebb away. Was tonight the night Florence would leave this mortal coil? She certainly hoped so.

The small flames forked the modest logs in the fire.

After a short while, she mustered enough energy to open her blanket. Beside her, she picked up a pile of photos, newspaper clippings, and letters. The bundle contained remnants of her previous life, moments encased in print and ink. Some happy, most not. There were pictures of her two children, Gladys and Bobo. Both were gone from her life for good and never to be seen again. The last time she saw them was just before she was locked in her bedroom at Michael's command, having been accused by him of the murder of her husband.

When she was in prison, she knew exactly where the children were. However, she was not allowed any contact. It didn't stop her from trying to send letters. None got through, of that she was sure. Michael saw to that. The children went to live with Michael's doctor for a while before joining him on the Isle of Wight where, laughably, he somehow was able to become mayor!

Florence's failure to reunite with her children after her release weighed heavy on her. She had become aware of Bobo's tragic death from a newspaper report confirmed by relatives soon after.

She was unaware he even went to Canada. As for Gladys, Florie had no idea where she was now. She began to sob as sadness overwhelmed her. Her poor, beautiful children.

After a while, she stopped crying. Florie could feel something changing in her. The tiredness was becoming more and more. It felt like a wave building. Her thoughts were beginning to slow right down. It was like a steam train coming to a slow and shuddering halt.

In that instant, her mind wandered back to May 1889. James had just revealed to her in his stricken and sickly state that he was actually Jack the Ripper. Florence remembered how she did not believe him. She recalled how she thought he was trying to frighten her.

That was until she slept on it.

How he spoke sent shivers down her spine. What was initial disbelief quickly manifested into realisation once she took the time to think about it thoroughly. The pieces began to make sense. Things started to fit into place. All those weekend trips to London on the same days these poor unfortunate women died. Why did she not see it? How did she not see it? How could she have not known that she was living with a monster? Was he not monstrous to her?

If she had noticed the signs sooner, could lives have perhaps been saved? That guilt had lived with her for so many long years, buried deep within her soul.

However, she felt no guilt for his murder. She remembered how she took laudanum from her cupboard that day and laced James's beef tea. She must have put about a third of the bottle into the hot liquid. She could even remember the secret delight she had in knowing this would finish "Sir Jim" off for good. It wasn't long after that James was dead. No more women would have to suffer at the hands of Jack the Ripper, or James Maybrick.

The court was right. The verdict was correct. Florence did murder her husband, but not through arsenic but with laudanum.

Florence recalled vividly that moment when she almost told the court. She stood in the dock, holding the rails tightly, nervous and with her heart beating out of her chest.

"Much has been withheld which might have influenced the jury had it been told."

Just before she was about to reveal the truth, she looked around the room and felt no one would believe her. They would have just observed a woman who was sentenced to hang, trying anything she could to avoid the noose. Instead, she denied her guilt.

"I am not guilty of this crime."

Florie knew she was, but she had also stopped any more innocent deaths.

She had ensured justice was served for all those poor lives James had destroyed. There was a kind of comfort in that. Even if she could prove at the time that she had indeed stopped London's most notorious killer, what difference would it have made? She was sentenced to hang, and nothing she could say would change that. She was still a murdering whore in the eyes of many.

Florence's fate was sealed the moment James died. Deep down, she knew that. Nobody would have cared about the truth. A sacrifice had to be made by the justice system, and that sacrifice was ultimately her own life. It was not just fifteen years of liberty that was taken from Florie. It was everything. Her entire life had changed beyond recognition. Even when free, she spent her life imprisoned in her own mind.

Florence often wondered if Michael knew the truth about his brother. His behaviour after James's death was so clinical. Perhaps he felt by assisting so forthrightly in her demise, he might ensure the name Maybrick would never be connected with that of Jack the Ripper? The fact that he eventually became her children's legal guardian was somewhat even more insulting in the grand scheme of things. This man was paramount in taking everything she had. Bitterness served no purpose now though. Michael was almost thirty years dead himself. The Maybrick ghosts still haunted her. Hopefully, no more.

Florie gently lay back in her blanket and closed her eyes. Her mind was clearing. The only sounds she could hear now were the slow breaths leaving her lungs. Slowly in, slowly out. The gap in between breaths was starting to take longer and longer.

Then pure, unadulterated silence. One long exhalation of air rattled through her chest and out into the ether. It was her last one on earth. The nightmare had ended.

The tortured wife of Jack the Ripper was finally at peace.

* * *

9 March 1992

Riversdale Rd., Liverpool

It was Monday morning. The indulgences of a Sunday night drink up at the Saddle were still being exorcised.

"Come 'head, Ed!" shouted a voice from behind the hedge.

Eddie didn't initially recognise it. Within a matter of moments, a face appeared to match the vocals. It was a face Eddie knew.

"Get your finger out of your arse, lad," bellowed the speaker.

Eddie had worked with Jimmy on several jobs for Harbers and Rose Building contractors, and this was another one. However, this job was taking a little longer than the bosses would have liked, and they sent Eddie, a jobbing electrician, over to try and speed things up a little.

"Start pulling up the floorboards in the living room, Eddie. We need you to run the cables for the new storage heaters along the joists."

"Sound."

Eddie made his way upstairs to the first floor of this creaky and slightly creepy Victorian house. He found the living room just off the corridor right at the top of the stairs. Most of the furniture was covered with dust sheets and moved to the room's edges in anticipation for the floorboards to be lifted. He did a quick review of the floorboards to see where the nails were placed so he could pull them out. Eddie took his trusty claw hammer from his tool belt and started to prise up the various nails. Most came up with ease. Some needed some extra elbow grease. Then he reached one such board, loose with no nails securing it down at all.

That's weird!

As he lifted the floorboard, something glinted in the sunlight. A sharp reflection of something metallic.

"What the . . . ?"

As Eddie moved in closer, he could see it was some kind of large metal box.

Is this some type of biscuit tin?

Whatever it was, it was old. The lettering and decal had all but faded away completely. He reached down and pulled it through the tight gap now left by the vacant floorboard. In doing so, he heard a slight rattle. This was no empty tin. The lid was on tight. It took some prising from his hammer to get the lid off. When the lid eventually did budge, Eddie was shocked to see several items inside.

Inside this old tin box was a dark-blue scrapbook around A4 in size, a small gold watch, a ring, and a suede drawstring bag with the initials "I. M. JACK." Inside the suede bag, Eddie pulled out what looked like a really old door key. He put the key back in the bag and took a brief look at the watch. The hands had stopped, frozen in time. It had an engraving "J. O." on the face. Then he picked up the old book and gently opened the pages. Eddie tried to read the first page, but it wasn't making much sense, so he flicked through to the end. He stopped dead in his tracks.

"What the hell is this?"

He read the last few lines and at first, it didn't register. To make sure he wasn't imagining things, he reread the words again—this time aloud.

"I give my name that all know of me, so history do tell, what love can do to a gentleman born. Yours truly, Jack the Ripper."

Eddie dropped the book in shock. "Holy f——"

THE END

AKNOWLEDGEMENTS

I found the resources below invaluable for learning the stories of Jack the Ripper, his victims, James Maybrick, and Florence Elizabeth Chandler.

BritishNewspaperArchive.co.uk.

Casebook.org.

FindMyPast.co.uk.

Harrison, Shirley. 1993. *The Diary of Jack the Ripper*.

Irving, H. B. 1912. *Trial of Mrs. Maybrick*.

Jones, Christopher. 2008. *The Maybrick A-Z*.

Maybrick, Florence. 1905. *My Lost Fifteen Years*.

Robinson, Bruce. 2015. *They All Love Jack*.

Rubenhold, Hallie. 2019. *The Five*.

Skinner, Keith, and Stewart P. Evans. 2000. *The Ultimate Jack the Ripper Sourcebook*.

PLEASE LEAVE A REVIEW

It would be enormously beneficial if you could take a few moments to give this book a review on Amazon. Thank you.

SPECIAL THANKS

I want to extend my sincerest thanks to *Tom Mitchell*. Without his support and feedback, I do not believe I would have completed this project. The world needs more of those willing to challenge long-held established beliefs. Thanks, Tom.

JAYHARTLEY.COM

I am a crime fiction writer with interest in history, pop culture and psychology. If you want to read more stories like this one, please visit my website and join my mailing list.

Printed in Great Britain
by Amazon